Short fiction
Book 2025

CW00819088

GRAVITY FLOW

THE JIMMY WHISTLER STORIES

GRAVITY FLOW

THE JIMMY WHISTLER STORIES

E.M. SCHORB

HILL HOUSE   **NEW YORK**

ISBN: 979-8-218-56470-4

Cover Drawing: E.M. Schorb
Cover Design: Selah Bunzey

ACKNOWLEDGEMENTS

The following stories included in *Gravity Flow* first appeared in these publications:

"Movie Money," The Bangalore Review

"How to Float," Short Stories Bimonthly

"The Liar," Chattahoochee Review

"The Girl Upstairs," Ginosko Literary Journal

"The Liberty Bell," Mudfish (only the first part of which was mistakenly published as a poem)

"Polaroid," Ginosko Literary Journal

The poem "The Orphaned," which appears in the story of the same name, appeared in The Yale Review.

"The Cartesian Diver" under title "Darkling, I Listen," Ginosko Literary Journal *for Patricia*

CONTENTS

INTRODUCTION

Whether you follow the page order or skip back and forth, smart & dear reader, this book will amaze you by the variety of what it offers, with sorrowful or merry stays in New York's Greenwich Village and environs.

In one story, "The Sandal Shop," we are taken back to the Village in the early Sixties. There, Jimmy meets his first beatnik, a character oddly named Marsayas— Marsayas complained that he could not live with his family. "Impossible!," he said, his whole family were "convention-racked lunatics" or "business fiends" or "materialist maniacs." Marsayas, instead: "I'm a Zoroastrian. I believe in the power of light to conquer the forces of darkness. I believe in universal love." A Zoroastrian! Those were truly the new, hip Sixties: something unexpected and far out at every turn.

Schorb has an ear for the manifold accents of American speech, and that adds significantly to the amazing variety of this book.

Schorb has a special touch, almost Dickensian, for depicting egoism in enduring ways and unforgettably despicable characters. Aunt Gertrude in "Movie Money" is one of them. She is a miser with mafia connections, who keeps Jimmy and his mother in thrall by the promise, not always kept, of giving them money for the movies on Fridays. Newark, however, is, for Jimmy, a sort of vile annex of the Village, as we surmise when we read "Candy Butcher," where people go to see "burlesque" — "to see at the Adams Theatre in Newark what Mayor La Guardia had banned from New York."

Schorb is not a writer to hand us happy endings. I'm not complaining. There are too many final-redemption stories in the market today, which is a cause for a demoralizing depression. That's something you, sharp reader, will not experience in reading this book. Schorb leaves Jimmy Whistler suspended, on the razor's edge.

Will he cower and submit to the logos that governs the bullshit world, so as to enjoy its rewards and prestige? Will he drop totally out of it? Or will he undertake the most difficult task, to change that logos from within? When I reached the end, I found myself praying for Jimmy to choose rightly, and I also found that actually I could not presume to know what would be for him the right choice.

Ricardo L. Nirenberg, Editor
Offcourse Literary Journal

PART ONE

THE LIBERTY BELL

I FROM THE CRIB

From the deep recesses of the universe, he woke to find himself gumming the blue lead paint from the top rail of his crib, blissfully unaware of the crack in the Liberty Bell, or the Liberty Bell itself, for that matter; Mussolini in Abyssinia, Schicklgruber, in Guernica or the Rhineland, Tojo in China, or any of the problems of the age into which he had been dropped. The lead paint was delicious and maddening, and would, no doubt make a mad poet of him.

He looked around and for the first time saw other humanoids (oops, hominids), much bigger, but basically the same. They, also, wobbled on two legs, holding drinks to their lips, as he held his empty baby bottle to his. One fell back into a faded, flowered easy chair, in what seemed, even to his innocent eyes, a flat, shabby and small, compared with whatever had been before.

Years later, photographs would tell him who they were. Someone had taken several Kodak snapshots. Here was his young Aunt, a fourteen-year-old schoolgirl, who hookied to the City of Brotherly Love to help with her new nephew, the young Master, her big sister's first child. An older boy would have noticed the beginnings of her breasts—in five years his father's big hands would be lifting the full version of them—and that she was a pretty young thing with startling blue eyes and chestnut waves piled up, but he was unaware of these uplifting attractions.

3

The woman was his Mother. Later he would under-stand that at that point in her life, made-up and Marcelled, people said that she looked like the actress Mary Astor, ex-cept for her harlequin-shaped glasses. He learned that in a dry town you get booze from a man who winks at your Mother.

The central figure, the one who had collapsed in the armchair, wearing what then he, himself not much more than an homunculus, would eventually discover—by these presents—looked like the famous-at-the-time Arrow Collar Man.

Well, that was his old man, tall, dark, and handsome alcoholic, Depression-fallen from stocks and bonds sales-man, to selling *The Book of Knowledge* in the territory assigned him by the publisher.

His young Aunt stuck a rubber nipple in his mouth and quickly the picture faded and never came back, 'til now.

II DENIAL

When he was about three feet tall, the gray streets of Philadelphia in winter were very long and tiring and slowly climbed uphill toward a dark sky. His mother dragged him along. Where were they going? Their arms were empty. Not shopping? Was there no money? Why were they walking, walking so far? He began to get very cold. Then, on the deserted street, a stranger appeared before them. His mother knew the man, yes, and they laughed together, startling echoing laughter, too high above him for him to have any idea what was funny, but something obviously was, for their laughter tinkled down upon him like sprightly snowflakes, like tinsel and sequins, a glittery sprinkling of fairy dust. He tried to get between them, where it fell most heavily. His mother yanked him back and away, toward her

4

own back. Then the man seized his mother in his arms and dipped her back toward where he waited, and kissed her hard and long. It was wrong, wasn't it? Because this man was not his father. His father was up ahead somewhere, somewhere at the end of the long gray avenue, somewhere up several flights of stairs, in a small ugly flat that looked down on the avenue, drinking. It was wrong, wasn't it? Because his mother did not struggle to be free. Instead, she simply held him behind her, away from them. He thought he might cry. The man seemed to lift his mother off the pavement and to place her back on it, her high heels clicking, then firm. She pulled him from behind her and around to her side, her other hand held out to the man as he stepped back, back, and turned and went a little way, and stopped, and turned again, and winked, and blew her a kiss, and turned once again, and went on down the long slowly sinking avenue. Who was that? He wanted to know. His mother dragged him forward up the hill.

"Who was that man?" he asked.
His mother climbed on, up the hill, pulling him along with one hand and wiping tears from her eyes with the other.

"Mommy, who was that man?"

His mother ignored him until he screamed his question at her, in his tiny, shrill, hysterical voice. The question and its answer had become imperative, like the bearing down of traffic at the intersection. Finally his mother said, "What man?"

He looked back and saw the receding figure of the man who had kissed his mother, no more than a dot now, a dot in time. He tugged his mother half around and pointed—

"That man," he said.

"I don't see any man," his mother said. "I haven't seen anyone since we began our walk, and neither have you."

He looked back again, desperately, but the man was gone, only eternity, only infinity remained to see. "You see," said his mother, "there is no one on the street but us."

She was lying, wasn't she, or could he not believe the evidence of his own eyes? From then on he struggled to keep his hand free of hers. From then on he believed what he had heard, that there was a crack in the Liberty Bell.

MOVIE MONEY

Aunt Gertrude had had no education—had been, due to the poverty and ignorance of her family, virtually a waif—but possessed noticeable innate intelligence. She kept several sets of account books, some of dubious public record and some honest, illegal, and secret. The house of her dominion may have been a rooming house in a Newark slum, but it was papered green with numbers racket hundred dollar bills that had to be accounted for.

She had been a buxom girl who had swollen into an enormous woman and subsequently shrunk back to a two-hundred and fifty pound mere shadow of her former self, leaving her sallow, inelastic skin loose and hanging. Jimmy's earliest memory of her—he was about four or five—was of that enormous middle-aged woman of sixty.

She sat across from him and his mother in a restaurant booth and he counted her seven ballooning chins. Tactlessly, he asked about them, though he was just as fascinated by the even larger balloons that rested side by side on the table top, that were deep-trenched and powdered and seemed to roll about of their own volition. Of the chins, Aunt Gertrude told him that each represented a daughter and that, collectively, they indicated that she was the seventh daughter of a seventh daughter and was therefore possessed of magical powers, such as the gift of the evil eye.

Later, his mother told him that Aunt Gertrude had been stolen by Gypsies as a little girl—actually, farmed-out as a helper—and had lived in a Gypsy camp somewhere in the Watchung mountains of New Jersey for over a year, when

7

finally her father had—reluctantly, for she had been a demonic child even before being "kidnapped," and some said that she had been given away—gone to retrieve her. Into her early sixties, she had developed ghostly cataracts that added impact when she gave you the evil eye, which she often did, and either had or feigned to have a heart ailment. By now, this doubtful heart condition had been present for as long as anyone could remember with no more dire consequence than that if anyone crossed her she would go spinning off across the room like a top on her little horny feet, her great, low bulk knocking a swath in the furnishings, and dive into a possum faint. This was called "swooning," and Jimmy's mother said that Aunt Gertrude had "swooned" or was about to "swoon." In truth, it was difficult to tell if her heart or her temper was the true culprit. She took—suitably—nitroglycerin for this condition, and smelling salts were always advisable. The smelling salts were carried in the pocket of another enormous, though much younger, woman, named Charity. Charity was Aunt Gertrude's flunky. She had culled Charity and Charity's husband, Donald, from the mildly-challenged ward at the mental institution at Vineland, New Jersey. Charity and Donald lived, as it were, by Aunt Gertrude's leave. Charity was a low, wide three-hundred pounds; Donald a high, narrow one-twenty-five. This couple existed upstairs and would plummet down a back stairwell at Aunt Gertrude's ear-splitting behest. Charity did all of Aunt Gertrude's domestic chores, more or less ran the roominghouse, including keeping in supplies—slow or not, she was a sharp bargainer—and Donald did the toting and fixing. They were well content, and even protective of Aunt Gertrude, who needed protection no more than did her favorite wrestler, Gorgeous George. Far from the least important member of this odd ménage was a canine. Wiggles was a very old bitch with tumorous, pendulous breasts. Aunt Gertrude, who had been

8

at various times in an otherwise amoral career immoral on a professional basis, had been unable to have children, and had always felt the lack of a daughter. Wiggles served her as such. Jimmy took it that there had been other doggy-daughters before the obscene Wiggles, but for as long as he could remember Wiggles had been about, door-scratching and spitting horrid barks at any intruder, himself included, being dragged back and shushed, and traipsing off down the hall ahead of the menagerie, like an old woman who has just given a salesman an earful, nails clicking, upright stubby tail stiff, broad hindquarters naked, unappetizing. Jimmy was a fastidious little boy and Wiggles deeply disturbed him. She sat at table, wrapped in a bib, and ate from a dinner plate. Because she was an old dog and couldn't chew, all were subjected to the spectacle of Aunt Gertrude, or sometimes Charity, masticating morsels before placing them in Wiggles' worn-down chops. And often, not being content with her own portion, Wiggles would heave her clattering bulk to the floor and beg Jimmy's, which he must forfeit or incur Aunt Gertrude's wrath.

"Isn't she a sugarball? Give her some of your meat. Don't forget to chew it for her!"

Friday was the big day of the week. Fridays, Aunt Gertrude prepared to go to Long Branch, New Jersey, where she would be met by her paramour and dominant partner, Tony "Ice Pick" Scarpia, a nearly four-foot tall man with a twisted spine, her "little giant," who ostensibly sold live bait, hence, "Ice Pick," to the fishermen on the pier there, but who was actually a mob-sponsored bookie and runner with the need of getting large sums of money out of his possession and back to Newark, to the roominghouse he owned and which existed under the absolute dominion of Aunt Gertrude.

* * *

When Jimmy's nervous mother rang the doorbell on Fridays, sending Wiggles into a conniption fit, Aunt Gertrude would usually be applying a sulphur-based solution, which she used instead of a razor, to her jowls and chins and pulpy, varicosed legs, of which, no pun intended, she was very vain, and every recess of the house would reek of sulphur, like a brimstone pit. Jimmy's mother would adjust herself to the powerful, rotten-egg fumes while Wiggles was being calmed and sent on her haughty way. On recovering from the spinning heart-seizure his mother's entry had caused, Aunt Gertrude would tell her to get herself some breakfast (coffee would suffice for Jimmy's mother in such an atmosphere); then Aunt Gertrude would carry on with her toilet like Susannah herself, if sans Susannah's everything including the intrigued elders. If Jimmy's mother could manage to be pleasantly helpful during the course of the day on Friday, and Jimmy could join her after school, and do the same, Aunt Gertrude might give them the money to go to a movie and buy some popcorn.

What was required was that they take her to the station and wait with her until train time. Jimmy would carry her bags and his mother would make chitchat, larding her comments with compliments.

"What a lovely dress, Aunt Gertrude!"

"I don't care for it that much!"

"Don't you?"

"No!

"Well, maybe it is a bit . . ."

"A bit what? Don't you like it? You just said you did!"

"I *do!*"

"Well—" Huff-puff!

Jimmy invariably arrived at a crucial moment, for with Aunt Gertrude there were no non-crucial moments. By now her beard and leg-hair would have been peeled heartattackingly off with the sulphurous pancake crusts that had mummified various parts of her anatomy, her top-hair would have been freshly dyed—this was Jimmy's mother's specialty—either jet-black or fire-engine red, as Aunt Gertrude's mood would have it, her too-small shoes force-fed by horn her horny feet, and, corseted, frocked, and fully decorated, she would look like a Woolworth's Christmas tree. But Wiggles would have to be left in the care of Charity and Donald, whom Aunt Gertrude did not trust to do right by her doggy daughter while she was away (albeit so in awe of her magic were the poor serfs of her household, that she had little to fear), and therefore had to be bathed and prepared for the weekend before Aunt Gertrude could take her leave in confidence. The galvanized tub would be on the kitchen table and Charity would be turning Wiggles fatly and stiff-leggedly about in it, soaping and scrubbing her under Aunt Gertrude's close scrutiny. Jimmy's mother would answer the door, lead little Jimmy back into the kitchen, and stand aside, eager to please, afraid to offend, baffled and thwarted, it being understood that she was not competent to be involved in this splashy task.

"Is there anything to eat?" Jimmy asked.

"Not now," his mother said, meaning of course not that there wasn't anything to eat but that Jimmy should keep quiet. Aunt Gertrude shrieked, grabbed her fat-buried heart, and fell back, knocking pots and pans from the stove. Charity had lost her soapy grip on Wiggles and the ungainly animal had slopped about in the bubbles.

"I thought she'd drown," cried Aunt Gertrude. "For God's sake, Charity, be careful with her!"

Jimmy sniggered.

"And just what do you think is so funny?"

One ghostly evil eye was on him, the other tightly shut.

His mother pinched him.

"Nothing, Aunt Gertrude."

"I should hope not!"

Charity got Wiggles rinsed, spread a bath towel out on the table, patted her dry, turned her over, powdered her tumorous breasts, and put a nice clean jockstrap on her. These jockstraps served as double-D doggie brassieres, holding Wiggles' pendulous powdered breasts in place. There were several other elongated jockstraps hanging about the kitchen on towel racks, drying. Wiggles stood upright now, a small whale on four toothpicks, jockstrap at sway. Charity sweatered, harnessed and leashed her.

This was where Jimmy came in. He could not fathom what gave Aunt Gertrude the idea, but she was firm in her conviction that it was good for Wiggles to be walked after her bath, and it was his delightful duty to walk her, and not just in front of the house, where he would frowningly skulk, if he were not urged on, but all the way up to Broad Street and under the Lackawanna overpass, where the bus stop was, and many people were, and back. If not conscious, was it subconscious sadism that compelled Aunt Gertrude to force Jimmy to do this? On more than one occasion people had laughed out loud at the sight of the red-faced, embarrassed little boy in short pants and the enormously overweight, pendulously jock-strapped dog that seemed in charge of their direction. It happened again on this particular Friday, and one woman even pointed at them from a passing bus. Jimmy's face burned red as a tomato, and tears of shame and temper rolled down his cheeks. But Jimmy consoled himself with the prospect of the movie that lay ahead—maybe.

They couldn't be sure. Aunt Gertrude was capable of not coming through on her part of the unspoken bargain, just to show them. There had been sad times when they left the station with empty pockets and had had to be satisfied with just looking at the bright marquees, to imagine how good it might have been to see the pictures and to talk about how

12

much they would have enjoyed them. Then they would go home cursing Aunt Gertrude a little but mostly laughing about the mishaps of Wiggles and Aunt Gertrude's swoons. Later, they would listen to the evening radio programs and look forward to next week, the eternal optimists—for, after all, being dirt poor, they had no choice.

Aunt Gertrude loved gin rummy and Jimmy was the only soldier in her small army who knew how to play it. But she had a method. She would set up the card table next to the television set, then a relatively new device with a huge, rabbit-eared antenna, and turn on wrestling, which she loved—Jimmy noted her adoration of Gorgeous George—and then, when in trouble with her cards, would shout for him to look at what was happening in the ring, and, while his attention was diverted, would cheat by changing cards or stealing extras. One time he caught her at it, though he had suspected her of cheating before this. Boldly, he accused her, and she accused him of being a thankless ingrate like his no-good drunken father. Jimmy sat fuming, about eight years old, then charged across the room like a little bull, goring her with his cowlick horns. She was terrifically strong, even then, and he could believe the family tales told of her by nieces and nephews whom she had lifted into the air in her lustier youth and thrown clean across rooms. This time she easily finessed him into a half-nelson, boxed his ears red, whirled, and, having subdued him, promptly fainted. Charity brought out the smelling salts while Wiggles and Jimmy's mother had hysterical fits of their own. No one was concerned with the crushed, defeated little heap under her—Jimmy. That Friday they did not get their movie money.

So Jimmy's eyes sucked back his tears and he held himself in and brought Wiggles back to the house.

"What did Wiggles do?"

"Sniffed at things."

13

"Was she cute?"

"Yes, Aunt Gertrude."

"Did she pee or poop?"

"No."

Thank God! That would have required removing the jockstrap in public and replacing it afterwards (he was always required to take extras along). It had happened before and was perhaps worst of all.

"Well, we are all ready to go then. Charity, get my pocket book! Donald, get my bags!"

When they took a taxi, the trip to the station wasn't so bad. Then it was just a question of stuffing Aunt Gertrude, her bags, and themselves into the back seat and setting forth. But sometimes she couldn't get a cab to come to the house at the right time; or else, for other reasons, preferred to take a bus. Jimmy thought she preferred to take the bus sometimes so that the passengers could get a load of her, all dolled up and, as she no doubt believed, dazzling. But this bus ride with Aunt Gertrude was nearly as much of an embarrassment to him as were the afterbath walks with Wiggles. Indeed, Wiggles and Aunt Gertrude had much in common. Aunt Gertrude's legs, however, were of stouter stuff than those of her doggy daughter. Jimmy watched her now, as they climbed the great wide ramp that led to the trains; and, though he could scarcely drag the suitcases that were attached to his weakening hands and weight-sloped shoulders, he giggled to see the bowed, varicosed, mouth-down megaphones of her legs triumph over the upgrade. Side to side she heaved, as if the whole station, and the whole world, were tilting.

As usual, she had bought them chicken salad sandwiches and coffee in the lunchroom down the ramp behind them, where everyone had seen them before, for many Fridays. As usual, she had complained about the expense. As usual, she had been rude to everyone, and as usual

14

Jimmy felt a little sick. But it was a good sign. It showed that she was in a giving mood. Perhaps she was in a good mood because she was looking forward to making love to her little "Hot Pepper." He loved her, they all knew that, if not why. Perhaps because she seemed oblivious to his deformity. Perhaps because she only heard his deep voice or saw his handsome head. But then, there was the gambling money she would be bringing back from Long Branch to Newark on Monday, and perhaps she feigned her obliviousness to his deformity, and her orgasms, which were occasionally overheard and commented upon by the horror-struck tenants of the roominghouse, as she feigned her heart attacks. Who knew?

They boarded the train with her, as was their practice, and sat with her, waiting for the train to show signs of life. Jimmy wondered if she would give them their movie money, which he felt they had earned, and if it would be enough, and if they would be able to get off the train in time, and not be swept off with her, away from the many glittering marquees of Newark, while she strung it out, cat and mouse. She bullied. His mother strained to be dutiful. He perspired. Aunt Gertrude's perfume was dizzying. The train jerked with coupling. Steam hissed.

"We'd better get off, Aunt Gertrude," his mother said.

"You have plenty of time. You're awfully anxious to get away. Where are you going?"

"Nowhere," said his mother, cowed.

"Well, then, sit still! Oh, by the way, here are a couple of dollars. Why don't you go to a movie? 'Gone With the Wind' is playing at the Adams on Branford Place." But she did not hand over the bills.

"All off!" cried the conductor.

Aunt Gertrude sighed, and handed the bills to Jimmy's mother.

They kissed her and got off the train. Now they must stand and dutifully wave until the heavily laden train puffed out of sight. If they did not stand long enough, she would call them on it next Friday, and they would not get their movie money then. Finally, the train completely disappeared, and they could leave the station and walk back to the center of Newark and study the other worlds of the magical marquees. In those days you really had a choice.

Or so it seemed.

CANDY BUTCHER

*By the time La Guardia was re-elected, the word
"burlesque" had been banned and, soon after,
the Minsky name itself, since the two were
synonymous.*
                                      —*Wikipedia*

This was a new kind of burlesque, Harold Minsky's
burlesque of 1952, with big production numbers reminiscent
of the great follies of an earlier era; and this was the
Saturday night crowd, middle-class and wealthy people,
husbands who had brought their wives, respectable theater-
parties, even an occasional clergyman, come across the
Hudson or in from the suburbs to see at the Adams Theatre
in Newark what Mayor La Guardia had banned from New
York. Now, for the sixth and last time of the day, the oily,
tuxedoed singer leaped from the wings singing the theme
song, a variation on "The Most Beautiful Girl in the
World"—

> *Oh, they're handy—*
> *Oh, they're dandy—*
> *And Minsky girls*

are the most beautiful girls in the W-O-R-L-D! The strip-
pers did a bump-and-grind, twirled the tassels on their
pasties, snapped their G-strings, and strutted off in their
spike-heels. The chain of chorus girls disappeared into the
wings with a sequined kick from its last link. The singer

17

took several bows and stepped off into obscurity. The great purple curtains rushed from the wings, met center-stage, ballooned, and settled.

*   *   *

In his first week at Minsky's Jimmy had his hair cut into a ducktail and bought himself a white-on-white shirt, like the ones the older candy butchers wore. The second week he cut his penny-ante tonk rummy bets—the novelty of the ongoing game was keeping him up till all hours—and managed a pair of blue suede shoes. He had begun to smoke, holding his corktipped cigarettes between his teeth in imitation of Stoney, the hard-faced ex-Marine who was the chief candy butcher for Lou Schenk, the concessionaire. He even attempted to imitate the bitterness Stoney had acquired in an apparently brutal life that had been capped by the Korean War, without quite understanding it to be bitterness, taking it for worldliness, a kind of crude sophistication. But Stoney disliked innocence, and delighted in persecuting it. He practiced his persecution of Jimmy during the all-night card games in the little concession room in the basement of the theater with a form of verbal abuse that had its origins in Marine Corps boot camp and in the black street kids' game of "The Dozens"—piling up ingenious metaphorical insults about one another's mothers. Stoney was the great white hope of "The Dozens."

"My balls itch. Whose Mama can get here first with a good ball-scratcher? You're young, Junior. Maybe your Mama's the fastest runner."

Jimmy thought it prudent not to offer a rejoinder. Stoney was big and raw boned and quick to temper, as Jimmy had observed. No one said a word. Tex and Big Jim, both of whom had at least five years on Jimmy, just sat patiently on their deep, upended trays and played on.

18

*   *   *

Jimmy leaned on the plateglass of the candy stand, smoking, and saw sloe-eyed Marge, the counter girl, staring up at Stoney's hard, handsome face. Jimmy saw her sad eyes and wanted to divert them to himself. He gripped his cigarette in his teeth and swaggered a little in his mind. Marge and Stoney were talking about someone named Sunny.

"Who's Sunny?" he asked.

"A tramp," Stoney said.

"She's not a tramp, Stonewall!"

"Sunny used to be my old lady when she was in the chorus in Bayonne," Stoney said.

"She never was!" cried Marge. "She was a lot too nice for you!"

Stoney ignored her. "She's an usherette," he said, "just hired."

"She's waiting for an opening in the chorus," Marge said, "like me."

Stoney snorted contemptuously. He took Jimmy's elbow and said, "C'mon, Junior. Let's find her." They pushed through the heavy red padded doors of the lobby and into the auditorium. On stage, Flame O'Hair was strutting her stuff. Stoney led Jimmy toward a blonde in an usherette's uniform. "This is Sunny Day, Jimmy. She asked me to introduce you."

Sunny Day smiled, and said: "Hi! I've seen you around and thought we should get acquainted." She had small, pretty teeth and gray eyes. "I'll be off duty in a half hour. I'm going up to the box on the left side to watch the show. Would you like to join me?"

"I don't know," he stuttered. He realized that his knees were beating unrhythmically against the orchestra's drum gambade and that his heart was beating only between

19

cymbal crashes and then in great, breathless gallops. He could feel his pointed ears burning and guessed they were red, perhaps enlarged.

When Jimmy joined Sunny in the dark, brass-railed box she was in street clothes and had undergone a transformation from the cute usherette into a woman of mystery. In the dim stagelight that rose up to them, he could make out the way her knitted dress clung to her voluptuous body. She said, "Hi, again!" as he sat down. Her wide-brimmed hat angled back to the stage. Feathery hopes, fears, and doubts fluttered Jimmy's heart. He was glad that he had stopped to comb his greased, ducktailed hair, and had put on Stoney's suit jacket. His scuffed leather jacket—which he had worn for several years as a Western Union boy, and which had grown much too small for him since he had taken up bodybuilding—would have been out of place, in what he now thought of as this formal setting. It would have completely hidden his white-on-white shirt as well. His knee-bulged dungarees were dark and dirty, but didn't show. He resented the lower darkness, though, for hiding his new, pointed, blue suede shoes.

On stage a long curving sweep of powerful powdered thigh rippled and flexed. From spiked heels two seams ran up mesh-covered flesh, were accented at the round hips and nearly met at the tiny, arching waist. Each gambade shifted the weight of the body from one jutting hip to the other, a pulsing, upside-down heart. Sunny put a hand on his knee and squeezed in rhythm with the music and the stripper's bumps and grinds. Jimmy sat, afraid to move, staring at the stage. Sunny unzipped his jeans, and in a few seconds there was a crescendo of music and motion. She pressed a piece of paper into his palm. "My address," and got up and left him alone in the dark box. He saw the comics come on but had no idea of what they were saying. He heard, "My address, my address, my address. . ." over and over, like the

20

refrain of a song. He had never before had a woman touch him like that. Never before had such a thing been done, he thought, not in all history.

*   *   *

Jimmy waited for two weeks before going to see Sunny. He wasn't sure whether he had avoided the encounter for two full weeks because he didn't want to seem in too much of a hurry or because he was afraid. He was not afraid, he told himself, he just didn't want to seem too eager. Nuts! He was scared to death.

Sunny took Jimmy's leather jacket and woolen scarf and put them over the back of an armchair. She was just out of the shower and her hair was wrapped in a big yellow towel. She was wearing a quilted pink robe and pink pom-pommed slippers. Her feet seemed incredibly small to Jimmy, and the nail polish on her toes glittered like enamel roses. She made him breathless, yet he tried to breathe evenly. He wanted to be cool and smooth.

"Sit down," she said, indicating the couch. "That thing opens into a bed." She smiled at him. "Are you horny?"

"No, I ate. But I'm thirsty."

She laughed, shaking her head, said, "I'll get some beer," and went into the kitchenette.

Jimmy sat like a collapsed puppet on the couch and clumsily fingered a pack of cigarettes. Finally he tore the pack open and stuck a corked tip between his teeth. This was the tenth brand he had tried in as many weeks. So far, these were the best for biting. He took a drag. The smoke got into his eyes and he wiped them quickly with his sweatered sleeve. He heard Sunny getting the beer, the clinking of bottles. The kitchenette had an oilcloth across its doorway. The walls wore faded flowered wallpaper. There was a metal dining set with a plastic top and maple end-

21

tables and a mahogany dresser with a mirror with cards and letters stuck in it. One of the items stuck in the mirror was a picture of Sunny in G-string, pasties, and spike-heels. His sixteen-year-old lust, which he had carried about in him like an overstuffed piñata, felt a near-bursting blow. Sunny came back with a tray, beer, and two stemmed glasses. She smelled of exotic perfume, passion flowers, his nose told him, not that he quite knew what they were.

"You've got a nice apartment here," he said.

"What, this dump? I rent it by the week."

"Isn't the furniture yours?"

"No, it's furnished. I just took it to tide me over when I came in from Bayonne." She saw his extended cigarette ash. "There's an ashtray." She sat down beside him and her quilted robe flapped open, exposing a neat, pale knee. "I never know how to open these things," she said, clinking a bottle-opener on a cap.

"Here," Jimmy said, opening the bottles with shaking hands.

"You're strong," she said. "I can see your biceps through your sweater."

"I lift weights," he said. "I've built myself up from a ninety-eight pound weakling, when I was thirteen, to my present size—almost six feet tall and a hundred and seventy-five pounds—in just over three years. I work out three times a week at the Y, and for the past few years I've done a lot of bicycle-riding. I was a Western Union boy. That really develops your thighs."

"Well, I understand that," she said, "being a dancer."

"I can see you have strong legs, too," he said.

"I have something else. I have something to celebrate tonight. I got a new job. I'll be shuffling off to Buffalo in a few days. A chorus job." She removed the towel from her head and shook out her damp, curly hair.

Jimmy could not connect with her words. He looked at her dark-rooted, orange hair, that looked to him like Rapunzel's golden locks, and wondered how old she was. Thirty? He couldn't tell about women. Then he realized that she was leaving town.

"I wish you weren't going away. I'll miss you."

He could never understand how women got their clothes to fit them as they did; how, for instance, they got their full hips through the narrow waistbands of their slacks. He had pondered these things.

"Why didn't you come up and see me sooner? I might not have taken the job in Buffalo."

"Well, I was kind of—"

"Scared? You've never been with a woman, have you? C'mon now, tell Sunny truth." She laughed, touched his cheek, and pushed back some of his fair hair. "I wish you'd change the way you wear your hair. It'd look nice without all that grease in it, loose and curly."

"I will—if you won't go away." He bounced his glass on the table and put his hand decisively on her knee.

She shuddered. "Oh, your hand's still cold!"

Jimmy held his ground for a moment, his eyes widening, then withdrew.

Sunny smiled, and affectionately added to the rumpled state of his hair. "That's all right," she said, putting his hand back. "Go ahead."

"Sure is hot in here."

"Why don't you take off your sweater?"

He stood up and pulled his sweater over his head, tousling his hair in a wild, electric disarray.

"My," she said. "I think you've got something for me."

*   *   *

A few nights later, Jimmy groped through the littered outer cellar of his parents' basement home, which was the superintendent's apartment of a rooming house, guided only by the demonic red eyes and teeth of the roaring jack-o'-lantern furnace. He reached out before him in the dark, acutely aware of his new gloves. They would protect him should he touch something sharp or hot. Sunny had come to the theater to pick up her final check and had brought them with her.

"For my curly-head," she had said. "Your hands looked red and raw when you visited me. But I shouldn't give them to you."

"Why not?"

"Because you told me a lie."

"What lie?"

"You pretended you had never been with a woman. But I know better, don't I?" She had kissed him quickly on the cheek and hurried off.

Now the tight smile of light from under the door of the basement apartment stirred mixed feelings. He wanted to tell somebody about himself and Sunny, but there was nobody to tell, nobody willing to listen. Once inside, he'd be doing the listening. He loitered in the dark, shadow-boxing without shadows to box. "Take *that!* Stoney—and *that!*" He wondered if Sunny had told Stoney about them. She had sworn to him that she had not told Stoney, but Stoney seemed to know and had been ragging him unmercifully. As he boxed there in the dark, it occurred to him that Sunny was probably in Buffalo. Would it ever happen again? His gloved hands dropped to his sides. It would never happen again—never, never! And he loved Sunny, *loved* her! Emotion shook through him. He wiped his eyes on his sleeves, the backs of his gloves.

Inside, his father sat at the table, wearing his mother's

kimono. He greeted Jimmy with: "Quoth the Raven, Nevermore!"

Immediately echoed by: "Quoth the Raven, yourself!" Jimmy's mother rose from a bed in a corner. She was wearing his father's overcoat. "He's been like this for hours, Jimmy. *Quoth the Raven! Quoth the Raven!* I can't stand it anymore. He's been drunk for weeks. He's supposed to sell books. When was the last book you sold? Look at us, here in this hole in the ground! Look!" Jimmy looked at the dripping, crisscrossing pipes, the painted-over, black-speckled bricks of the walls, where the bedbugs lived, the faded linoleum roses. . . .

"The Wizard of Oz!"

Jimmy looked at his father. "Mom's right, Dad. Look at us! Look at this place! We can't live here. Nobody can!"

"That's what I've been telling him. That's what I've been saying. What I've been telling *you!* Nobody'll listen to me. It's mid-winter and we have no back wall, just a rug slung up to keep out the cold. If it weren't for the furnace outside the front door, we'd freeze. In fact, we ought to knock out that beaverboard partition so we can get more heat."

"Mom's right, Dad. This is the worst yet."

"Just one minute, young man," said his father, raising a finger. "Since when do you decide policy?"

"Since he sees his mother in this terrible condition."

"People can't live like this, Dad."

"People can and do. But let me propose the biblical solution to you both. If your home offends you, pluck yourselves from it!"

"He doesn't know what he's saying, Jimmy. Don't pay any attention to him."

"It is *you* who never knows what you're saying—or doing," said his father. He gave Jimmy a conspiratorial

25

look. "Did you know that she found a woman's photograph in your suitcase?"

"Sunny's picture?" Jimmy looked at his mother. "Mom, you didn't have any right to go through my things. I have a right to *some* privacy."

"No, you don't! Not when you're only sixteen and might be getting into all kinds of trouble."

"Where is it?"

"I tore it up. What do you think? A picture of a half-naked tramp with 'I'll never forget you' on it! I only hope you didn't have anything to do with her. You might have a social disease."

* * *

It was Saturday night again, the big night, and the last show was over. Jimmy sat with his friend, Tex, in a bar that was catty-corner across the intersection from the theater. Through a soft, steady fall of snow he saw the Minsky marquee-lights dowse out. He had plugged the jukebox with a nickel to hear his favorite song, "Rags to Riches." The crooner understood how he felt.

"Look, Junior," said Tex, "the lady's got to live her life. She's got to take a job when she gets the chance. You can't go moping around like this—'taint good for you. Go on, now—drink your beer. The chorus line's full of girls who would be glad to sleep with you."

"Nobody else is like Sunny. She made me feel like somebody cared about me."

Stoney and his ne'er-do-well buddy, Big Jim, emerged from the backroom, where they'd been shooting pool. "How's the virgin?" said Stoney. He was drunk and disgruntled, having lost a game and a five-spot to Big Jim. "Poor Jimmy Junior! Does he miss his ladylove? You dumb shit, Junior! Playing romance with these whores

26

makes me sick. Haven't you figured out that I put her up to it?"

"What do you mean?"

"He don't mean nothin'," said Tex. "Don't pay no attention to him."

"I mean I told her to make a man out of you."

"He didn't, neither," said Tex. "He's just teasing you, Jimmy."

"Butt out, Tex!" said Big Jim.

"She liked me," said Jimmy. "She gave me these gloves."

"Let me see those," said Stoney. "Look!" He held the gloves out for Big Jim's inspection.

"These are *my* gloves, Junior. I lost them in Bayonne a year ago. Now you turn up with them. I must have left them at her place."

"They're brand-new," Jimmy protested.

"They were brand-new when I lost them."

"Put them on," said Tex. "If they fit, then we know."

"I told you to butt out, hillbilly," said Big Jim.

Stoney threw the gloves on the bar. "I don't have to prove anything to a punk like you, Junior. Keep the damned things." He gave Jimmy's shoulder a scornful pat. Then he smiled. "*C'mon!* She's just a whore. Hell, Junior, they're all *whores.*"

Lou Schenk, their boss, got up from a booth and came over, tough and bulky. "Push off, Stoney," he said. "You're drunk. Go home and sleep it off."

Stoney looked at Jimmy and laughed ridicule, shrugged indifference, threw an arm over Big Jim's shoulder, and allowed himself to be walked to the door. Jimmy picked up the gloves and pulled them on, tenderly.

Suddenly he convulsed, his eyes making a small shower of tears. Standing, he gripped the bar-rim hard in his gloved hands and hung his head between his arms. He

27

looked down at a brass rail and a tin spittoon filled with floating butts.

"She was a *pig*, Junior," Stoney called back from the door.

From deep in Jimmy's throat came a sound like the howl of a wolf, and he ran out into the black-and-white lacework street after Stoney. "You bastards!" he screamed after the snow-curtained figures who walked ahead. "You liar, Stoney! She *liked* me, you rotten son-of-a-bitch!"

Lou Schenk and Tex had followed Jimmy into the street, grabbing after him. In his hurry the heavy concessionaire slipped on the iced-over sidewalk. Jimmy was only vaguely aware of Lou's curses and Tex's nervous laughter. Ahead, Stoney detached himself from Big Jim and turned back. "Apologize, Junior, or I'll come back there and teach you some Marine Corps manners. I warn you: *Apologize!*"

From somewhere Marge had appeared. "Stop it, Stoney!" she called. "Stop it!"

"Shut up, bitch!" Stoney yelled. He stalked forward, eyes glittering drunken anger, intent on Jimmy.

Jimmy hesitated. Then Tex said: "Go to, Junior! Git 'im!" Jimmy took a step forward.

"No, no!" cried Marge. "Stop them, somebody. You'll all end up in jail!" She held a cigarette and her gesticulations tracked up and down in the gloom.

Then Stoney slipped on the ice, and Jimmy pounced on him, pummeling him with his gloved hands, hitting his face, his shoulders, his flailing arms, sometimes just hitting packed ice. It was his life he pounded. Then he felt hot flashes on his face: Marge was burning him with her cigarette, sticking it in his cheek, his temple.

"You bitch!" he heard Tex say, and felt Marge being pulled from him. He heard her scream in short, shocking spurts. But he was in a dream, a nightmare. He pounded his life until he felt himself being pulled from Stoney's inert

28

form by Lou Schenk, heard the concessionaire's deep soft calming voice commanding him gently to stop, to be still. Then he was being manhandled by a pair of burly blue policemen.

*   *   *

Jimmy's father said, "I have the shakes, snakes, and the dancing bears, but I'll be all right in a few days."

"I know you will, Dad."

"Now, what's this you want me to do?"

"I want you to sign me up so I can go in the Marines."

"You can't go in the Marines," said his mother. "You're not old enough."

"Always the nay-sayer," said his father.

"I'll be seventeen on my next birthday. That's old enough, if I have your permission."

His father looked at his mother. "He can do what he wants to do if he has the courage to do it." He smiled blearily at Jimmy. "I'll sign you up."

"And be rid of you," his mother said. "That's all he wants. He'd like to sign me up, too, but I keep the rooming-house going."

"I'd like to sign up your voice," said his father.

*   *   *

Stoney, Big Jim, Tex, and Lou Schenk were in the concession room getting ready for the matinee. Jimmy felt a nervous embarrassed pride at seeing that Stoney had a black eye and a blue bruise on his jutting jaw. His stomach shook as he did a stationary swagger that said: Don't tread on me.

"Here he is," cried Big Jim. He looked at Stoney. "Aincha gonna do nothin'?"

Stoney shrugged, morose, subdued, sober.

29

"No," said Lou Schenk, "he ain't gonna do nothin', an' neither are you. I don't want no trouble among my butchers. I got a business to run. If it wasn't for me all of you'd be in jail right now." He turned his attention to Jimmy. "I like you, Junior. You got a lot of guts, showing up here. I didn't think you'd have the nerve to come in today. But I got to let you go. Stoney's my number one butcher. I need him."

"That's O.K., Lou. I figured. I just came in to say goodbye, and no hard feelings to anybody. O.K. Stoney?"

Stoney nodded.

"So—well—that's it."

Tex walked Jimmy out of the concession room and through the theater. "What are you going to do?" he asked.

"I'm going to join the Marines, Tex. The Marines build men. Look at Stoney. If he'd been sober, why he'da beat the crap out of me. And right, too. I don't know what got into me."

"You really mean to join the Marines?"

"If they'll have me."

"Oh, they'll have you, Junior, don't worry about that." He thought for a minute, as if remembering. "Well, it ain't nothin' here," he said, indicating the darkened theater. "It's the big burlesque out there. Hell's bells, Junior, it's all a big burlesque. You do it all."

HOW TO FLOAT

They found the coast of China colder than Kobe, the straits full of frayed fog, like a gray curtain, a fine, wet, disheveled lace, that seemed to rise from the gray ship's pregnant sides, and up into a threatening sky. About them distances opened like hall doors, and then they could see where they had been, or might be going, which was, a low, colorless land too distant to see clearly, too close and ominous for comfort. Oh why had they joined the Marines? Not for this murky ocean and that misty land. Their feckless rifles were aimed toward imagined Chinese hordes. Later, they read in the papers of how near to war they had been; the whole world was in fact near to war. But once more diplomacy resolved the terrible threat, at least for the time being, and, after two nerve-wracking, sleepless weeks of hazardous duty, of crisscross cruising, the ship took a scudding turn in the Straits of Formosa, making a long, curving wake, followed by swooping, screaming gulls, famished for the jetsam and trying to land on the blurred, floating letters of farewell the Marines had written home. With hosannas of thanksgiving, their lucky ship set course for Hawaii, O happy day!

The 3rd Shore Party Battalion of the 4th Marines, Fleet Marine Force Pacific, Kaneohe Bay, Oahu, Territory of Hawaii, got a new education officer. Lt. Bland was assigned directly to Jimmy Whistler's outfit, Company B, and immediately held a white-glove inspection. Bland stopped at Jimmy's footlocker and dug into his books.

"You read Faulkner?"

"Yes, sir!"

"What's this?"

"Paradise Lost, sir. Milton."

"You're half through it?"

"Yes, sir."

"I read it at Stanford," said Bland, in cultivated tones. "I took engineering, but I read a lot of literature. I'm a Catholic—have you read Dante?"

"Not yet, sir. He's next—after Milton."

"I understand you box."

"My box?" Jimmy looked down at his footlocker—was something wrong?

"You're a boxer."

"Oh, yes, sir. I'm on the boxing team."

"And you're a weight lifter?"

"Yes, sir."

"How much can you bench press?"

"About three-twenty-five, sir."

"Not bad. I can do about three-fifty."

"That's very good, sir."

"You know I'm the new education officer for the battalion, don't you?"

"Yes, sir. I've been told that."

"I want you to report to my office after inspection."

Jimmy duly reported and was told to sit down across the desk from Lt. Bland.

"Now here's the thing," said Bland. "I've looked over your records. I see you have a unit citation for hazardous duty in the Formosa business. I've never been in any kind of action. What was it like?"

"Boring—when we weren't scared, sir. We were put on three LSTs and sailed down from Japan and into the Formosa Straits. We sailed back and forth along the coast of China for about two weeks, then we got an order for our ship to peel off and come here to Hawaii."

"Go on."

"That's about it. We didn't know what it was all about until we got here and read it in the papers. Then we found out we were close to war. Ike—President Eisenhower— threatened the Communists with atomic weapons and they backed down. And we were given the medal."

"I bet you were glad to get here."

"Yes, sir. It was good to know I was back in the States."

"Do you think Hawaii will ever be a state?"

"Oh yes, sir! No doubt about it."

"Do you have any close buddies in this outfit?"

"You don't have friends in the service, sir, just military acquaintances."

"You're a bit of a loner, aren't you?"

"There's not many guys to share Milton with, sir." Jimmy thought Bland was a very impressive fellow, friendly but sharp. He felt that here at last was a guy he could hit it off with—too bad he was an officer. He wondered what Bland was after. He suspected that there was a method in this apparently random questioning.

"What did you do before you joined up? I see you dropped out of school."

"Sir, I was a Western Union boy for a few years. Then I was a candy butcher at Minsky's Burlesque in Newark— hawked candy, orange drinks, popcorn, girly magazines, like that, sir."

Then Lt. Bland said, "How would you like to be a Naval Air Cadet? NavCad? You could become an officer and a pilot. I want to give you a series of academic and intelligence tests—are you willing to try?" Jimmy figured he had nothing to lose and said, "Yes, sir."

Jimmy wrote home and told his parents about this. His

mother wrote back, saying that his father completely disapproved and she agreed with his father. Elliot Whistler had lost a son by a previous marriage, an RAF pilot, shot down in 1941. He would not have another son flying. So both were against him becoming a pilot, as his mother had been against him becoming a writer, a boxer, a weight lifter, a Marine, or just about anything. Even his father called her "The Negative Force." But his father joined her in being against flying, so it was two-to-one, or two-to-two, if he could count on Bland.

Night after night, Jimmy thought about his parents, often dreamed of them. They seemed always on the run from a bad check or an overdue rooming house bill, or in search of better sales territory or an even cheaper rent. Sometimes they moved twice in a week: twice a month was ordinary. Jimmy rarely attended school, and then it was usually only for a short time. Now they were superintending a rooming house in Newark. His mother had written because his father was on a three-month drunk. Someday Jimmy would come home, and go to work in a factory, and help support them, she suggested. Nothing must happen to him in the meantime. That was his future as they saw it. It seemed a very bleak future to Jimmy. He planned to go to school on the G.I. Bill. He intended to become a writer. Becoming a Naval Air Cadet would eliminate a good many steps in his progress. But soon a second letter came, this time from his father, who had sobered up: by no means should he follow this dangerous course. Look at what had happened to his half-brother! His father was a fairly good writer when he was sober. He had been a W.P.A. writer, and once wrote speeches for the mayor of Newark. Jimmy remembered his father walking him along the little wall that fronted the Newark City Hall, holding his hand. He must have been about five then, and so proud of his father. These days his father was a door-to-door salesman, and fancied himself an

34

expert in making people agree with him. His father's letter put a damper on Jimmy's enthusiasm for cadet training. But the more tests Jimmy took, the closer he and Lt. Bland became, and Jimmy felt torn between the ideas of the two.

Despite the rules against fraternization, Jimmy and Bland began to meet at Waikiki. They would sit in their bathing suits in the shade of the Banyan Court at the Royal Hawaiian Hotel, drink Mai-Tais, and watch the waves and the surfers roll in. Bland loaned Jimmy a book on tank warfare, another on fighting the Huks in the Philippines. "We must never get into a land war in Asia," he told Jimmy. "Read the book and see why." Bland was probably about twenty-five, but he seemed a fountain of wisdom, which was why Jimmy did not want to disappoint him.

"Think of it," said Bland, "you'll be flying the newest jet planes! Pretty exciting, eh?"

Jimmy thought of his mother and father, and Bland noticed his frown. "Look what I've brought along," he said, digging into a duffle bag. "I'm going to teach you to play chess. I give us a week and you'll be beating me."

As a Shore Party Logistics man, Jimmy had made many beach landings, jumping out of the landing craft in helmet-high water while loaded down with a fifty-pound pack, rifle, cartridge belt, canteen, medical kit, bayonet, etc. Many times he had gone under, only getting his head back above water with the greatest effort, despite his strength. Even if he could swim, he couldn't swim in such a getup. And the truth was, that, in spite of all the time he had spent in YMCA and other gyms, he had not learned to swim. He was taught again in the Marines, but it didn't take, and, though the Marines said he could swim, and had certified him, he did not believe it. He tried at the Armed Services Y in Honolulu, but could only keep from drowning by the most strenuous effort, which, despite his strength, he could not maintain. It was as if his forever negative mother was

35

there to say, "You can't learn to swim at your age," as she had said, on his sixteenth birthday, when asked what he wanted to be and answered that he would like to be a writer, if he could.

"You can't be a writer. You have no education." She seemed to stand by the pool, scorning his efforts—and he sank, and sank again, and again.

Another beach landing was coming up. He wasn't a malingerer, but the redundancy of these landings was getting to him. He decided to goldbrick on this one, go to sickbay with a minor ear infection—why he had misheard Bland at the inspection—and spend a few days on his rack, reading and smoking Lucky Strikes. He had just started *The Revolt of Mamie Stover*, when a group of MPs appeared at the empty squadbay doors and called his name. He called back, and discovered that he had been assigned to a military police unit called the HASP, for the Hawaiian Armed Services Police. He stuffed *Mamie Stover* in his back pocket and found himself walking into her world of prostitution and violence. This is what he got for trying to get out of something. Served him right, he guessed.

HASP headquarters was on Ala Moana in Honolulu. The HASP itself was composed of a patrol section, a motor-cycle section, an AWOL apprehension section, an investigative section, an aid station, and several lockups. All services were represented. Training was on the job. There was a barracks area on the second floor where Jimmy was assigned a bunk. This was something of a come-down from the beautiful surroundings at Kaneohe Bay, across the enchanted Pali mountains. Jimmy felt as if he had returned to Kobe, Japan, or, worse, Newark. He was assigned to the patrol section, which meant that he had to walk about like a street cop with a forty-five pistol on his hip and a nightstick in his hand, and break up fights and arrest trouble-makers. Apparently, he had been chosen for this select outfit because

36

he was big, strong, smart, and, most of all, available. If he had gone on the beach landing this would not have happened, he reasoned. But it was a lucky break in a way, too. Now he didn't have to decide between Bland's and his mother's and father's versions of his future. Not for the present, at least. That very night, he found himself patrolling Hotel Street, part of which was known as "Hell's Half Acre." This was where all the action was, bars, fights, killings, prostitution, etc. It was the job of the HASP to keep it under control.

He had been on the job for about two months, when one night he saw a transvestite followed into a men's room by two sailors. Suspecting the sailors of being up to no good, he followed them in in time to stop them from completing the beating of the transvestite that had already resulted in a long-lashed eye being popped out. One of the sailors had the transvestite's money, in an initialed clip. He arrested both sailors and took them to Ala Moana, where they were charged. An ambulance had taken the transvestite away from the bar. Next day, Jimmy received a letter from the Chief of Police, honoring his work. It turned out that the transvestite was a relative of the Chief's. Jimmy found himself to be something of a hero. Several other incidents added to his reputation. A bottle across his face also added a broken nose and several minor scars. But he was beginning to like being a cop—you could do some good, he thought. Jimmy was not what he called "a badge and a whistle man," self-important. He avoided seeing as much trouble as he could.

He wrote to Lt. Bland and told him he would not be going to NavCad. Bland wrote back, telling him he had passed his one year college equivalency test, and that his I.Q. score was very high indeed. He would be crazy, wrote Bland, to miss this opportunity. "It will change your whole life."

Up or down, which way would he go? Which way *should* he go? He wrote to his parents and told them he would not rise into flight, but continue to walk the soiled if solid ground of Hotel Street. It'll be Newark next, and Minsky's Burlesque house, back where I started from. Or a by-the-hour worker at the scissors factory on Halsey Street, or the chewing gum factory in Bayonne. That's what you really want from me, he thought. But still, he harbored dreams of his own. He thought he might go to a drama school, become an actor, and later a playwright. He filled his secret notebooks with poems and plots. He would think of lines he thought beautiful while patrolling among the low-life on Hotel Street, in the heart of "Hell's Half Acre." Above the street, with its tawdriness, was the sky, blue and cloud-scudding by day, and full of stars by night.

He would check into the Armed Services YMCA, when on liberty, and spend the weekend in his room, reading. He read the Pocket Bible straight through on one weekend. Occasionally, of a morning, he would try to swim the length of the Y's Olympic-sized pool, from the deep end to the shallow, just in case his strength began to fail. He could do it with the power of his arms and chest, but nothing would allow him to float. He had to use all his strength or he would sink and drown. It wasn't that he couldn't swim but that he couldn't float. Bland seemed to have given up on him. His parents seemed to have forgotten him again. No letters came. He had no girlfriend. There had been a whirl of military activity and travel that precluded getting to know any women, and he had no taste for prostitutes or even B-girls, both of whom he worked among. He was lonely a good deal of the time, even in the middle of the noise and activity of Hotel Street.

And wherever you looked, people caused you trouble, or betrayed you. Jimmy had been sending money home, so that he might have a nest egg to start out on, and had recently written to his parents asking if his financial records matched theirs. They flat out denied ever receiving a cent. They had stolen his money—probably used it on booze— and didn't even have the good grace to be honest about it. If they had asked, Jimmy would have given them the money. It was the betrayal that hurt, the lying. They were all he knew of love and they sided together against him.

Suddenly he couldn't breathe. He was drowning in murky water, held down by an enormous weight, something on his back, a man or a woman, holding him under. His scream was a gurgle, and he waked, sitting up on his bunk, his whole body wet. What was he going to do?

Then, in the usual mysterious way of the military, Jimmy was transferred out of the HASP, and assigned back at the Kaneohe Brig to be a prison chaser, one who takes prisoners from one locale to another. The HASP had to keep their limited lockups cleared, so they would send mixed batches of Army, Navy, Marine, Air Force, whatever, to any brig or stockade that could house them, then sort them out, and the chasers would take them back to their own base lockups. Jimmy took the dog-faces to Schofield, the swab-jockeys to Pearl, and the flyboys to Hickam, shotgun at the ready.

One bright morning, Jimmy had to report to the Provost Marshal's Office over an incident in the mess hall. The prisoners had a schedule, and there was some pressure of time to get them fed and back to the brig. Jimmy had ordered about fifty prisoners to the head of the line. He had the authority to do this, but usually the prisoners had to wait their turn, along with the non-prisoners, all of whom ate in the same mess hall. There was a gung-ho corporal named Dunkel who was interested in getting ahead in the military police, another chaser, like Jimmy, but with more brig experience, though he lacked Jimmy's background in the HASP, and may have been jealous of it. Dunkel made a big stink about what Jimmy had done, demanded his sidearm and his armband right there in front of everyone, and made a virtual arrest. Now the question of who was right was going to be settled by the Provost. Jimmy didn't give a damn who won. If he won, things would go on as usual. If Dunkel won, Jimmy would probably be placed back in his Shore Party unit, which he missed. If he could get himself back under Lt. Bland's control, he might re-think the NavCad idea. After all, he had a right to his own life, especially after his parents had stolen his money, their latest betrayal. But the question was settled in Jimmy's favor. He had been thinking of the well-being of the prisoners and the safety of the situation. It was not a good idea to keep a large group of prisoners, anxious to eat, and to get on with their day, waiting for other units to go through ahead of them. He had used good judgment. On the contrary, Dunkel's actions had been considered over the top, extreme, generally not very sensible. Dunkel did not hide his hatred. Outside, he spit at Jimmy's feet, and Jimmy would have to work with him for God knew how long! Sometimes winning was worse than losing.

There was scuttlebutt about what was going to happen at the brig. For reasons beyond Jimmy's understanding, there was a dearth of rank on the base. The Turnkey was going stateside. He was a staff-sergeant. There were no more men of that level, only corporals, like Dunkel and himself, and privates first class and buck privates. The scuttlebutt was that one of the corporals was going to become Turnkey. Jimmy did not want the job. Let the gung-ho Dunkel have the job. Jimmy was content to ferry the prisoners about. But now he feared that the incident between himself and Dunkel might put him in the lead position to get the job. That was the last thing he wanted. He had a low opinion of power-seekers.

In an effort to get all his troubles off his mind, he took

off by himself. He thought he would go down to Hotel Street, have a few drinks, and then go to a Chinese restaurant he favored and have a good meal. He was wearing slacks and an Hawaiian shirt. Blond, bronzed, and athletic, he passed the entrance to an upstairs dance hall. In his experience, these countless dance halls started young girls off as hostesses and quickly turned them into prostitutes. This was ordinarily none of his business. Bad things were always happening in Hell's Half Acre. But this time his attention was caught. A youthful female voice had cried out. An angry male voice had responded. Jimmy turned back and looked up the stairway. A man with the body of a Sumo wrestler had a pretty young Hawaiian girl pinned to the wall about half-way up a wide, twenty-foot stairway.

"What's going on up there?" Jimmy called.

"Help me," cried the girl. "I want to go home!" The girl was crying, and trying to twist loose from the big ape's grasp.

"Get lost," said Sumo, "this is none of your business." He was a bouncer type, part Polynesian, part Oriental, or some such mixture. But it was hard to tell. The light was dim in the upper reaches of the stairway. "You came here," he said to the girl, "now you stay."

"Let her go," said Jimmy.

"Mind your own business." The big man showed Jimmy his full face. Jimmy felt a cold chill run up his spine. The man's face wore a full tiger head tattoo. Jimmy got a grip on himself.

"I'm military police," he called up, and waved his wallet at the man. "Now let her go." To locals, the Military Police was the same as the Civilian Police, since they worked together. The man let go of the girl. He seemed to be waiting for orders. Jimmy said, "Miss, you come down here." He pointed up at the man. "You stay right where you are. Got it?" The man gave Jimmy a surly, but assenting

41

nod, and the girl broke free and stumbled, tears streaming, down the ten or so steps to join Jimmy.

"Stay put," Jimmy warned again, pointing at the man, and took the girl's arm and walked her briskly to the corner. "There," he said. "You're free."

"Please, don't leave me," she begged. "I'm afraid they'll come after me, and I don't have any money." Now Jimmy saw that she was a beautiful child, perhaps sixteen or so, an exquisite Polynesian girl with eyes like black full moons. Sweet Leilani herself.

"What did you do, run away from home?"

"Yes. But it was a big mistake," she said, through tears. "I want to go home."

They walked a little way and Jimmy hailed a cab. "Tell the driver where you live." It was some place Jimmy had never heard of.

"What's your name?"

"Leilani Kona."

"Sweet Leilani?" he asked, opening the cab door.

"Another one. Not the original. She was a white girl."

"Have you been—uh—molested?" he asked, slipping in beside her.

"No. But it would not be so, if you hadn't come along. I have only been here today. I have heard stories, but I didn't know how bad it was down here."

"Pretty bad," said Jimmy, looking out at Hotel Street.

"Oh, but it is beautiful. You mustn't think that it is all like Hotel Street. It *is* paradise."

"I guess I've just seen too many of the wrong places."

"You'll see, when we get to my village—you'll see how beautiful it is."

"Then why did you leave it?"

"I was full of curiosity about the wild side. You're young. Aren't you full of curiosity?"

42

"I come from a tough town in New Jersey called Newark. I left there to go to a tough town in Japan called Kobe. I ended up here in a tough town called Honolulu. They all seem the same to me."

"You are a tough guy, aren't you?"

He looked at her. Was she kidding him?

"Not so tough, I suppose."

"No," she said, "not so tough, I suppose."

When the taxi finally pulled in to the bamboo village, it reminded Jimmy of the Jungle Jim movies he had seen as a boy. He half expected to see Johnny Weissmuller in his white hunter outfit emerge from one of the grass huts. What appeared to be the whole village of at least two hundred souls gathered around them, speaking a clicking, excited Polynesian tongue. It appeared that Jimmy's runaway girl was not just ordinary, but a celebrity of some kind. She began to translate for Jimmy's benefit.

"They are relieved and happy to see me," she said. "Here come my father and mother." They came open-armed and seized their daughter in a loving embrace. Leilani told Jimmy that her father could be called "the Chief," so that was how Jimmy thought of him. He was the apparent head of the village, his wife the Queen Bee. Now Jimmy saw that his Leilani was a sort of Princess.

Jimmy had expected to let the girl out, and have the cabbie take him back to Honolulu, but the Chief pulled Jimmy from the cab and sent it off without him. For a moment, Jimmy thought he was going to be lynched, but then he realized that everyone was smiling. Then he thought of cannibals, but he had never heard of any on the islands. Finally, Leilani told him that her parents, indeed, the whole village, considered him a hero, who had saved her from a fate worse than death, and the big luau being prepared was now, that very evening. So he would eat, not be eaten. He was much relieved, and told Leilani so, who at first laughed

43

at his apprehension, and now laughed at his flushed embarrassment.

"But I didn't do anything," he said. Leilani turned to her father and said a few words, then back to Jimmy: "Yes you did! I told them all about it, what the tiger-faced man was trying to do to me, and how you stopped him and brought me home." Jimmy received the first of many affectionate pats on the back from Leilani's father, who told him that the luau had been planned for Leilani's sixteenth birthday, but that now it was for him, Jimmy, her savior, as well.

"You are going to have a real feast. We've been working on it for days." He put an arm over Jimmy's shoulder. "Leilani is going to be punished for running off like this, but we'll see to that later. Right now we're so happy to have her back, we don't intend to do anything to spoil her birthday, and we intend to honor you, young man, so please enjoy yourself." A busy man, he vanished into the crowd. A band—guitar, bass and ukulele—struck up and a few people began dancing. The Chief appeared out of the crowd and handed Jimmy a cold beer. Jimmy had no sooner finished that one when he was handed another. The party was in full swing. Leilani sat with Jimmy and showed him how to eat the pork and poi in the proper Hawaiian way. Through the interstices of the trees Jimmy saw the sky over the sea explode in reds and blues and trailers of white and the moon become huge and gold and close. At last, morning light showed through the jungle fronds and fans, but the luau was still in full swing—deep drums now and grass skirt dancing—and the Chief forced bowl after bowl of a powerful Polynesian drink on him. He shrugged and chugalugged and the party continued right into the full red dawn that came to that true paradise, blue Hawaii.

Jimmy woke slowly, only gradually realizing that he lay on a beach, safely up from the surf. He saw Burt

44

Lancaster and Deborah Kerr rolling around together in the surf, making passionate love. Had he got inside the movie screen, for the beach rose right up to him, where he lay? He looked behind him and saw a seaside village nosing out of the vegetation: a little grass shack, or the corner of a little grass shack, prow emerging as if to slide down and into the water. Fleecy clouds were passing the sun's brightness down to him. The blue Pacific's horizon rose to the left of him, a tilted picture. Far off an outrigger seemed to ride on its side. He sat up with a start, and things straightened out. Lancaster and Kerr became driftwood. He took a few deep breaths of the wonderful salt sea air, and his head began to clear. But where was he? Then he heard high, tinkling laughter, and almost immediately Leilani emerged from the direction of the grass shack, carrying a tray. He smelled coffee—Leilani, of course. The luau. Her father's potent brew.

"Good morning, Mister Jim. You want some coffee?"

"Thanks. That smells wonderful." He took a few sips of black coffee. "What am I doing here?"

"You passed out. I thought you were safe enough—besides, I sat beside you until early dawn."

Jimmy drank more of the coffee. "You know," he said, "I never knew there were villages like this—I mean, a hundred years ago, maybe, but today . . . "

"There aren't too many of the real thing left. Kona Village is my father's idea. Did you like the luau?"

"I did. And I seem to remember people saying that it was in my honor, for bringing you home safely."

"That was a last minute change. They dedicated my birthday luau to you."

"What do you mean about the village being your father's idea?"

"This is a commercial venture. This was all an old sugar mill. My father bought up a big patch of the land,

45

including the old mill, to make a hideaway hotel and restaurant. Visitors can come and see how the sugar mill worked. They can enjoy a luau with entertainment, dancers, etc., and sleep in a modernized version of a grass hut. It's a business. It'll be open for tourists in a few months. My father owns a number of businesses. You didn't take all this seriously, did you?"

"But they *were* speaking Hawaiian. I couldn't understand a word they said."

"They were giving you the atmosphere. Everybody here speaks perfect English. Honestly, Jimmy, I didn't think you were fooled. It wasn't our intention to fool you. We, I, at least, just thought you were playing along, for the fun of it."

"What a dope I am. It must have been all that kick-a-poo joy-juice."

"Do you feel better now? The best thing to do is to take a dive in the ocean. Come on, Kimo, take your clothes off."

"Who's Kimo?"

"You. Kimo is Jim in Hawaiian. Come on, Kimo, into the ocean with you."

Jimmy stripped down to his skivvies and ran into the water with her, the trill of her laughter higher than the waves, echoing back from the taut cyclorama of blue-drum sky.

*   *   *

The secret machinery of the Marine Corps had decided. Jimmy received orders to report to the Provost Marshal's office to receive orientation. He was to be the new Turnkey at the Kaneohe Marine Corps Brig. Jimmy had just finished reading *From Here to Eternity*, and ugly visions of Fatso, the Turnkey at Scofield, who had brutalized Maggio in the novel, came to mind. How could he, Jimmy Whistler, have gotten himself into such a situation? He bet Lt. Bland was behind this unwanted advancement. Bland knew by now that Jimmy was not going to take him up on his offer to send him to NavCad training. This was either his way of advancing Jimmy, or perhaps his way of punishing him. As he had always proclaimed, people either betray you or get you in trouble, even when they don't mean to. Shun friendship, stick to military acquaintanceship. Keep people at a distance! Jimmy went to the base Chaplain.

"Isn't there some way you can get me out of this, sir?" he asked.

"Why should you want out?"

"I don't want to be a Turnkey, sir. I'm not right for it."

"The Marine Corps thinks you're right for it."

"They're wrong."

"I doubt it. Now, if you have any other problems . . . ?"

"Don't you see, sir, this is a mistaken attempt to help me along in my career. Lt. Bland is doing this because he thinks I ought to be in charge of something."

"I doubt if Lt. Bland has anything to do with this. This is probably the result of the incident that brought you to the attention of the Provost Marshal's Office in the first place." Jimmy returned two more times to state his case and received the same answer: "The Marine Corps thinks you're right for it. You can't outguess the Marine Corps, son. Now just go and do your duty."

There was nothing to be done. Jimmy was Turnkey of the Kaneohe Marine Corps Air Station Brig, and he would have to like it or lump it. He promised himself he would be the most humane Turnkey in history. He would not allow the chasers to pull any rough stuff, especially Dunkel, who was always eager to use force. Dunkel was the kind who, if given free rein, would end up as a war criminal. But Dunkel was not going to get his way in any brig run by Jimmy.

"I'm not going to let him push those guys around," he told Leilani on one of his many visits to her village. They

47

held hands and took walks through the jungle to the nearby beach. Leilani was teaching him to swim, as others before her had.

"There is so much tension in your body. You must relax. It is because you are so tight inside that you can't float. Try to forget about Dunkel and your mother and father and even your friend Lt. Bland. Now breathe in slowly and ease back on my arms."

"You can't hold me up," he told her, but found himself floating on her brown arms, and looking up at her great dark eyes that reflected the sunset over the horizon. "You're so beautiful," he said. She took her hands from beneath his back and pushed him under.

"You'll learn someday," she said, when he had shaken the water out of his ears.

"Learn what?" he said, laughing.

"You are like a rock, but you will learn to float. You will learn to be a floating rock. That's a rare thing."

"Impossible," he said.

"No, the islands have lava that will float."

"I don't believe it."

"You don't believe anything. That's why you can't float. Look," and she leaned back into the water and swam into the sunset, so that his eyes couldn't find her, and then she rose up beside him, sleek, like a seal, lithe and laughing.

Months went by, and under Jimmy's supervision the Brig ran smoothly. But it *was* a responsibility of nightmarish proportions. Sometimes it got the better of him and he'd spend the night in an Hotel Street bar, drinking into forgetfulness. One night a couple of HASP patrolmen made a routine stop in a dive and, recognizing him, started a conversation.

"Hear you're the Turnkey at Kaneohe now," one said. "Look, do you need a ride back to base? We'll get you one." They seemed concerned about him. Perhaps Jimmy looked too drunk to maneuver. One of them said, "We better get him back to his brig."

"No, no," Jimmy protested, then everything went blank. Next thing he knew, he was brought to the brig barracks and dropped off. It was late, after lights-out, and he found himself deserted. He stumbled his way through the bay's faint, indirect light, moonlight and watchtower light, thinking sleep, and more sleep, but there was a surprise awaiting him. Dunkel was sitting on Jimmy's bunk, holding a glittering bayonet in each hand. Dunkel said, "I've been waiting to cut you up, you son of a bitch." Jimmy couldn't be sure, in his condition, but he thought Dunkel was drunk, too. Ah yes, beside Jimmy's bunk glittered a bottle of booze. Jimmy tried to summon whatever alertness remained to him. He sized the situation up this way. If he turned and ran, Dunkel would surely pig-stick him with one of those bayonets. But Jimmy was a boxer. He knew that if you can get in close to a long-armed opponent, that opponent's arm-length, otherwise an advantage, becomes a handicap. Dunkel would find it impossible to turn those bayonets around on him.

Jimmy dove at Dunkel, between his arms, and hugged the flailing chaser up and back into a metal wall locker. One of the bayonets went through a metal door and stuck, the other bounced from Dunkel's hand. They struggled there, and suddenly the wall lockers, the whole row of them, went over. Somebody turned on the lights, and Jimmy and Dunkel got a first clear look at each other. Both were bleeding. Jimmy swung, connecting with Dunkel's chin, and Dunkel sprawled on the floor, out for the count.

"He tried to kill you," someone said.

" He's drunk," Jimmy said. "A couple of you guys put him on his bunk. And don't mention this to anyone. Nobody says a word, hear me?"

*   *   *

Jimmy was going home, leaving blue Hawaii and bound for the Golden Gate. The emerald islands of paradise were disappearing from view. He stood on the bow of the troop transport, smoking a cigarette. There was a lot that he would never forget, but, alas, a lot that he would. He knew that. After all, he was a writer, wasn't he, and knew things beyond his years?

Leilani had finally taught him to float, but he doubted if he could do it without her. He hoped that he would come back and see her someday, in the not too distant future. He would come back and she would be married to some local boy and have a couple of cute little brats. He had never laid a lustful hand on her virginal beauty. He loved her; she would always be his sweet Leilani, his sweet dream forever, his sweet little sister.

He looked along the gangway and saw a queue of young men that seemed to vanish in perspective. The first in line stepped up to him. "We don't want to bother you, sir, but we want to thank you for the way you treated us when we were in the brig. You could've made it very tough on us, but you didn't. Thank you, sir." Brig orders had required that the Turnkey be called "Sir."

Jimmy said, "Don't call me, sir. I always hated it."

That one stepped away with a nod and a smile, and another stepped up, saying much the same thing. And they just kept coming. Jimmy was overwhelmed. "Thank you, thank you, thank you." They ignored the fact that his eyes had dampened. Then Dunkel stood before him.

"I owe you," he said. "You could've had me court-martialed and sent to Leavenworth. You knew I wanted to make a career in the Corps, and you gave me the chance to do it, even though we never got along. Semper fi, buddy."

"Semper fi, Dunkel." Jimmy looked out at the ship's wake and the long waves beyond it, the white tops floating

50

with leis, and the island, green and paradisal.   On an impulse, he reached out and seized Dunkel by the shoulder. "Dunkel, you know, I learned something while we were here."

"What's that?"

"How to float."

THE LIAR

She came in to the cafeteria three or four times that week, would sit with her older friend, a kind of watchdog, but pleasant, in his section, and would smile at him when he came near. He was a busboy. No, he wasn't. He was an acting student. No, he wasn't. He had run out of money. But he was going to have more money some day, and then he would go to New York University and take dramatic arts.

He was about her age; but, somehow, in the circumstances, and quite un-intentionally, she made him feel younger. She looked like she had money, and he did not, look like he had money, that is. Of course he did not have any, or why would he be a busboy in a cafeteria? She must have been in her late teens, early twenties, but she had a mature way about her, serious, intelligent. He lived in Greenwich Village, but not quite. He lived on the great wall of Greenwich Village, 14th Street, in a shoebox of a room with a sagging single bed which he shared with a friend as poor as himself, a Puerto Rican boy of intellectual bent who had been in the Marines with him. They were not out very long, a matter of months. They had a G.I. Bill coming, but had to get tuition money together first, and be reimbursed. They seldom had car fare. They had few clothes, which they shared, on a first come first serve basis, so that neither of them could be sure what he was going to wear at any particular time. Who knew what would be left? First one up and out was best dressed. Now he wore a white jacket supplied by the restaurant, an apron stained with food, old baggy fatigues, split in the crotch from squatting to pick up under the tables, and down-at-heels muddy shoes of military issue. They had white soap stains at toe and heel. He owned no others. It embarrassed him that this beautiful young woman, who looked like a movie star, kept smiling at him. The smile was sweet, intelligent, and kind. The smile was warm and friendly and respectful. But it hurt his pride, because she was so beautiful, and poised, and well-dressed, and obviously well-off, and established-looking. He would have thought that she was making fun of him or teasing him or something, but somehow he could see that she wasn't. She and her friend sat and smoked cigarettes after eating and he had no choice but to go to their table and collect their dishes. and he hated it, because of the way she looked and smiled; but he had no choice but to do it. The older woman said, in a pleasant voice, "We've been watching you. My friend thinks you're very attractive." This horrified him, horrified him. What was he to say? He nearly spilled the stack of dishes. "Careful," said the older woman, and laughed a little in a friendly way.

"You take your break soon," said the younger one, "you take your break about now, I noticed. Won't you bring us all some coffee and sit with us?"

"I can't sit with the customers," he lied. Nobody would care. It was a cafeteria.

"Of course you can," said the older woman in a pretty full-throated voice. She was a bit overweight.

"Please bring us some coffee and sit with us," said the beauty.

"Can't you see she's smitten," said the other, and the beauty looked actually embarrassed herself. "She wants to meet you. She thinks you're very handsome. What do you do? I mean, beside this."

"I'm an actor," he said. Was he lying?

53

"So am I," said the beauty. "My friend, too. Are you studying?"

"Yes," he lied.

"We thought you might be," said the older woman. "Get the coffee and come and sit down. We want to talk to you."

So he sat with them that time and again the next time they came in. The beauty seemed nicer and more cultivated the more he saw her. She was so young, it had not occurred to him that she might be working, but it turned out that she was already pretty well-known. She was in a play on Broadway. So was the other one. They made him feel like a roach. It wasn't their fault, of course. They were as sweet as could be. He knew it was himself, his pride, but he couldn't help it. They made him feel like a poor ignorant slob, bussing dirty dishes, his old stained shoes stinking under the table. And yet the beauty made him melt, just melt. She was nice and nicer and it frightened him. It embarrassed him. She wanted him to ask her for a date, but where could he take such a girl, a girl rich and famous and successful? He didn't have any clothes to wear, let alone an extra dime to spend on her. Why did she have to pick on him? Where could he take her? Oh, where could he take her? And as if she knew what was in his mind, she asked him if they couldn't take a walk together sometime. "Just go for a walk," she said. "You don't have to take me any place special. I'd just like to be with you. We could go for a walk in the park. To the zoo."

I have no clothes that I can wear to walk beside you, he thought. I am only a busboy, not even a real actor. But he *was* an actor, for he said, "No. It will do you no good to know me."

"Because," he said, looking down at his stained apron and muddy shoes, "because, you see, like so many actors these days, I don't like women, I mean not in that way."

"You mean," she said, "you're gay?"

"Yes," he lied, and watched her gather up her things and leave, her friend consoling her; watched the most beautiful, wonderful girl he had ever known walk out of his ridiculous lying failure of a life forever. He gathered up their plates with deep sad relief, swearing to himself that he would get himself some new clothes, so that the next time this happened, he would be ready.

THE GIRL UPSTAIRS

Jimmy had met Vera at the famous 46th Street rehearsal studio. He was there because an acquaintance of his was playing piano for a dance troupe, of which Vera was a member. She sat down next to him on a bench and dried herself with a towel. Next thing he knew they were making love at her apartment. When he thought of it later, he could not remember having said or done a thing to get himself there. Nevertheless, he was complimented by her attentions. He asked himself who wouldn't be? He was a lucky dog. Everybody who met them together said that he was a lucky dog. And a dog he felt, for he suspected an invisible leash had been snapped on his fifteen-and-a-half inch neck. He discovered very quickly too, that her strong dancer's body was a very fit instrument of aggression, even violence, and he began to pull back from her emotionally only to discover that such withdrawal led to even greater aggression. She was more of a hot potato than a hot tamale, as he'd first thought, but he *was* an ex-Marine and he wasn't going to be intimidated. Even though he had read Sartre and could see no exit, he was still proud of this prize, this beautiful energetic dancer.

West Seventy-first Street in Manhattan was a shabby, low-rent neighborhood in Nineteen Fifty-eight and they lived in the worst building on the block, a big, ancient brownstone warren. Vera had complained for months that the apartment was dark and dingy and Jimmy calculated that a coat of paint might just cozy the place up enough to make

56

her feel more at home—to subliminally contribute to cooling her on the idea of striking out for Hollywood. Jimmy was a drama student and his mentor, a famous European dramatist, had pulled strings and had practically set up a very promising film gig for him. But Jimmy, who was of a studious bent, was also attending N.Y.U. on the G.I. Bill, and had deep misgivings. He wanted an education. Something solid. Not the shimmering mirage of tinseltown.

Vera liked pink, so they went out and bought several gallons of pink paint. And one day when they were standing with rollers in their hands and the door open for air, the new young lady from upstairs, whom they had passed once or twice in the hall, stopped at their door, introducing herself as Lola Sherrill. She was eighteen, from Missouri, a singer, and was looking for work. Vera invited her down for supper. Lola said that she wouldn't dream of eating supper with them unless she could help them with the painting. Jimmy took a break and went into the kitchenette, a curtained, wall-debouched hall with a small bathroom to one side, to get a can of beer. He discovered that Vera was whipping up a big gourmet spread, to impress their new neighbor. "Paella," she said. "It's Spanish."

Jimmy drank his beer, listened to some jazz, thumbed through *War and Peace*, and after a while a knock came at the door. He opened the door, and there was Lola, in skintight, see-through tights. "I've come to help you paint."

Vera called from the kitchenette: "Ask Lola to come in."

"Well, come on in, Lola," Jimmy said. He felt like an endangered species. He knew that, somehow, Vera would blame him for Lola's state of undress. He said, "I'll just break out more paint."

Vera popped out. She was hot and bedraggled from cooking, paint-smeared: had been hitting the bottle. And there was Lola, dipping her cello-bottom this way and that

57

as she painted, her see-through tights displaying with perfect clarity the flexures of each ample adorable cheek. Vera stopped short in the doorway of the kitchenette, the curtain tangled over one shoulder, took Lola in with a deep inspiration, and looked at Jimmy as if he had pulled off Lola's knickers. Jimmy stirred paint so fast that it spattered on his shirtless torso, turning his taut tummy pink.

Lola said, "I'm helping your husband." Jimmy thought: "Either this is the dumbest dame I've ever met, or she has more chutzpa than a vacuum cleaner salesman in a marble hall."

Vera said, "Well, Lola, I think we should call it a day on the painting, now." Jimmy thought it was about time for him to put his two-cents in. He said, "Maybe we can get this wall done before we quit. Why don't you just go ahead and concentrate on supper. It smells good." He meant it. They could use the help, and he didn't care what it wore, or didn't wear.

"Yes," piped Lola, "I'll help Jimmy get the painting done. I'm a good painter."

Vera went back to cooking. Pots and pans could be heard whizbanging in the kitchenette. Jimmy was having a good afternoon, even though Vera kept popping in and out; and every time she caught him looking at Lola, which he couldn't help doing, gave him one of her You'll-pay-for-this looks.

Vera came out, Merlot in hand, finally, to survey the job. She stood with Lola and admired the wall. Jimmy heard Lola say, "I'm glad I could be of help." Vera had the table set and told them to wash and come and eat. At last, Lola's behind was out of sight, on a chair, and her legs were under the table.

"Oh, this Paella looks delicious," she said, and Jimmy felt her pink-nailed toes walking up his leg. No shoes,

58

either, of course. He moved his leg away to see if the walk wasn't an accident.

"Yummy!" cried Lola. "You are a *wonderful* cook, Vera," and back came the tootsies.

"She sure is," said Jimmy in a disturbed voice. No doubt about anything now. Lola was pure brass. It seemed to Jimmy that Lola certainly knew how Vera felt, maybe could tell that Vera wasn't too stable, and was actually trying to make her crack. He did not know how else to explain Lola, a stranger, sitting there wearing next to nothing, running her chubby little toes up and down his leg while his wife looked on! Vera didn't show it, but Jimmy thought that she must know what was going on under the table. "Why doesn't she blow up?" he asked himself, and kept moving his legs away from Lola's groping toes; but he couldn't well dodge Lola and not be obvious about it. The table was too small. Then, through his alcoholic fog, he could see that Vera was on to Lola. He could also see that Lola knew that Vera knew, but didn't care what Vera thought.

They were all getting drunk. Vera slammed down her fork. "Whatever you're doing, Jimmy, I want you to stop it."

"Really, Vera, your Jimmy hasn't done anything to deserve the way you're treating him."

Jimmy got up and went to the bathroom. He took a long freedom-loving pee. "Hell, no!" he said to himself, stepping out and zipping up.

"What have I done?" He was crocked, and not at all sure of what had taken place during the course of the evening.

"But if you feel that way," Jimmy heard Lola say, "I'll go up to my own place."

"Go ahead, you ungrateful little bitch!" said Vera, tears squirting from her eyes.

59

Lola said: "But not till we clear the air."

"You *want* him!" cried Vera. "You *desire* him!"

"I don't want your stupid husband," Lola shouted, then looked at Jimmy apologetically. "You're just crazy, that's all! Everybody in the building knows it. You're crazy. We *all* hear you!"

Jimmy went back to the kitchenette to fix himself a drink. Now Vera was crying, Lola consoling. "Vera's about to be violent," he thought, remembering how she cried, like a bird of prey, before she swooped; and just then she flew by him, like a great mad bird, and locked herself in the bathroom. Lola pursued; pulled at the door knob.

"She's going to kill herself!" Lola cried. Jimmy told her not to worry. "She loves every ounce of herself. She's a performer."

Vera heard him—"I heard that!"—and flew out wielding her little pink Princess safety razor. She went straight for him. He fended her off, and she kept on going into the front room. Then swaths of pink paint came back, like watery cotton candy. *Swash! Swash!*

Lola had got more than she'd bargained for. She cowered behind the freshly pinked refrigerator. *Crash!* they heard the front window break. Vera had thrown an open can of paint through it.

In two seconds, sirens sounded through the shattered glass.

Vera heard them. She was scared now. She had done something fairly serious this time and it panicked her. She charged back into the kitchenette and then locked herself in the bathroom again. "This time I really *am* going to kill myself," she shouted through the door.

Jimmy noticed that she still had the razor with her. Maybe she *was* going to do it this time. She had had enough to drink, meaning too much even for the survival instinct.

Lola put her arms around Jimmy's neck. "What should

we do?" she said, rolling big brown eyes.

He put a hand on that behind he had wanted to touch all evening, and said: "I don't know." He didn't.

Lola said, "Shall we break the door down?"

He told her that he couldn't; he had had occasion to try.

Vera screamed. It was the worst fit of many. Jimmy was more than a little scared himself. He put his drink down and put another hand on another cheek. What a behind!

The hall door was being pounded. "Open up, police!" He went to the door and opened it.

"What's going on here?"

He tried to explain the situation. The building super, who was gay, stood behind the police. He liked Jimmy, disliked Vera. Jimmy could see that the super had been talking to the cops. They gave Lola the twice-over, but there was too much confusion. "Come on out of there," one of them called to Vera.

"I'm going to kill myself."

"Do you think she'd do it?" one of the cops asked.

"No," Jimmy said.

"Yes," said the super. "She crazy bitch. Oh, I sorry, mister, but I hear."

"I think she would," said Lola. Jimmy wondered if she wasn't hoping so.

"I will!" cried Vera.

"In that case," said a cop, "I'm calling Bellevue."

"No," Jimmy said. "Don't do that." He was weakening, as he often did, beginning to feel sorry for Vera. This was how he always lost his wars with Vera—pity.

"This is out of your hands now," said the cop. "Have you got a phone?"

"It's in here," said Lola.

The bathroom door flew open and there stood the wild woman herself. She had pink paint all over her, and looked pitiful.

61

"Don't let them take me to Bellevue," she cried. "Please don't let them."

"It's out of his hands," said a cop, grabbing her. "You're nuts, lady."

"They'll help you there, Vera," said Lola, nursily.

"You little. . ." fumed Vera, speech failing her, and *wham,* she threw her Princess safety razor at Lola. *Zing!* It missed. Both cops seized her arms.

Then the men in the white suits showed up. "We'll help you," they said.

Jimmy fixed himself a drink. He looked away while Vera was carried out in a straight jacket, screaming and kicking. He was not allowed to go with her. He went to the radio and turned it on. Music! Lola had assumed the role of hostess. She saw the whole menagerie out. Suddenly it was very quiet in the apartment.

Jimmy went to the window. Vera had cleared the glass out of it, but for a few jagged pieces. He leaned out and saw that there was a lovely long swath of pink paint down the front of the old brownstone. Below, there was a fracas. A small crowd watched as Vera was dragged, kicking and screaming, to the nut wagon. Lola came up behind him and put her arms around his waist. "You poor man," she crooned.

A bitter little laugh caught in his throat. "She certainly brightened the old place up," he said. "Did they say when I can see her?"

"They said you could visit her tomorrow morning. Now you come over here and sit down. I'll fix you a fresh drink. Then, later, I'll sing you to sleep. I'm really a very good singer, you know. I'll be a star in no time."

The next morning Lola left him to find herself a singing job. She kissed him goodbye and promised more delights upon her return. Vera, however, was released to him at ten that morning. So there wasn't much chance for

Lola to get at them again and Vera made it no chance at all. Jimmy was to accept that Hollywood offer immediately. After a few phone calls, she insisted that they leave for the west coast that very afternoon.

After all, what could be better than Lola than La La Land?

PART TWO

THE SANDAL SHOP
Or
How, while Being Pursued by the Divorce Demon,
Jimmy Whistler Discovered the Beats,
and was Saved by Marsayas, the King of the Beasts

1

The office of Magazine Subscriptions Unlimited was a bustling place, filled with telephones, none of which had time to ring for being dialed. Men and women of all races, creeds, ages, and costumes kept them leaping to their ears and slamming back for an instant's cradling before another leap and dialing. Jimmy Whistler estimated that at least fifty people crowded the place: workers, that is; aside from those, like himself, who waited to be interviewed for a job. Smoke hung heavy in the air, an ectoplasm.

There was a man seated across the table from Jimmy, a man with great broad shoulders, made to appear broader because of the heavy overcoat he was wearing. (It was February, and bitter weather: a fine time to come to New York from California; but nothing Vera and he did made any sense!) The man was big, but not fat. On the contrary, one could see—for he sat pushed back from the table in a sprawling, easy posture—that, where his coat fell open, his waist was neat and narrow. His legs were long and delicately shaped, seeming to be of a lighter bone structure than his upper body. Jimmy could see them plainly through the thin,

67

blue, much-too-shiny summer slacks he wore. But what greatly interested Jimmy about him was that he wore a beard—a rarity in the clean-shaven Fifties and a pronouncement that the hirsute Sixties had arrived—every strand of which was thick as wire and glittery, coppery red. It was nearly a foot in length, and all of a piece, so that it moved with his jaw. It rayed from his chin like a Blakian sun. All this blinding hair began directly under a sensual, long lower lip, flexible and pink as the innertube of a bicycle tire. His kinky hair puffed over his ears and down to his frayed collar. On top he was nearly bald; though Jimmy was to learn that this, his first Beatnik, was only twenty-eight. The big fellow seemed ill-at-ease, perhaps because Jimmy had been studying him so intently—and rudely, too, for that matter—or perhaps because he was waiting, in a place he did not wish to be to do something he had no wish to do.

In any case, after completing his application form, he behaved restively, crossing and uncrossing his legs, smoking cigarette after cigarette, thumbing through magazines, and throwing them back in the pile with a look of irritation on his benignly satanic face. Finally, he started fishing with very long, delicate fingers in an empty cigarette pack. He crumpled the pack in his fist, and startled Jimmy out of his contemplation of him by leaning across the table and, with a show of white teeth and a whisk-broom movement of beard, nearly sweeping away several magazines, asking if he could have a cigarette from him. Jimmy said, "Sure," and gave him one.

He told Jimmy he had just come back from Germany, where he had left his German wife and his two children, a boy and a girl. He had been a language teacher there, for Berlitz: had taught English to the Germans. He was in the process of breaking up with his wife, by his description a stuffily middle-class Hausfrau. He was staying with an aunt

68

and uncle, a staid old couple, out on Long Island. They had ordered him to look for a job; and so, to appease them, he was making this half-hearted effort. But he had other things in mind, for the long run.

He told Jimmy that he had picked up a young woman on his first day in town, while wandering about in Greenwich Village, a big, strapping Fraulein, with an enormous bust and a Madonna-like face. Not the least of her virtues was that she had a sister and a brother-in-law who were "really hip, swinging." They ran a sandal shop in Brooklyn Heights, had a baby who never cried, never wore a diaper, and who was allowed free use of the floor for urinary and defecatory purposes. The brother-in-law plunked the bass fiddle, studied Zen, kept a Mulligan stew going for a month at a time, made sandals, and did odd jobs in his neighborhood. The sister was a mysterious beauty who smoked pot and sang lullabies. And in many other ways, apparently, this couple led an idyllic and primitive existence of which Rousseau would have voiced his approval. "Call me Marsayas," he said.

Marsayas told Jimmy that he was going to work his way in down there (which wouldn't prove difficult, as Rolly, the brother-in-law, had already accepted him as his guru), and stay with them for a while, at least until he could get Joan (his girlfriend) to get him a studio of his own. He was a painter, you see, and a poet, too. "Any old how," he said, "I've got to get out of my uncle's house. The old folks are driving me up the walls. Too much, too *much*! *When are you going to get a job? What are you going to do about your wife and those dear little kiddies of yours? Life is real, life is earnest. You must look to the future.* Would you believe it? They want me to be in the house by midnight!"

Jimmy agreed that that was a bit much to ask of a grown and married man, and especially one with two kids. Marsayas said that his whole family was that way,

69

"Impossible!" His whole family were "convention-racked lunatics," or "business fiends" or "materialist maniacs."

Not Marsayas. "I'm a Zoroastrian. I believe in the power of light to conquer the forces of darkness. I believe in universal love." Jimmy was impressed, even impressed with the holes in the heels of the argyles of this gleeful gargoyle as he walked to his interview as one walks to the gallows.

2

They were hired, and started the next evening at six.

Jimmy worked as fast as he could, thinking of Vera, of their latest peace pact, and worried that he might not be able to find a good, full-time job before the next rent fell due. But Marsayas, though Jimmy had heard him try a few times at first, had already given up the outlined pitch, and was engaging in long, relaxed conversations with, as the boss called them, "the Zombies."

Jimmy discovered that, though he had a certain talent for making people say yes, by the next evening, when the supervisor called them back to verify the sales, his customers had often changed their minds. They'd claim that they had not agreed to buy a subscription at all. They'd claim that they had only accepted his offer to send them a free dictionary.

Well, either he hadn't heard right, and had pressured the "Zombies" too hard in his financial desperation, and they had changed their minds as soon as his persuasive voice had clicked from their receivers; or his supervisor was a swindler, as some claimed, and was simply stealing his sales by canceling them in Jimmy's name and putting them in his own. This Jimmy suspected, but had no way of confirming, as the sales were checked by others and the order forms were out of his hands.

Rightly or wrongly, his sales were being canceled faster than he was making them. And this was the sort of thing that just could not be explained to Vera. He confided his plight to Marsayas, whose own sales hadn't added up to enough to get a cancellation from, and to his amazement Marsayas was surprised that Jimmy should be worried. "For Chrissakes, Jimmy, I thought you were just working here for beer money, like me. Why don't you get that Frau of yours off her ass and out into the labor market? She an invalid?"

After work they stopped in a midtown bar and had a few beers. It was one of those dives that have a food bar, and smell of corned beef and cabbage, stewed potatoes, cheap wine, draft beer, and sour people.

As they had agreed to do the previous evening, they had brought their poems to work with them, and now they sat and read each other's work. "GuraaaAH!" Marsayas sounded, and sipped his beer, leaving a broken ring of foam in the bristling red wires around his mouth.

He slammed Jimmy's little, stapled booklet on the table, chug-a-lugged his remaining beer, and vanished. Then he was back through the crowd like an ecstatic Bacchus with four huge mugs of slopping broth, two in each hand. He shouted: "You, you poor fool, are among the elect, the elite, the only *true* elite on earth. You are a *poet!*"

"Do you like them?"

"*Like* them? They're real *poems*, good as anybody going!"

Jimmy was thrilled. No one but Marsayas had ever encouraged him in his yearning to be a poet, everyone else thought he was foolish—especially Vera. It would be quite a let-down, after such stimulation, to have to take himself home to Vera and her cranky, middle-class bohemianism. Midnight was looming, Marsayas's curfew hour.

"Well, it won't always be like this," said Marsayas. "I'll be out of that bourgeois scene before the week-end.

71

I'm moving into the sandal shop. Then we'll be able to drink and talk all night."

"I wish Vera would help me with tuition for school," Jimmy said, dreamily. "I'd like to be a writer, but I need more education."

"There's all kinds of writers, boyo—and all kinds of education. If you want to write, first read, read, read, then write, write, write! But if you want to go to college, well, that's a different story. I've got a masters, but I can't write poetry like your stuff." He drained a mug. "Chrissakes, Jimmy, who the hell is the boss in your house? Look at the lion. The king of the beasts! The lioness goes out and kills the quarry, then steps back and guards the old man while he eats."

"That's lions—not people."

"Well, people then. Do you know that the Indian brave never worked. He sent his old lady out to do it. *He* stayed at home and talked, talked *war* and *peace*," he shouted, and the whole bar, which seemed to be filled with middle-aged, unshaven men, turned to look at him, interest in their eyes, even hope.

"That's what women are meant to do," he roared on, after a bow. "Let them make the nest pretty and wait like the votary bird to be impregnated. Then you take over until the egg is laid. *Only* until then. And then you go back and keep the nest warm with wine and good conversation while they go and forage for worms. Worms of milk for the baby and worms of wine for you. I tell you that is their biological role. *They* know it, so why don't you? Don't they all want to go to work nowadays? Don't they? Well, for God's sake, let them!

"This guy Rolly I've told you about, he makes sandals—because that's art, but Jean, his wife, chews the leather. That's right. She *chews* the leather—makes it soft so Rolly can work with it. Rolly only makes one pair of

72

sandals a week, he tells me; but Jean, with those beautiful sharp little white teeth of hers, chews enough leather for him to make twenty! He keeps her at it all day—chewing, chewing—except when she's nursing the baby, or turning on. Now that's a *wife* for you! They're in the battle for survival together—it isn't all thrown on *his* back. That's *life*—and listen, that's *love*! I tell you, Jimmy, once I get to Brooklyn, I'll never work another day in my life. That's my oath. I intend to dedicate myself completely to the muses."

Jimmy wondered if Vera would chew leather for him. Marsayas was opening new vistas. He was an inspiration!

3

Jimmy got an idea. Friday night, pay night, he would have next-to-nothing coming, so over the weekend he would need all the moral support he could get. He thought that the hard edge of the weekend might be softened if Vera could hear Marsayas present his version of things before he presented his own. So they made a date for Marsayas to come to Jimmy's place on Saturday and help him out.

Marsayas didn't mind telling Jimmy that he thought he was quite a coward for being so afraid of a woman, and over such a little thing as not having any money. He had never heard of a wife who wasn't at least willing to help her husband, if asked. But Marsayas had no idea what Vera was like, or what she was capable of, if angered. And Jimmy had to admit that it was more than a modest proposal that had induced him to ask Marsayas over. He was also interested in finding out what would happen when these two forces of nature came into contact. Perhaps they would vanish in a clap of thunder, and leave only a little mushroom cloud behind.

Marsayas showed up at noon on Saturday, toting a case of beer and a gallon jug of purple wine. Jimmy saw him through the window, striding down Horatio Street. He had told Vera a little about Marsayas, and that he was coming, but he did not, could not, do him justice. He went over and stood by the expensive new coffee table (which Vera had bought the day before with the last of their savings, and upon which she had laid out all the tea-time and cocktail-hour delicacies a Happy Homemaker could conceive), and waited to enjoy the immediate impact his wild man find would have upon her.

The knock came, and Vera, who was near the door, opened it; then stood, as if transfixed, gripping the knob until her little fist turned white. Jimmy thought for an instant that she was going to slam the door in his friend's face, and start screaming. But she collected herself, asking:

"*Marsayas?*"

"Vera, I presume?"

"Ha—yes!" said Vera, looking up into the aimed ends of his red rays, and finally bethinking herself to step back. "Please come in—come in, please—*please!*"

Marsayas gargoyle-grinned, and slippity-slapped into the apartment on shower shoes. His naked feet were dirty, and red-and-raw-looking with the cold. Jimmy saw Vera eyeing them distastefully as the guru set his burdens down in the midst of the hors d'oeuvres. Jimmy had hoped that it would take Vera longer to get her wind back. He had hoped that from first sight this imposing giant would keep her off balance. But, plain to see, she was coming around, resilient as ever.

He indicated a chair for Marsayas, and Marsayas seated himself, moving Vera's tidbits aside and putting his feet up on the table, between a bowl of cheese dip and a platter of cold cuts. Vera looked at him wide-eyed; at Jimmy, narrow-eyed; then pulled a tight meager smile back to her downy ears, and sat. Jimmy had received the first dirty look of the day. And he knew something about Vera. One dirty look meant more to follow, and maybe even along their trajectory one might find, in an hour or so, a vase, or a bottle, flying.

The thought flashed that he had better move quickly to prevent Marsayas from saying what he knew Marsayas intended to say. But then he was distracted. Marsayas said, from his recumbent position, "I hope you kids don't mind, but I took the liberty of inviting some friends of mine down—my girlfriend's sister and her husband. I thought it might do you good to meet them."

Vera stared at Marsayas, as one might stare at an oddity, trying to figure out what to make of him. "Do us good?" she said.

"Yes. They do everyone good."

"How do you mean?"

"They're an example, an inspiration."

Marsayas removed his feet from the table long enough to fill two glasses with wine and stick them before Vera and Jimmy. He waved aside Jimmy's apology for not having done the honors, placed his horny heels back in the cold cuts, jug neatly draped on an elbow which he raised in salute, and yelled "PROSIT" loud enough to make Vera blink. They picked up their glasses and yelled "Prosit!" back at him. It seemed like the right thing to do.

Then Marsayas made his gleeful gargoyle face, which put on display for Vera his big, beautiful white teeth, and said, "Why didn't you tell me you had such a pretty wife?"

Vera perked up. "Why, thank you," she said.

"Yes—yes—I must paint you some time. But first you're going to have to become more natural. These are the new, hip Sixties, Vera. Hang loose! You're the very personification of the uptight Fifties. You seem . . . . *constrained*—yes. Even your hair—is it dyed? A Lana Turner helmet.

75

You'll have to get that stuff out of your hair and let it down—let it be natural—yes—" He moved the thumb of his free hand in a painterly gesture of measurement. "And you stop Jimmy from being a wage-slave and help to develop him as a poet. He's the real thing." The wine bottle remained cradled in his other arm, like a baby.

Fortunately, for Jimmy could see Vera revving up for a reply, a knock came at the door. It was the Reuters.

Rolly Reuter was a little fellow with big, lugubrious brown eyes, long black hair, and a long, silky black beard. Jean, his wife, was a striking young woman, with chatoyant greenish eyes, and beautiful long ebony hair that swam, like a dark, glittery stream, down neck and chest and out, over a more than ample, T-shirted bosom, to twin falls, stippled by nipples.

Marsayas picked up the thread of what he had been saying. But the atmosphere was irrevocably altered. Vera was discontent. She no longer listened to Marsayas, but interjected odd, pointless questions, as if only to attract attention; and the conversation became forced and jittery. Even so, Jimmy was able to attend to the Reuters enough to see what Marsayas had meant about them. It was simple. They were in love.

He looked at Vera, popping off about something or other, that hard, mean look about the mouth, those hurt, jealous eyes, and he knew what was going on in her mind; knew that she wanted this pleasant vision of love out of her sight. It was too much for her, too uncomplicated.

Jimmy envied Rolly his beautiful Jean—and he saw that Marsayas envied him, too—but tried not to show it. If Jimmy let on to the slightest admiration, Vera would make him pay—make them all pay, possibly.

The Reuters stayed for two hours and then went on their way. But Marsayas sat on, like a great blood-bubbling fixture. He finished off the last of the wine and started

76

whittling down the case of beer he'd brought; then he dragged Vera up and danced her about to the phonograph. Vera's mood brightened after Rolly took his beautiful Jean away. When Marsayas went to the bathroom, she kept on dancing by herself, whirling about the living room like the ballerina she had been trained to be. Once, she stopped, and tried to pull Jimmy to his feet to dance with her. But he refused. There was even something in her gaiety that made him nervous. He knew all too well how quickly it could change into angry hysteria. Yet she seemed happy, now; and if it hadn't been for all the misery she had caused him he'd have been glad to see her so. He'd have got up and danced with her, but for that.

4

Marsayas slept, head hanging forward, in an antiquated easy chair near the lumpy couch on which Jimmy woke. A young woman sat on the floor at his feet, propped up against his legs, asleep, with her head in his lap. She wore a quilted kimono, and one breast bulged into view where the kimono fell open. She was a bigger, heavier version of Jean. Jimmy looked around, through puffed, uncertain eyes. There were sandals, belts, pocketbooks, all manner of leather goods, hanging in festoons from walls and ceiling. He must have moaned; because, then, from somewhere up near the ceiling, in a dark corner, in the rear of the shop, a soft, purring voice drifted down, asking, "Got a headache?"

It was Jean. He could see her now, or see her eyes, like a cat's, high up, glimmering in shadows.

"Are you levitating?"

"I'm on a platform. This is where Rol and I sleep. How's your wife?"

Jimmy looked around, and there behind him, under a heap of coats, was Vera. She looked a mess. Her lipstick

77

was smeared, there were Mascara-tear-stains down her cheeks, and her hair looked like a burning bush.

Well, was it paradise? Was this absurd little sandal shop a heaven on earth, a sanctuary? No, he guessed not; it was just that he had come from a small, unimportant hell. And why have anything to do with any hell if you can stay in a little, bright heaven? It was just too bad that there wasn't one more of these plump, lovely creatures around, another sister, for him.

He had been drinking beer with Marsayas for two hours before Vera grunted and woke up. She had a hangover, was angry, had slept badly (so she claimed—been mashed by him), and wanted to get out of this (whispers, harsh, in his ear) "filthy place." She would not have Jimmy drinking again today. It was Sunday.

"What *are* you, an alcoholic, like your so-called friend, Marsayas? He's a filthy beast and the sandal shop is a stinking zoo." She stomped outside "to get some clean, fresh air."

"She walked out on you last night—do you know that?" Marsayas seemed much amused by Jimmy's pickle. "You fell asleep in the car—I dumped you there, on the couch, and she got into a temper tantrum trying to wake you up. Feel your leg."

Jimmy felt around, looked at the place on his calf that hurt, and there was a large purple bruise. "It'll soon be time to go back to California," he said. "D.D. is catching up with us."

"Who's D.D.?"

"The Divorce Demon. He's been pursuing us since we got married."

"She gave you quite a pummeling before I could stop her." Marsayas laughed. "You were inert—wouldn't, or couldn't, move for love nor money."

78

Jimmy was beginning not to like the way Marsayas looked, the beast. He seemed to think that Jimmy's problems were a joke. But then, who could blame him? It was the truth, after all. Vera and he were a joke. They had been making public fools of themselves for three years. Why shouldn't people laugh? The thought occurred to Jimmy that maybe he had finally come face to face with the Divorce Demon. Then Marsayas broke the news: "Your phonograph and your TV were stolen last night. Some of your clothes, too."

Rolly came in from the back and sat down, looking lugubrious. Now he reminded Jimmy a little of Chico Marx. "That's the trouble with having possessions," he said; "it's not that they get stolen, but that it should hurt when they are. *Things!*" He sighed. "It's no good basing a life on *things!*" He wore such a sad face. It struck Jimmy funny that he should seem to be suffering more over Jimmy's loss than Jimmy was.

"Oh, but it's true," Rolly said, as Jimmy laughed. Then he looked at Jimmy's feet. He had given him a pair of sandals to wear. Jimmy had them on over his socks. Quite a bumbling novitiate beatnik he was. "Do they fit?" he asked. Jimmy said that they did, quite comfortably.

Marsayas went on to tell Jimmy that, after he had pulled Vera off him, she had run out into the street and stopped a car by standing with outstretched arms, like a crucifee. The car had gone off with her. Marsayas said that he had been too drunk to follow, but that after taking a nap he had driven up to Manhattan to see if he could get her to come back. He said that he had found the front door wide open and Vera hysterical. She told him that the man who had driven her home had threatened her, and that she had given him everything he asked for and was afraid to call the police.

Trouble! *Trouble*! Four hundred, maybe five hundred, dollars worth of his hard labor stolen! His most prized possession—his typewriter. More disorder! More chaos! Well, Rolly was right. He was a fool to work for *things*. He wasn't angry; he was just disgusted, with himself and with Vera. What a dreadful pain in the ass they must always seem to people! Ah! He thought to himself that he would go right ahead and get just as drunk as he damned well pleased; and he would start right now to demand, through an iron-clad indifference to anybody's harangue, his *rights*!

But just then Vera appeared at the door, eyes shooting hot tears like sunstruck diamonds. "I want to speak to you," she said, choking in temper.

Marsayas bent down and buried Joan's neck in the red excelsior of his beard.

"Do you hear?" Vera shouted. "I said I want to speak to you!" Her smeared lips were pursed, her grim, green eyes on Marsayas.

Rolly peeked in through the curtain, from the back, but withdrew his scared, comic-Christ face when he saw Vera.

"Step outside, please," said Vera, and Jimmy felt as if he were being called out by a barroom bully. Her breath was hot, and he thought he saw a flame leap from her mouth. He got up and walked outside, onto Henry Street, a pretty, quiet, Sunday view, reminiscent of Utrillo. He could hear tugboats tooting in the harbor, beyond the esplanade.

Vera had her coat on. He was in shirtsleeves, a little chilly. He shivered. He thought that he must look like hell, unshaven, disheveled. So did Vera.

"I want you to come home with me," she said. "I've been waiting in that church over there for nearly an hour. I was not going to step one foot back in that filthy zoo of a sandal shop, with that smell of dead skin, but I did, for *you*. Now you come along with me, do you *hear*?"

"I'm staying here for a while," Jimmy said, affirming his rights. "You go ahead. I'll be along."

He was a bit tipsy—not much, but a bit; enough to think he was going to get away with facing her down—enough to think he was going to win, this time.

"No!" she said. "You come now!"

"No!" he said. "Later! I am a lion."

"You are not the king of the beasts. You're a pussycat. I suppose you'll want to grow a beard now."

"You just listen to me roar," he said.

"If you don't come now, I'll kill myself!" she shouted. The sentence rang down the hollow, empty Sunday street like a ricocheting bullet.

"No," he said; but he was weakening.

"You'll see," she yelled at him, turning, and running around the corner. "You'll see," she yelled again, farther down, out of sight.

He stood still for what seemed a long time, determined not to give in, determined to hold his ground. But then he heard her yell, *"You'll see,"* from far down, toward the docks, and he thought of the harbor and the water.

It came to him. She means to throw herself in. But then it occurred to him that she had won medals for swimming. How could she drown herself? And what could he do if she did take it into her head to jump into the drink? He couldn't swim at all! But he had lost already. Even to think about it was to lose.

He started running down the block, around the corner, to the river. He slowed down, occasionally, wondering what he would do when he got there. He couldn't save her! Three years in the Marines hadn't taught him to swim. He wasn't going to learn in the next five minutes. And she couldn't drown, was an expert! He stopped running once, and began to laugh. The absurdity of what was happening struck him. He had a stitch in his side. What kind of

81

damned crazy show was this? And what part was he intended to play? The clown who gets fished out of the drink by his wife? But, then, in an instant, he was frightened again. What was she going to do? She was capable of anything.

He started running again, and he got to the dock just in time to see Vera take off her coat, and, looking back to make sure he was watching—he felt she would have waited for him to catch up had he taken longer—jump in.

He walked the next hundred or so feet. He wondered what sort of expression he wore. Whatever it was, that miraculous crowd that gathers out of nowhere at public events such as the one taking place under the esplanade in Brooklyn Heights did not like it at all. He did not move a wee bit faster, however. In fact, he sauntered. Meantime, until three or four burly firemen, who were stationed on a fireboat docked nearby, swam in three or four strokes to rescue her, Vera swam gracefully about, doing a lovely backstroke of the sort that had won her the medals. Then she allowed herself to be saved by the florid knights of the fireboat. Unfortunately, thought Jimmy, it wasn't even necessary to knock her out; they swam back to the boat in a beautiful formation, like well-trained frogmen, Vera on point, and the knights of the fireboat took her aboard.

As for Jimmy, he just stood where he was. He may have been laughing, or he may have been crying, but whatever he was doing, it roused no sympathy for him in the heart of the crowd. It was thumbs down for him. Then one of the big, fire-colored knights stepped up to him.

"You that young lady's husband?" It sounded as much like an accusation as it did a question.

"Yes," Jimmy admitted, "I am."

"Well, whatsa matter widja? Why dinja jump in after huh?"

"I can't swim."

82

"Call that a 'scuse?" the fireman demanded.

Jimmy thought that he had best be careful now. He might be lynched.

"No," he said meekly.

"Well, now . . ." the fireman said, thinking. It must have been quite a search that went on in that big head, but he came out of it empty-handed. All he could say in his state of indignation was "Get aboard!"

There was a cop on the boat. "Are you prepared to take your wife home?" he asked, adding, "Otherwise I'll have to take you both to the station." Jimmy wanted to ask what he had done, but thought better of it. He said he was. He looked at Vera, who was sitting wrapped in blankets, three or four firemen asking her questions, consoling her, and no doubt condemning him. Vera saw him, then, and stood up, stretching her arms out to him through the blankets.

"Oh, Jimmy," she cried, "take me home."

Sure he would. What did it matter now? Something had happened, something had snapped. Vera thought she had won again, but she hadn't. This time he had won. And so had protean D.D., the Divorce Demon, in the form of Marsayas, poet, painter, prophet, and king of beasts.

POLAROID

Jimmy Whistler was visiting his parents over the weekend. On Saturday morning, sitting around the tiny kitchen table in a tiny apartment in Baldwin, the mad house—as Jimmy thought of it; most of the tenants were sent to them from the Vineland looney bin— rooming house his parents superintended, his mother Fay showed Elliot, Jimmy's father, the Polaroid photo she and Jimmy had had taken at a local bar, the Juke Joint, where they had danced their first Chubby Checker "Twist" the night before. Elliot examined the photo, his horn-rimmed, taped five-and-dime magnifying glasses at the tip of his pink nose. "You both look drunk," he said, who had stayed home with his dignity and a bottle of sherry and a pack of Chesterfields.

"I have a hangover," Fay said, holding her head in her small hands as if she had just caught a football. She had had three cups of coffee and was coming awake.

"I need a pick-me-up," said Jimmy.

"A hair of the dog that bit you," said Elliot. The idea of them all getting drunk again was appealing to him. After a few pick-me-ups and increasingly enthusiastic calculations, Elliot and Jimmy decided to buy a used Polaroid themselves at Kelly's Newark Pawn Shop, which was near the Hudson Tube Station, and take pictures of customers in the bars and night spots around Greenwich Village. "After all, that's the place for exhibitionists who love to have their pictures taken," said Elliot, employing over a half-century of sales wisdom to the case. Jimmy reasoned, too, it was the weekend and he was entitled to a little recreation. He did love his father, in spite of the fact that he had grown up with the difficulties of dipsomania, and it would give them some time together, an adventure. He didn't take the idea seriously. It was a lark.

Elliot was always ready to go into some kind of scheme, the crazier the better. Recently he had been talking about opening a phrenology parlor in Greenwich Village. To supplement his social security, he had been managing an Angel's Own thrift shop, where he came upon a porcelain head, the kind with the skull mapped off in sections, the sections conforming to mental and character qualities such as Conjugality, Inhabitiveness, Alimentiveness, etc. He had read up on the subject, bringing home books by or about Gall, Spurzheim, Combe, the Fowler brothers, and others among the famous bump-readers of the world. No one knew if he took the subject seriously, or if it wasn't just something to talk about.

The photography scheme, or Jimmy's slightly inebriated view of it that Saturday morning, was that Elliot would put up the capital for the camera and Jimmy would run around like Weegee, the famous candid photographer, taking pictures galore all over Greenwich Village, making a fortune, of course, which he'd split with Elliot, and at the same time making himself a famous Village character, like Maxwell Bodenheim or Little Joe Gould. Everybody would know him; and when he flew, busy and vigorous, in the door of a Village dive, they'd say, "Hey, there's Jimmy Whistler, the famous candid photographer, and he's packing his Polaroid!" Fay was to stay behind, and, as Elliot advised, "Keep the home fires burning" (which suited her fine, for she still had, that morning, "an awful hangover"), while Elliot (who phoned downtown and got himself a leave of absence from the Angels' Own stores on the grounds of receiving medical treatment) and Jimmy went to the Village to make their fortune. As soon as they could afford to move into a Park Avenue apartment, they would send for Fay. Then she could pack up all her cleaning paraphernalia, pay back whatever money she had embezzled from Baldwin's books to its owner, Howard Burns, and give up superintending forever. She could be like the Society Ladies she was forever reading about in the columns of Dorothy Kilgallen and Cholly Knickerbocker in the newspapers.

On the train Elliot got up, his big overcoat heavy upon him, and swung and swayed his way to the end of the car; and turning toward the wall, in full view of his fellow passengers, who believed he was about to pee, perhaps disappointed them by removing, with what he seemed to think was great stealth, a half-pint bottle of Haig & Haig from his hip pocket, and slugging—judging from the number of times his head bobbed—three good! stiff! drinks! He returned the bottle to his back pocket, patted his ass; and, returning down the aisle of the racing, rocking, underground-going train, smiling and nodding in a most cordial manner at the frowning or giggling faces he passed, proceeded to sit down on the wrong side of Jimmy, placing himself slowly and carefully on a young woman's lap; even having time, in his *sang froid*, to pull up the sharp creases of his shiny trousers, and to cross his legs, before the dumbstruck victim could figure out whether to scream or push or what. Fortunately, she was a good-natured young woman, and only tapped him on the shoulder from behind with her dainty rose-tipped fingers, saying, "Sir—oh, sir—you're sitting on my lap, sir—" Elliot finally got the message, removed himself from her lap; and, with many a courtly flourish of apology, tried to undo his ungentlemanly wrong. Jimmy shrank in embarrassment, especially now that Elliot strap-hung over the poor, sweet kid, grinning at her, his handsome, debauched old face sometimes not an inch from hers, and his breath smelling mephitic, like a tub of hooch. They pulled into the station that way, like a sideshow.

They began their career in photography, as they had planned, by making the rounds of the Village bars. In five hours of steady drinking (they *had* to have a drink in these places; it wouldn't look good to just walk in and out—as Elliot put it, "You have to spend money to make money."), they ran across one prospective customer, a tattooed sailor in a bar over near the docks who had a couple of bimbos with him and wanted them to go to a hotel and take porno pictures. He wanted to show his shipmates what a good time he had had on shore.

Elliot and Jimmy held a conference and decided not to do this because the sailor was drunk and rowdy and they didn't want to get into trouble with the law. Too bad they didn't take the gig, however, because they never got another offer of work. Their drunken dreams of fame and fortune in the art of photography were shattered that snowy evening, as was the lens of their camera (the disappointed sailor had knocked it from Jimmy's hands). But they were resilient; they'd find another way to make a fortune. Elliot was keener than ever on the phrenology parlor and he decided to stay with Jimmy in Manhattan while he solidified his plans.

During the next few days, big Denise, a graduate student at Columbia and Jimmy's upstairs neighbor, would come downstairs to his breadbox of a room at Miss Bee's single-rooms-for-rent establishment around the corner from a riotous gay bar, and create a crowd of three. They would hold long philosophical discussions, Denise touting Locke or John Dewey and whatever liberals she had in her bag, Elliot being legalistic with Coke and Blackstone and Roscoe Pound, and Jimmy spouting Bergson and the *elan vital*.

Denise and Elliot turned on and off like a couple of blinker-lights. "Here," Denise would say, "try some of these little reds, Mr. Whistler. They'll bring you down a little."

"I've never seen any little red ones like these before," Elliot would say, like a connoisseur, studying the bottle by holding it up to the light while pulling his broken glasses down to the tip of his rubicund nose. "What are they?"

"They're a downer, Mr. Whistler."

"I don't like barbiturates, Denise. They always leave me with a headache."

"Oh, these don't, Mr. Whistler. Go ahead and try one. It's just a gentle trip down. Nice and smooth, like a sliding board."

"Well, I'll try one—I'd like to come down just a little;" and he'd flip it in and wash it down with a shot of Haig & Haig. "By the way, Denise, I was reading DeRopp on hashish. Do you suppose you could get some?"

"Oh, I don't know, Mr. Whistler, it's kind of tight right now. But I'll try." And they'd sit there, a handsome, unshaven, grizzled old man in his fart-stained underwear, and a big, unkempt young woman, not much more than a kid—he on the cot, and she, cross-legged, in the lotus position, on the floor at his big pink feet, fingering through her box of goodies as if they were chocolates—exchanging pills and popping them, until neither of them was talking to the other anymore, but just talking—talking to the hooded mystery guest.

After a couple of weeks, Jimmy and Elliot were having a bit of trouble, what with Jimmy trying to work during the day and Elliot walking up and down his back all night. In fact, they were a little sour on each other. Jimmy slept on the floor and Elliot slept on the sagging single bed, really only a cot; and they hardly had room to turn around in. Jimmy's peaceful existence was fading a little more with each day that Elliot stayed, as were his joys of a single life, because with each sleepwalking night he was almost run out of his room. It was maddening to Jimmy. In the middle of the night Elliot would wake up from his rumbling sleep, throw his huge pink feet over the side of the cot and right onto Jimmy's back, and wobble down Jimmy's spine like a tightrope walker. Then, Hey, Presto, the lights would come on, with a *"FIAT LUX!"*

"Dad," Jimmy'd say, "for Christ's sake, do you have to walk down my back?"

"What?" Elliot would say, oblivious. "Oh, I'm sorry, my boy. I just wanted to take another Miltown and have a couple of spoonfuls of peanut butter."

"Miltown! You're like a zombie already!"

But Elliot wouldn't pay any attention to that, or perhaps couldn't.

"Have you seen that bottle of sherry I bought yesterday?"

Jimmy'd have to get up and look for the bottle, which was usually on the bed-table, right under Elliot's nose, among the dirty litter of pill bottles, sticky glasses, left-over, skin-topped clam chowder cups, and the always delightful-looking sets of false teeth. Then back to sleep for an hour or two, if there weren't other trips up and down his spine, and off to work Jimmy'd go, at some temp job of the moment, feeling like Quasimodo. He wasn't doing any writing (his secret passion) at all.

After a few weeks, at some vague, pilled-up point, during one of their evening conversations, Elliot, feeling grandiose, told Denise that he had written a history of Rome. He was honest enough to say, "I didn't quite finish it, but what I did of it exceeded Gibbon, if I say so myself."

"I didn't know you were a writer, too, Mr. Whistler. Oh wow!"

"I'm a professional, Denise. The W.P.A.—you know what that is, or was?"

"Of course. My folks were New Dealers. The Works Project Administration."

"Exactly! You are a very wise young woman. You not only know ancient history, you know modern history. If it weren't for the fact that you were a woman, I should call you a gentleman and a scholar."

"Women are scholars today, Mr. Whistler. I'm working on my master's degree."

"And Denise is very much a gentleman," said Jimmy. She gave him a pilled-up look and he smiled back, nodding approval. Then she nodded back in a sort of salute.

Elliot said, "I wrote many a speech for Mayor Parnell of Newark. I wrote the great anti-reefer speech."

"But you didn't believe it—?"

"We writers sometimes have to say things for the public consumption. You're sophisticated enough to understand that, I dare say."

"Certainly! Oh, Mr. Whistler, you could help me so much! "

"How could I do that, my dear?"

"It's my thesis for Columbia. I've tried and I've tried and I just can't seem to write it."

"Try cutting back on the pills, Denise," said Jimmy.

"Nonsense! I find them a tremendous help—don't you, Mr. Whistler?"

"In getting the mind operating with full cargo and at full speed, indubitably, yes. Now, how can I help you?"

"I'm supposed to write a thesis on John Donne."

"I'm not sure I'm—"

"John Donne, Dad, the poet," said Jimmy.

"Of course, John Donne. The poet!"

"I'll supply you with all my notes, over two year's worth."

"And I shall have to read them. I mean—"

"I'll pay you five hundred dollars."

90

"Five hundred dollars?"

"I'll give you fifty to start you off."

"Yeees, I see. Now when would this thesis have to be completed?"

"As soon as possible!"

"And you say you've been trying to do it for two years?"

"Yes, but I just can't get started."

"We have an agreement. Jimmy, you stand witness. I shall write this thesis before a month is out. Now, about the fifty dollars—" Denise pulled fifty dollars from her wallet and slapped it into his big hand. "We're on our way," she said. "We're on our way," Elliot repeated, grinning darkly. His grinning, approving teeth floated in a glass at his elbow.

When Elliot got the chance to pick up the fifty from Denise, he already had it in his noodle to blow, and the night after she gave him the money, he vanished, leaving Jimmy to convince Denise, who had been a good friend, that he knew nothing about what his Dad was up to. The double-dealing old con-artist! Jimmy was sore. Elliot had been living on him for weeks, and Jimmy was behind in the rent, and the Miss Bee was swooping down like a vulture on him for it.

Jimmy had a hunch that Elliot wouldn't return; but he wasn't sure yet. So, when she asked him, he told Denise he thought his Dad had just gone to Newark for a few days to check in with his Mom; for her, Denise, not to worry; that Elliot would probably get started on her thesis while he was over there and bring it back with him when he came. That kept Denise happy for a day or two, then she started getting worried again. Jimmy called Fay. Elliot hadn't showed up. Fay was a little worried, but not too. After all, she knew Elliot. He was probably parked in some hotel room, either in New York or Newark, having a maid run his errands for him. After about a week Jimmy called Fay again and Elliot was there all right, sobering up. He had been hiding out in a Philadelphia hotel.

"What about Denise's paper?" Jimmy asked him. "Or her money?"

"Tell her I'll give her her money back as soon as I get my social security check," he said. He sounded sick, as he always was after a binge, so Jimmy didn't push it too far. Only thing was, Denise was after Jimmy now. So he said: "Denise wants to know where you live. Should I tell her?"

"For God's sake, no! I'll send her the money when I get it. You can't get blood from a turnip, can you?" Jimmy realized that he must be broke and waiting for his check.

Elliot sounded beat; so Jimmy said, "O.K., O.K.," and let it go at that. He knew that Elliot was going to dry out for a couple of weeks, take long hot baths, eat, and take vitamins, and sleep, until he was his old ruddy, rosy sixty-eight year-old self again, detoxified and sober as some judges. He figured Elliot would pay Denise off, now that he was getting sobered up. What he had not reckoned was that Fay had been living on the owner's house-money all this time, juggling the roomers' rents in the books like a champion embezzler. Elliot would have to replace that money, so he might not be able to pay Denise back. A few more days passed, and Jimmy couldn't hold Denise off any more, and he didn't have enough money to pay her himself, having to fork over every extra cent he earned to Miss Bee, who had become a double-barreled bitch since Elliot had taken off, Elliot having apparently given her reason to believe that there might be something between them (the old goat); so Jimmy gave Denise the address in Newark, and his blessings into the bargain—let the principals fight it out; Jimmy was only an agent, an unwilling broker. Denise took off for Newark, angry now, and hurt, and determined, and formidable as a sumo wrestler, too.

Elliot's pomaded, neatly-combed hair stood right up on end when he saw her come in the door. She said: "Mr. Whistler, I'm surprised at you. I thought you were a gentleman, and I discover instead that you can't be trusted. I should have remembered what Jimmy told me once about how you stole his money when he was in the Marines."

Fay smelled Elliot's blood and wanted some of it herself. She chimed in: "I know; it's *terrible*. Elliot, you've got to pay this girl what you owe her." Fay was only on Denise's side because she was angry at Elliot for leaving her to steal from the landlord.

Elliot had been caught off guard. His social security check was sitting on the table, right under Denise's nose. She saw it through her hornrims and said to him: "I'm going to stay right here until you pay me;" whereupon she sat down, opened her *The Brothers Karamazov,* and began to read with great concentration. Elliot considered running her out, but she was too big. Fay offered her something to eat and began to prepare a little spread. Denise began cutting slices from a leg of lamb that was on the table, and that decided it. Elliot figured if he didn't get a move on to cash that check Denise would devour the whole larder. He hurried up to the supermarket on the corner, cashed his check, and hurried back, forked over the five tens to Denise, and sat down, fuming.

"Thank you, Mr. Whistler," Denise said. "I cannot say that I have enjoyed our dealings. Good day."

"Goodbye," called Fay, from the front porch, waving her to the bus stop on the corner. "Come back and see us— any friend of Jimmy's is always welcome."

A month passed and Jimmy regained his solitude. Though he was working at physically demanding jobs during the day his mind seemed strangely alert and ambitious at five o'clock. Even the rejection slips that he'd taped to the wall seemed to inspire him because he'd just won a five hundred pound prize from an English anthology for his poem, "The Poor Boy." He wished he still had that Polaroid. He'd take a picture of that check and pin it up at the top of all his rejections.

SPARROW

Both living at the same rooms-for-rent joint, Miss Bees', a long barracks-like brick building with twenty cubicles in the heart of Greenwich Village, Jimmy and Denise, mostly one might suppose, to ward off loneliness, had become literary pals, what with her working on her Columbia master's thesis on John Donne, and him trying to write a novel, or whatever it was he was pounding his typewriter about night and day. One afternoon they shared a joint in Jimmy's room. Denise rose from her lotus position to study Jimmy's British poetry prize check, xeroxed and framed on a wall.

"What are you writing, Jimmy?"

"Part of a poem, part of a play, part of a novel."

"You know John Donne, Jimmy—"

"No man is an island," he broke in, and his words swirled away in a tide of pot.

"—and no woman, either" Denise said, thoughtfully. She told Jimmy about a friend of hers, named Phyllis, who'd recently broken off with her boyfriend, Reginald, "a real cool black cat, so she's lonely," and asked if Jimmy'd like to meet her. He said he would; and they walked over to the then-ominous Lower East Side one hot summer night.

Houston Street; big ugly old apartment building; Phyllis at the apartment door in a slip: a thin pale little wraith, with pale little curves of breasts and hips, and pale little legs just missing being curveless, womanly shapes so subtle that a change of light could have caused them to vanish. She had long fine hair, pale and no-colored, but with a soft sheen, a luster that, when it was noticed at all, was more an emotional response than a fact.

They talked, Jimmy feeling rather formal and incongruous in the starched dress shirt and pressed summer slacks he'd worn to work, sitting on the edge of a floored mattress, a pad, in a room lit only by stub-ends of drooling candles stuck anywhichway on the low night-cum-coffee table before him, observing the walls, painted scarlet and bright green and deep purple, and the mobiles made of coathangers, and the jet-black cat with golden eyes that kept leaping up from its dreams to squirt short shots of piss like a squeezed wine-bag in any direction it found itself aiming, then smugly curling up again to nap; him watching the cat, and watching Phyllis and Denise, too, and listening to them drawing—*ss-eh, ssss-eh*—on the little corn-cob pipe they passed back and forth, a pipe with a strip of tin-foil on top held by an elastic band and punctured for pot; Jimmy watching and listening and drinking the green Ballantine ale he'd brought along; and thinking, while eyeing those thin little legs like a girl-child's, how tenderly he would hold a girl like Phyllis in his arms. Gently, gently, or she might break.

But then it was time to go and he took the frail little hand proffered him and gently squeezed it; and he looked back from the door that Denise in her big ambling way was closing and saw the small pale wraith in a slip fade, withdraw into the rear darkness of the apartment with trembling, unsteady steps, the dart-dart of retreat, like a pale butterfly into dark and ancient woods.

Jimmy liked Denise, and he liked Phyllis. They supplied all the female companionship he felt he could handle. They were both of a studious bent and were a welcomed and refreshing change from his Ex, the beauty-queen dancer, Vera. Their discussions of art and music and poetry lent a lively diversion to Jimmy's rather monastic life of work, study and writing. Sometimes the three of them would get together for a movie or a Chinese dinner. Jimmy began to look forward to their meetings and to feel a certain affection for Phyllis. Though he had sworn off women, Phyllis was a definite balm to his nerves. She was an opposite number from Vera, all right. Phyllis had had a childhood of illnesses and confinements which had molded her into a person of imagination and observation. She was thoughtful and somewhat timid. Vera, on the other hand, had been a veritable physical force. She'd had plans for her life, and Jimmy's too. She was going somewhere in the world. She was a beautiful professional dancer. She was going to point her pretty toes and kick life the way she wanted it to go, like a soccer ball. She was going to kick the poetry right out of Jimmy, but she hadn't been successful, thanks to Marsayas, a man who knew something about bliss.

One night, Jimmy decided to take his last quart of ale over and see Phyllis. He tapped on her door and she invited him in to that dim psychedelic haven, her apartment. They sat side by side on the mattress and split the ale, talking and gazing into the flames of a couple of giant oozing candles stuck on the stained coffee table. Jimmy slipped his hand under Phyllis's bony bottom and pulled her closer. She did not resist. She did not resist anything for about the next half hour. Indeed, he was surprised by her boldness. She stood up and stripped in the candlelight as he lay back waiting to see. His interest was not merely sexual, and certainly not sensual. He was curious. What were her clothes hiding? She appeared in them so frail, bodiless, whispy. She had told him that she had broken up with her boyfriend, that his overtures were welcome. But the boyfriend's picture sat on a table near the mattress, overseeing the scene, a good-looking black fellow—named Reginald—of about Jimmy's size and build. What had he seen in her, this whispy girl-woman, this pale, thin girl? She was naked in the candle-lit

97

room, all dark out of the candles' range, and small and white as a Roswell alien, as the body of a flying-saucer creature taken from a crashed spacecraft. She stepped forward, so that he could see her face again. She had removed her glasses and her eyes looked large and dark and upward slanted, but he knew them to be pale, the palest blue, and her let-down hair was just a glow of soft light, waving about her narrow, bony shoulders, that had no meat on them, no muscle-mass at all, and tugged at his shoes, clump, clump, and his socks, and his blue jeans, and his jockey shorts, tug, tug, tug, off, off, off, and she eased herself down astraddle on him, and he held her back and rolled them over and found that he could feel himself through her paper-thin back, could almost grip his own organ, as he thrusted in his gentlest slow-motion. But he found that there was no sensual response in her at all; she seemed merely to want to please him but did not have the strength nor the passion to be anymore responsive than to wait for his orgasm and in the most off-key way whisper, "That was good." It was all a terrible letdown, an anticlimax, so to speak, and, as he withdrew, he began to laugh, a low and sorrowful laugh it was, more pain than pleasure in it, and she asked him what he was thinking.

"Thinking," he said, "I believe that's what you've been doing." But she flung herself against him and clutched at him.

"Oh I love you," she cried. But he, used to the physical passion of Vera, the athlete, the dancer, and others as physical and passionate, tried to grasp what she had got from the encounter. Her tears were genuine. He could feel them welling up in her thin breastless breastbone, throbbing in her throat, a vibration in the vein in her neck. He held her back and looked at her and everything he saw looked genuine.

"I never come," she said. "I can't come. I guess I just don't have the hormones in me. That was one of the problems Reginald and I had. He was very hurt that he couldn't make me come. He said that he just knocked himself out trying. He gave up on me. Please don't give up on me, Jimmy."

And later, when Jimmy stood and put his crumpled jeans back on, he extended his hand to Phyllis, pulled her up, and hugged her. He patted her soft, no-color hair and remembered ruefully his vow to remain unentangled with women, their demands, their needs, and sometimes, their due. He walked back to his room through the hot, humid New York night filled with city lights, vaguely trying to discern if he was sinking or swimming, or merely floating. Maybe, he thought, it was the residual pot.

* * *

It happened three months later, as they were driving cross town. Marsayas, Jimmy's friend and guru, had picked them up. Phyllis and Jimmy were sitting in the front seat with him. Butterworth, a visiting friend of his who'd fallen out with his wife, and was a former Marine education officer, sat in the back seat. Then, suddenly, the whole front seat of the car was filled with blood.

"Jesus Christ!" Jimmy cried. "What's that?"

Phyllis had not noticed that she was bleeding, until that moment. She didn't appear to be in any great pain. But she was the color of flour-paste.

"Does it hurt, honey?" Jimmy asked, nonplussed, stupid, not knowing what to make of this horror.

"No," she said. "It's just cramping a little."

Giant Marsayas was shaken. "Should I drive to a hospital? St. Vincent's is just up town." He didn't like this sort of thing, no, not at all. Jimmy didn't like it any better than Marsayas did. It was horrifying to see all that blood, the blush drained from a ghost.

"No," Phyllis said. "I don't want to go to a hospital. Take me home. *Please!*"

"But you'll bleed to death," Jimmy said.

"No, I won't. I'll be all right as soon as I lie down. Please, take me home!"

They were closer to Phyllis's apartment on Houston Street than they were to St. Vincent's Hospital, uptown, and Jimmy could see a flickering look of relief dance in Marsayas's eyes at the thought of getting rid of them as soon as possible. This wasn't his scene at all. Jimmy'd have bet that the first thing Marsayas would do after dumping them would be to get numbingly drunk.

"Oh, I'm getting blood all over the car," said Phyllis, squirming around, pushing a tattered old newspaper that Butterworth had handed her from the back seat, under her little bottom.

"Oh, hell, the car!" said Marsayas, driving like he didn't know where he was going. "Don't worry about the blood; just worry about getting well."

"You see what you've done—taking her out in this condition? She's having a miscarriage," Butterworth said. "This is your fault, Jim."

"I didn't even know she was pregnant. She didn't show," said Jimmy. He had an arm around Phyllis; he turned to face Butterworth, who bounced about behind him.

"So help me, Butterworth," Jimmy shouted over the traffic noises, "as soon as I get this straightened out, I'm going to kick your shiny teeth in."

"I'll be glad to meet you—anytime," Butterworth came back coolly.

"Shut the hell up, Butter—both of you two stupid Marines!" Marsayas shouted. "What the hell's wrong with you? Is this any time for that?" Marsayas pulled the car to the curb in front of Phyllis's apartment house and Butterworth got out and held the door for Jimmy while he climbed

100

over Phyllis, who had been sitting on the outside, near the window, because she liked the breeze, and got out and picked her up in his arms and carried her into the building, leaving drip-drops of blood wherever he stepped. Behind him he heard the car door slam after Butterworth, and Marsayas, burning rubber, screech the car off—Marsayas, the doctor who couldn't stand the sight of blood.

Inside, he was about to put Phyllis to bed, but she ordered him to let her down. She staggered into the bathroom and shut the door. There was much flushing, a few moans and groans, then a long silence.

Jimmy knocked on the door.

"What is it?" she called weakly.

"Are you O.K.?"

"Yes. Come in and get me, please, Jimmy; I can't walk. The door's unlocked."

Jimmy opened the door and there she sat on the john, her little bottom so small she sank into the commode like a child. There were bloody towels all over the floor. Blood everywhere. He made up his mind, then.

"I'm going outside and get a cab," he told her. There was no nearby access to a phone to call an ambulance. "You stay where you are. When I get back I'll fix you up to go to the hospital."

"I don't want to go. Please, Jimmy; I don't want to go to the hospital."

"No, Phyl, you've *got* to go to the hospital, that's all there is to it. You'll die if you don't. You'll bleed to death." But she was unconscious now, stuck in the stool like a wilted little pale-green weed in a porcelain pot.

Jimmy ran outside and hailed a cab and told the driver to wait, explaining that it was a hospital case, and ran back in and lifted her out of the commode. It went crazily through his mind that she was being treated by life like something that was meant to be flushed down the toilet.

Even as he picked her up the blood poured from between her spindly legs, plopping in cherry-red gouts into the already overfilling, splashing bowl. He held her with one arm, like a rag doll, and flushed the mess away. It had to be gone. He couldn't bear it. Then he stuffed a big wad of towels between her legs and wrapped a blanket around her and carried her out to the cab. He'd had the good luck to get a sympathetic cabby. In fifteen minutes she was checked in at the hospital.

Jimmy waited to find out if she was going to be all right, and was told, eventually, that she was. She was being transfused.

He left St. Vincent's and bought himself a couple of sandwiches, a container of coffee, a six pack of beer, and went back to Phyllis's apartment (somehow he couldn't bring himself to think of it as his own, although he'd paid the last rent on it; maybe because accepting her apartment as his own would mean a final acceptance of his situation). There he ate his little meal, drank his coffee, and proceeded to sip the beer until the small hours of the morning.

Serious times were here. He had hoped for an education. He had hoped for peace and quiet in which to write. He had hoped that he'd have time to live through what had happened to him with Vera. He had hoped that somehow he'd get his guts back, and be able to deal with things again; he had hoped that he'd have time to live through his hurt and his sense of failure before life came at him again, swinging its big, clouting, medicine-ball fists. And now this. More chaos.

He sat deep into the night in that ridiculously painted apartment, with its psychedelic walls, its mobiles made from coat hangers, its filthy, furry, unframed mattress, and its mad, yellow-eyed, pee-squirting black cat, Phyllis's familiar, and drank his beer and tried to understand what manner of woman-child it was to whom he was obligated in grief.

102

What was at the center of that little soul who was carrying (or had it flushed away down the toilet?) a small pulsation of his own being, some of his own cells, his own actual life, living, living? Who was Phyllis? Did she hurt? Was she in pain now? Had he caused it? What was her unhappiness like? How felt? Like his own? Worse? Dreadful? Could she bear it? Was she afraid? Was there no way he could find in his heart her pain, her anguish?

There was a big stack of notebooks, wirebound books bought in stationery stores, books children use for homework, about twenty of them, stacked on the floor, next to the mattress, at its foot. Jimmy had seen them before, but had never paid any attention to them. He pulled the top one off the stack and opened it. It was filled with pictures of dinosaurs, tyrannosaurs, brontosaurs—all that pretty, Jurassic family—clipped from "National Geographic," looked like. He flipped back to the cover, upon which was hand-printed—

PHYLLY'S DIPLODOCUS BOOK,
awarded to her on her ninth
birthday, for being such a
good, brave, and patient girl while
being sick, with LOVE
from Mummy and Daddy

all in different colored crayons. It triggered something in him and he began to cry, sob out loud in the empty apartment. In a few minutes he got himself under control and put the book back. Shit, it was only a crying jag. "A crying jag, that's all it is," he told himself.

Jimmy had paid the last rent; the last one that they had paid, that is; which, to date, left them two months arrears. Why they hadn't been able to scrape together the paltry sum of seventy-five dollars a month for this mad, dingy pad, he didn't know. He guessed it was drugs and booze—expensive pastimes. He hadn't been making much, either, since quitting Barnes & Noble; where he had worked as a rare book librarian, only working for Strong Arm Labor or, 'til recently, at Tony's Halfway House, or as a dish-washer in Katz's deli, across Houston Street from Phyllis's building. It hadn't seemed important to him to have money. He had only needed enough to keep on reading and writing. But now?

Phyllis had been drawing a check of a hundred a month from her daddy, the pilot. He could have sent her a hundred a week, but he apparently had the idea of forcing her to get some kind of job, do something with herself. It would have been incomprehensible to him that she could have actually lived on only that hundred. She would write to him occasionally and tell him that she was working at this or that. Jimmy doubted if she had worked since she had been in New York. She had a reasonably good education, having completed three years at the University of Washington. But she had majored in English, and had no secretarial skills—could not type or take dictation—so there was really very little she could do to earn money. He thought of himself—a poet with a high school G.E.D. from the service. A year at NYU. Dramatic schools. Bah! Beatniks, bah!

Phyllis was likely to stay in the hospital for another week and Jimmy was absolutely broke, and the Marshal was coming around to put their things on the street. Aside from a few changes of clothes, his books and typewriter, Jimmy had nothing, his poetry prize money having run out. But Phyllis was a magpie, a nesting bird. Like those extremely introverted lunatics who are discovered dead by the police and are written up in the tabloids, Phyllis surrounded herself with all manner of junk. Her apartment was an hallucination extended into the physical world, a secret garden wherein she could shape her own particular brand of madness in safety. Conjuring up that early image of her pale form retreating into a candle-lit and madly-colored sanctum, Jimmy

104

thought of fear. She was like one of those soft little hermit crabs that scurry about in what appears to be terror, looking for an empty mollusk shell in which to hide. Hike, hike, get the thing up on your back, little side-walker, and, teeter-totter, off you go. But now Jimmy or life or something had caused little Phyllis to be yanked out of her shell. Here she was, soft and exposed.

It would have been easy enough to let the Marshal throw the whole works out into the street. A few months earlier Jimmy might have done just that—just upped and walked out on the whole crazy situation, split. But not now. Something had happened to him. For the first time since the early days with Vera, he was experiencing glad twinges of responsibility. But it wasn't quite a phoenix that was rising from such small sparks. Nevertheless. . . . Nevertheless. . . . Jimmy had to save Phyllis's little treasures, the whole pile of junk. And what he needed was money, "long green." That evening he went to the hospital to visit Phyllis. But before going in, he asked the doctor in attendance how she was.

"Your wife will be all right, Mr. Whistler, but I have some bad news for you." He gave Jimmy one of those steady-eyed, professional looks.

"Well, what is it?" If Phyllis was O.K., Jimmy couldn't imagine what bad news the doctor could have for him.

"You've lost the baby," the doctor said.

Well, for God's sake, of course they had! Still, it was odd to hear it put that way—"the baby." Was it really a little living thing, then? How strange it was to think of it that way! Jimmy wondered who it was, that little soul. He went in to see Phyllis. She looked very weak. She was being fed intravenously. But, somehow, she looked better. There was just the faintest tinge of pink in her cheeks. Relief, perhaps. Or maybe fever?

"Are you all right?"

"Yes. Oh, Jimmy, I saw it. I saw it when it came out. It had a little body and a definite head, like a little person."

"That's impossible," Jimmy said. The idea of its having a shape horrified him. "It was an homunculus of your mind."

"Oh, no. It really did, Jimmy. It had a little body and a head."

Jimmy couldn't stand this kind of talk, although it seemed to make Phyllis happy, somehow. Her cheeks had pinked a bit more, and her eyes were shiny. She was smiling—faintly radiant, really.

He changed the subject. "Listen, Phylly. I've got to get the stuff out of the apartment before they come and throw it out. Is it all right with you if I move it?"

"Oh, yes. Do whatever you have to."

"O.K.; now look. I'll come back tomorrow morning, if I can, but if I don't, it's because I'm getting the stuff moved. In that case I'll be here tomorrow night, O.K.?"

"O.K. But—Jimmy?"

"Yes?"

"Are we together?"

"Yes. Don't worry about anything. The doctor said you'll be out in a week. I'll have a place for you to come to, I promise."

"Do you have any money?"

"Yes," he lied.

"Oh, Jimmy."

"Don't worry, hear?"

"No. I won't."

"I've got to get going."

"Goodbye, Jimmy."

"Goodbye, Phyl. See you later." He gave her a kiss on the cheek and left.

*   *   *

106

The management of Phyllis's apartment were coming at almost any time now to dump her stuff on the street. What to do? Jimmy drained his beer and at the bottom of the can found a half-baked idea. Eureka! He thought he knew where he could get the money he needed. For several months, Marsayas had been working at home editing "How-To" books and had just received one of his editing checks. If he could get Marsayas to lend him fifty of it, he'd be able to find a furnished apartment, move Phyllis's clothes and papers and paraphernalia into it (maybe Marsayas would even drive him from one apartment to the other). He'd then get himself some work and pay Marsayas back and put a stock of food in, whatever Phyllis would need when she was released, and have a little nest all set for her to come home to and recuperate in. With this plan in mind, Jimmy hopped a subway down to Brooklyn.

When he got to the apartment, Marsayas and Butterworth were drinking. Jimmy was so relieved that he'd been able to put together some small vision of hope that, after a drink or two, he actually found himself in high (or slightly hysterical) spirits. Soon he was laughing and chatting away like an idiot. "Yes," he was saying, "Phyllis is going to be fine. Just fine."

"The poor little girl," said Butterworth. But Jimmy didn't pay any attention to him. He had to make himself particularly charming today. After all, he was going to borrow money. Then he noticed that there were suitcases out.

"What's up?" he said, giving a look.

"Oh," said Marsayas, "my boss at How-To Books is letting us have his cabin in Bucks County for a few weeks. We're going tonight, maybe, or tomorrow morning."

"Oh, Christ, Marsayas, that's great! But I wanted to ask a favor of you, and now . . I suppose—"

"What was it?"

Jimmy told him.

It might have been the perfect time to ask Marsayas for money—just when he most needed it himself—because, being Marsayas, he was fond of grand gestures. The idea of giving all his money away just when he would need it probably appealed to him. But, on the other hand, he really *did* need all his money, at this particular juncture. Jimmy could read his thoughts, the mixed impulses. He'd have loved to have responded immediately, for the sake of the shock value, and thrown Jimmy his wallet. But then Jimmy knew, too, that Marsayas was thinking of Butterworth, of the negative effect that would have on him. Jimmy's heart was sinking into his stomach. But, thank God, Marsayas came through. He reached back to his hip pocket, withdrew his wallet, and handed Jimmy five tens from it. Jimmy whistled like a kettle with relief; he couldn't help himself.

"But how are you going to live in Bucks County?" said Butterworth.

"I'll send him the money as soon as I get it," Jimmy said, "and more, too. Thank you, Marsayas, thank you, I can't tell you how much this means to me." Jimmy was weak and shaking with relief. Up until that moment, he'd been afraid to admit to himself how much he had been counting on Marsayas, but now he could.

"Hell, that's what buddies are for," said Marsayas, grinning his broad, gargoyle grin. He poured them each a great big waterglassful of the rot-gut he usually drank, and, beaming madly, toasted, "Prost!"

Jimmy Prosted him right back with everything he had. "Prost!" he said. "*PROST!*" he cried.

Marsayas looked as though he had shocked himself into a kind of hilarious madness. Jimmy thought he was already beginning to be frightened, have doubts.

"You have a hell of a nerve," said Butterworth, "coming here and taking money Marsayas needs for his trip."

"Leave him alone!" said Marsayas sternly. "This is my house and I won't have it!" Then he jumped to his feet, in that sudden way of his. "I'm tired of drinking this stuff," he said. "Come on. Let's go down to Chic's." There was a comfy Mafia bar on the first floor.

"I'm sorry," said Butterworth, "I'm not drinking with Jimmy."

"Stay here, then," said Marsayas; and, to Jimmy, "Come on, buddy." Down they went.

The day had gone wonderfully well. Jimmy felt positively blessed. All he had to do now was get out early the next morning and find a furnished room. He should have gone back to the apartment and packed, but Marsayas wanted a drinking companion, and Jimmy at least owed him that—some company. But, as it turned out, it was a bad blunder to have stayed with him. Marsayas had nothing to do until Joan got home from work, and, when he wasn't editing a book, usually drank the day away. Now, as a result of the shock of having given a chunk of his money to Jimmy, he began to get seriously drunk, fast. Jimmy was half drunk with relief himself, and a few drinks took care of the other half. In an hour, he was only vaguely aware of Marsayas's presence, what with the noise of the juke and jammed joint, and when Jimmy looked for Marsayas an hour after that, he was gone, and Butterworth was in his place, on the barstool next to Jimmy.

"Where's Marsayas?"

"Marsayas is upstairs. He sent me down to ask you for the money back. He said you can keep five."

"But I need it," Jimmy said.

"He needs it, too."

"But I gotta have it. He said I could've it. It's you, you sonofabitch, you did this to me."

"Whatever's wrong with you, you did it to yourself. Now, gimme the money."

"Oh, *God!*" Jimmy didn't care. He was beaten, beaten. "Here," he said, and slapped the bills into Butterworth's fat, pink mitt. Jimmy hated guys like Butterworth in the Marine Corps. He called them Goody-Two-Shoes. Butterworth walked out, winner and new champion, and Jimmy sat on his barstool, swivelling a little this way, a little that, beaten, drunk, sunk. He saw Phyllis's poor little skinny body under a sheet, and all her doodads being taken away from her, having no place to go when she was released from the hospital. He had got her into this mess and he had to get her out of it. He chug-a-lugged his beer, and thumped and stomped his way back upstairs to confront Marsayas.

When he knocked on the door, Marsayas asked who it was, although he damned well knew. That was by way of telling Jimmy that maybe he should just walk away and let it be. But Jimmy couldn't. He began to feel as though he were fighting for his very life. The whole damned thing had somehow got to be of monumental importance. He *had* to get that money. He didn't care now if he had to crawl around on the floor and beg Marsayas, licking his toes and barking—he'd have done it. He was half choking when he said that it was himself at the door. It came out in such a thick, broken little voice—"*Me.*"

"Come in," Marsayas called.

There they sat, around the table—Joan had come home in the interim. Joan and Jimmy had always been friends, so he could see how bad things were, because even she was giving him the fish-eye. He felt that they had been talking about him—his sad case—Oh, his shame was boundless!

"What d'ya want?" said Marsayas. He was zonked all right, even zonked Jimmy could see that Marsayas was zonked.

"Marsayas, please," Jimmy began, his knees shaking, "I've *got* to have that money. I don't know what I'll do otherwise. *Please!* I'll give it back to you in spades." His legs

110

were practically dancing out from beneath him.

"I can't give it to you. I need it myself. Didn't Butter tell you that?"

"Yes—but—"

"Why don't you get out of here," said Butterworth, "and leave these people alone?"

"You dirty bassard!" Jimmy cried. "You're behind this."

"I'm going to run you out of here," Butterworth said.

"Sit down, Butter!" Marsayas roared.

"Why don't you go now, Jimmy," Joan put in. And that really hurt; that was it; that was too much. Butterworth was standing there on the other side of the table like Smedley Butler—Big Marine! Jimmy had known so many like him, seen that stance so often. His legs were bobbing underneath him when he made the leap, just like he had been warming up for it. He went crashing across the table and grabbed Butterworth, and then the whole thing began to fall over sideways—Jimmy, the table, Butterworth, dishes, silverware, bottles—onto Marsayas, who was half risen, and took him along with it, like a big, multiplying slide of rocks, to go crashing and bouncing on the floor.

Jimmy heard Joan screaming behind him, but all his concentration was on Butterworth, whom he had by the throat. Butterworth was kicking, and hammering on Jimmy's back with his big pink mitts. Jimmy'd throttle the sonofabitch breathless before he let go. He wouldn't talk for a month. But something looped into the collar at the back of Jimmy's neck and pulled him up, turned him in a circle, so he saw three-quarters of the room go by, saw the terrible disapproving face of Joan, and headed him toward the door. It was Marsayas. Then Butterworth was opening the door and Jimmy was being shoved through it. Butterworth kicked his behind on the way out. The door slammed shut. Jimmy heard it being bolted. He stood in the hall for a few

111

minutes, getting his bearings, then wiped the tears from his eyes and, like a loose-stringed puppet, staggered down the stairs, through the hall, and into the street.

*   *   *

Jimmy woke, his eyes were photophobic; the glare of the sun coming in the window was an agony. He got up, moved into a dark corner, and sat like a mole in a hole and finished his coffee. He tried to think, but could not remember how he got back to Philly's apartment. In the blood-smeared bathroom, he took a beating hot shower, then a cold one, hanging on the tarnished old brass faucets for support. He shaved with a dull blade, patching himself with toilet paper. He went to the corner greasy spoon and ate fried boiled ham and wet eggs. He went to the corner dive and ordered a flat draft beer in a stained stein and begged change for the antiquated telephone, which he had just discovered. He called Marsayas.

"Hello?"

It was Butterworth.

"Hello. This is Jim."

"Oh, Jim. Look, I wanna tell you something. I'm sorry about last night. I was pretty drunk."

"Christ, so was I. And I'm sorry too."

"I suppose you want to speak to Marsayas."

"Yeah. Is he there?"

"Nope. They went to Bucks County last night—after the fracas."

"Oh."

"But look, buddy—Semper Fi—what's the problem?"

"I've got to get Phyllis's stuff out of the apartment and put it somewhere. The Marshal's coming to evict us. Then I've got to get some place for her to come home to."

"Hmmm. Well, I'll tell you—where are you?"

112

"In a bar near her place."

"Well, look, I'll get a cab and come over there—and we can move the stuff up here, O.K.?"

"God, yes! That'd be great!"

"O.K. I'll be right over. You wait at the house."

"O.K. I'll be there."

"So long."

"So long."

That was that. They moved all Phyllis's stuff into Marsayas's apartment that morning, making several trips in the cab. Butterworth paid for everything. He even helped Jimmy pack the stuff. After the last trip, they sat down and had a beer together. They shook hands and made friends. Butter really wasn't such a bad old egg after all. He even loaned Jimmy twenty bucks to maneuver on.

"Aw, shit, I told you I was drunk, Jimmy. We Marines have to stick together, don't we? Semper Fi."

"Semper Fi, Butter."

The day Phyllis was released from the hospital Jimmy checked them into a fleabag hotel in Chelsea. He'd got a few days work and had some money in his kick; but not much, not enough. They couldn't afford to go on paying high daily rates very long, not that, and eat in restaurants, too. Besides, Phyllis shouldn't have to go out to restaurants to eat. Jimmy could bring food up to her—but what would she do when Jimmy was working? The doctor told her to stay in bed for a couple of weeks. It wasn't just the miscar-riage—she was anemic and a dozen other things. There were prescriptions, vitamins, etc. Phyllis suggested that she might call her father and ask him for her check a little early. That was a good idea, but it still left them with problems. Then Jimmy thought of big, sprawling Newark, right across the river, where there were two giant transient apartment house-hotels he knew of, side by side, way down on Broad Street—The Margarita and The Celeste. One could walk

113

freely in and out of these joints. They were like hotels in that respect—with the check-in desks located somewhere on the first floor, just another apartment, only with Dutch doors, the bottom half shut, the top open, a registration book at belly height. Inside—usually a frowsy dame of middle age, with few and yellowed teeth, and a skinny bald man in shirtsleeves. Cans of beer. A TV set with bent rabbit ears—in summer a baseball game, in winter a Charlie Chan movie. There were large marmoreal bathrooms in the halls on every floor where one might find used condoms floating in the bowls, small packets of pills tucked away under the tubs, or decks of pornographic cards. All sorts of treasures might be found in these places, pelfs of monumental interest to pubescent boys, he remembered. And then, too, these bathrooms offered a safe location in which to smoke. The neighborhood hard rocks from ten to thirteen (the ones still young enough to have some small fear of the wrath of the public, authorities, or parents) would gather in these filthy latrines, stepping friskily over the inevitable pot-holed, sour-pee-puddles, and take their places along the rim of the tub to perform the ritual of lighting up and spraying the already foul air with Lucky Strizz streamers, which quickly broke into clouds. Then, as they smoked and talked, in the locally designed gutturals of their monosyllabic jargon, they would study the walls. It was from those walls that, as a shoeshine boy, Jimmy had learned about sex.

Jimmy decided that he and Phyllis should check out and go over to Newark to one of these half-way houses and get a furnished apartment by the week—there were always vacancies there, unlike in New York—and that's what they did. Jimmy vowed he'd build a little nest for Philly, his partner in sorrow; his little bird with a broken wing.

THE CUBAN (THESIS) CRISIS

In October, Jimmy Whistler and his girlfriend, Phyllis, received a visit from their friend, Denise. She sat monumental and Gert Steinian at a rickety table in their apartment at the Margarita. Beer and pretzels vanished before Jimmy's eyes. Between Rabelaisian mouthfuls, Denise stated her case. "I can't do this damned thesis," she said.

She was stoned on pot, or a lot of something else, but she looked worried too. "I have to have it in by November. I just can't get anywhere with it. Ever since you won that poetry prize, Jimmy, I've been thinking that you could write it. I don't know why I asked your dad. I should have asked you in the first place. Besides, I knew how much you loved Donne. I remember you telling me so when we first met. I could bring all my books and notes over here and you could put it all together. I know you could, Jimmy."

"I don't know . . ."

"My trust fund says that I can spend all the money I need to on education. I can give you three hundred dollars for writing it, five hundred if you type it up in good shape for me. You can type. I've seen you."

"Why can't you do it yourself? You've been reading Donne for years. You've been studying at Columbia—how long has it been?" Jimmy picked up an opener and double-popped a sweating can of Ballantine beer. He quoted Roethke:

> "I am my father's son, I am John Donne
> whenever I see her with nothing on."

115

He saluted with a can of beer and drained it.

"You know me, Jimmy—I just stay too stoned. I can't get my head together anymore. Please do it for me. Please. It would be the biggest favor anybody's ever done me. I'll owe you more than money—eternal gratitude."

"What do you think, Phyllis?"

"I think you should do it for her, Jimmy." Phyllis had had a childhood of illnesses and confinements which had molded her into a person of imagination and observation. She was thoughtful and usually somewhat timid, but this time she jumped right in on what Jimmy thought was a ridiculous proposition.

"O.K.," said Jimmy, thinking it over. "Get me the books. God knows, we need the money. But remember you're asking me to do in about two weeks what you haven't been able to do in well over two years. Don't expect too much."

"I have to get this done before the end of term, or they'll drop me. If you'll do it, and I don't get my master's, I'll still give you half. If I do get it, I'll give you a hundred dollar bonus. How's that? I know you love poetry. You're a poet. All you have to do is explain John Donne."

"Deal!" Jimmy reached out and took Denise's big mitt and shook it.

Phyllis was across the room in the Murphy bed where she had been reading *The Courtier*, and had several newspapers spread about her. "Do you guys know that there's big trouble in Cuba? They say the Russians have put in atomic missiles down there. And look at this." She waved a *New York Times*. Denise got up and took the paper. Phyllis looked at them with the huge anxiety of a child. "I just know the stupid bastards are going to blow us all to hell. Look at the upper left hand corner. "If you want to get your masters, you better let Jimmy get started right away, before it's too late."

116

"I don't think things are that dire, my little sparrow," said Jimmy.

"Fuck it," said Denise. "I'm stoned anyway."

The next morning Denise arrived with a sea-bag full of books and notes, which she helped Jimmy organize around his typing chair. He scanned the book titles, along with pounds of indecipherable notes on legal pads and index cards.

"Jesus Christ, Denise, you don't really expect me to read all this in the next two weeks, do you?" Jimmy popped open a beer.

Phyllis was down on the floor in her pink nightie looking, stacking and re-stacking the books as if they were boxes of candy. All this English Renaissance stuff squared with her Castiglione Italian visions of courts and courtiers and ladies of the courts. She loved it. "What are you going to write, Jimmy?" she asked from the enthralling stacks.

"It has to be an analysis of 'A Litany,' which is a long poem by Donne," Denise said. "Now this is what I want," she said, taking a long draught of beer, and Jimmy cut her off right there and then.

"I can't write that way," he said. "I'll dip into these books and put what I get together and you'll just have to settle for it. That's the only way I can do it—especially with only two weeks to do it in. Now you go ahead and get out of here and let me get to work."

"You better hurry, Jimmy," said Phyllis. "The Russian ships are heading this way."

"Will you shut up about the Russian fucking ships!"

"What am I going to do in the meantime?" asked Denise. "What happens if they blow us all to hell before I get my master's?"

"You'll just have to be one dead Donneian ignoramus."

"I'll be *Donne* for!" Denise laughed hysterically.

Jimmy sat down at his little typing stand and started work. In a minute or so, he tore the page from the typewriter and handed it to Denise. He waited, now sipping a bourbon, while she read "The object of this paper is the elucidation of John Donne's poem, "A Litany," on three levels: (1) to show exactly how the poem is, and how it is not, a litany; (2) to show that the poem is a profound moral statement of a very personal order; and (3) to show that the essential theme of the poem is John Donne's personal re-creation. I should stipulate here what is meant in this context by "*re*-creation," the word and the idea offering myriad interpretations. When I speak of re-creation in this context, I am speaking of that idea in Christian thought, the most succinct statement of which is to be found in St. Paul, in the Sixth Chapter of his Epistles to the Romans, that it is possible for the Christian believer to be re-born into life before he is dead."

Denise said, "John Donne, a born-again Christian?"

"Now that's what I intend to do. Satisfied?" Jimmy said.

Phyllis said, "Wow! That's amazing!"

Denise said, "Cool, man! Hit those keys!"

Jimmy said, "Now get the hell out of here so I can work! Go and catch a falling star!"

Jimmy went into total concentration and was not aware of just when Denise left or when Phyllis fell asleep, but when he stopped for a cup of coffee Denise was gone and Phyllis was snoring. Denise had been thoughtful enough to bring him a bag full of Benzedrine tablets and he began popping them down with coffee. He snapped on the little radio for a minute, just to distract himself. "Russian ships approach Cuba." The bullshit world of the Cuban missile crisis receded as the Elizabethan world projected itself again. He lived in Donne's world until a knock came at the door. Phyllis was still sleeping. But there was natural light

118

in the room from the window. He'd been working all night. He went to the door and opened it. His father, Elliot, stood there, drunk and disheveled, a hopeful, ingratiating look on his face.

"Dad," Jimmy said, trying to untie himself from his thoughts. "What time is it?"

"Must be around ten," his father said. "The liquor store was open. Oh, to hell with it! Your mother's driving me crazy. All she knows is what Walter Winchell tells her. I came downtown on some business and I thought I'd stop in to see you. No, the truth is, I'm desperate for some intelligent conversation. I have a nice bottle of Mr. Boston with me. Would you like a drink?"

"I'll put a shot in my coffee. What's wrong, Dad? You look kind of sick."

"It's this missile crisis," said the old man, sitting down at the rickety kitchen table among the books. "Don't you think we should all go to Denver?"

"The first place they'll hit is out west," said Jimmy, sipping his spiked coffee. "That's where all the missile silos are. They have to take them out first. We're probably safer here."

"I never thought of that. I guess you learn things like that in the Marine Corps."

"It's fairly common knowledge, Dad."

The old man looked around. "What are you doing with all these books?"

"I'm writing Denise's paper for her. The one she wanted you to write."

"Oh, yes, I rather disappointed her on that one, didn't I?"

"Look, Dad, don't be worried about this missile thing. I said that they'd have to hit our silos first, but that's not quite true. They want to hit the command centers first. That means that the stupid sons-of-bitches have each other in

119

their sights—I mean Kennedy and Khrushchev—and they're not going to pull the trigger. If they could kill a few million of us without killing each other, they would, but they can't, so you might as well not worry about it. Remember what Voltaire said—"

"You've read Voltaire?" The old man looked at Jimmy with new-found respect. "Of course I've read Voltaire. Remember what Candide says, about how he's going to deal with life? He said that if he heard that the world was going to end tomorrow, he would just go on tending his little garden. Remember that?"

"I do, indeed! Just go on tending his little garden." The old man looked as if he had been handed the key to happiness.

"This has been a very edifying little talk. Let me have just one more drink and I'll be on my way. I have business to do. Important business." And he was off.

Phyllis was up, eating something.

The room was dark. Jimmy hit the light switch.

Phyllis was asleep.

The room was bright.

He went on working.

As though heav'n suffred earth-quakes, peace or war,
When new Townes rise, and olde demolish'd are.
They have empayld within a Zodiake
The free-borne Sunne, and keeps twelve signes awake
To watch his steps; the Goat and Crabbe controule,
And fright him backe, who els to eyther Pole,
(Did not these Tropiques fetter him) might runne:
For his course is not round; nor can the Sunne
Perfit a Circle, or maintaine his way
One inche direct . . .

"Oh, Jimmy," Phyllis said, "Oh, shit, I hate these bastards! Why don't they do their stupid shit by themselves and leave the rest of us out of it?"

"No man is an island, Phyl. Let me work."

Jimmy wrote: *What could be more natural at this juncture, at this time in his life, and at this point in the age in which he lived, than that Donne should choose the litany as the form in which to address his God? But, while Donne is perhaps thinking of himself as a symbol for the confusions of his age* (Jimmy thought: Chaos), *his main concern—*

"Jimmy, when are you going to sleep?"

"I'm just about half-way through. I'll keep going until I . . . " He put his head down on the typewriter and the keys flew up.

"Jimmy? Jimmy!"

SOME SOVIET SHIPS VEER FROM CUBA;
KHRUSHCHEV SUGGESTS SUMMIT MEETING

"I told you once that we wouldn't blow each other up," he said to Phyllis. "Too cowardly. Remember?" But Phyllis had been scared into near catalepsy. She had stopped going out for the past few days altogether: sat in bed day and night, a valetudinarian, her pale hair veiled by the smoke of pot, and devoured her books on the medieval Royal Courts of Europe. She hated the present bullshit world, but adored the bullshit of the past. Jimmy lay snoring, exhausted. When he woke he heard distant voices: Denise and Phyllis, chattering.

"Oh, Denise," said Phyllis, "I've never seen anything like it. He was absolutely manic, like he was on a coke-amphetamine cocktail. First he got that typewriter stand out into the middle of the room, then he stacked all your books around him like a wall, then he'd dive into one, growling the title of this book or that, then another, back and forth, up and

121

down through the stacks. I don't know if he knew what he was looking for or what. He'd highlight, underline, dog-ear, tear out, bits from this book and that, and I don't know how he knew if he was making sense or not, but he seemed to because your thesis kept getting bigger, or then he'd cut and it would get smaller again and then bigger again, like an accordion, up and down, up and down. He'd swear, drink endless cups of coffee, take shots of whiskey, curse again, leap up and almost run around the room, and this went on for almost two weeks, I swear to you, without a break. He didn't sleep, he'd doze at the typewriter, then be pounding on it again. I've never seen anything like it."

"You've read it through?" asked Denise.

"Twice. It's beautifully organized. It's just what you wanted, you'll see. When he was done writing, he re-typed the whole thing as neat as a pin. He's a very fast typist. Very fast and very neat. He even tried to line up the edge on the right margin. He used a ruler. But look at him now. He's knocked out. I've seen him do this before. He works like a madman, in a fit, then collapses."

"Let me read it. If he's done it, it's amazing. I couldn't do the damn thing for two years and he does it in two weeks, without taking any classes."

"Yes, but he knows all about Donne, so it wasn't strange material to him."

"I know. He reads Donne for fun. That's why I thought he could do it." Denise buried her face in the thesis and Phyllis went back to Castiglione.

Jimmy slept for two days and nights. He showered. He was revived. He was hungry. "How are things in Cuba?" he asked Phyllis as he fried himself a couple of eggs.

"Thank God, Jimmy, it's all settling down. The Russian ships have turned around and are heading back. Looks like we're not going to kill ourselves this time."

"Yeah," Jimmy said. "But there's plenty of time. I only worried about somebody making a stupid mistake." He shovelled in his eggs. "This brinksmanship is idiotic. Two power-mad monkeys challenging each other over coconuts. So Denise liked the paper, did she?"

"She loved it. She's sure she's going to get her master's."

"And we'll get our five hundred bucks, right? And a hundred bucks bonus!"

"She'll keep her word, Jimmy."

"About as much as anybody, I guess," Jimmy said.

For the next few weeks Jimmy just rested and read the five novels of Dashiell Hammett. Then one morning Elliot appeared at the door, hand out, as usual.

"It's near the end of the month," he said, "and I'm running a little low. My social security check hasn't come yet. I'm flat. You couldn't lend me a couple of dollars, could you, Jimmy?" Gad, but he had the look of a revenant, eyes blood-shot, nose like a rose. The old fear for his father rose up in Jimmy, then the tenderness.

"Come on in, Dad, let's have a drink."

"Good thinking, my boy! And how is the wasp-waisted little lady of kindness today?"

"I'm fine, now, Mr. Whistler," Phyllis said, "but they sure as hell had the shit scared out of me for the last couple of weeks."

"They who?" asked Elliot.

"The bullshit world! Cuba and all that, that's who!"

"Of course. I myself even considered a tactical retreat. He who fights and runs away lives to fight another day, you know. I think that was the Scarlet Pimpernel. Douglas Fairbanks, Senior. The real Douglas Fairbanks, not that skinny son of his."

"But you decided against the tactical retreat, eh, Dad?"

123

"As unbecoming an officer and a gentleman. Cannon to the left of them, cannon to the right of them, and into the breach rode the six hundred. Tennyson. I'll just sit down right here on the bed, if you don't mind." He leaned backwards wearing an expression of faith and fell across Phyllis's skinny legs. Jimmy took his free hand—the one not holding the king-sized Chesterfield—and pulled him into a sitting position. "Now where's that drink?" Elliot said. "Ho, someone's gently rapping, tapping at your chamber door."

Jimmy went to the door and opened it. "Oh, how a gala begins!" he said. Denise stepped in wearing a smile as wide as the moon and carrying innumerable packages.

"Hail to thee, Jimmy Whistler!" she cried. "You're looking at a newly minted Master of Arts! And all hail to thee, Jimmy Whistler!" She saw Elliot. "And no thanks to you, Mr. W.P.A writer!"

"May I have my drink, please?" said Elliot. "Garçon! Garçon! A drink over here, and high time. Let's have a little cheerio-chin-chin!"

"Mr. Whistler," said Denise, unloading her bundles and wriggling out of her coat, "I've got something better than a drink for you. And you too, Philly. You're gonna love this."

"What is it?" cried Phyllis.

"Hashish! Number One Tangier hash! Hashish—food of the assassins!

"Voici le temps des assassins!" piped up Jimmy.

"Rimbaud—right on—now is the time of the assassins," Denise translated. Remember, Mr. Whistler, you wanted me to get you some? I had no idea you'd be here. I brought it for Philly. I know Jimmy doesn't care. But Mr. Whistler, you're gonna love it. And I've got a check here for you, Jimmy. Five hundred smackers."

124

Jimmy shook his head for her to be quiet, but alas, too late. Elliot smelled money. "It appears that my visit is serendipitous," he said, raising his eyebrows.

"Do you have any cash, Denise?" asked Jimmy.

"Some," she said.

"Have you got fifty to give me? Or that bonus you promised?"

"Yes," said Denise, looking through her big leather bag. She handed Jimmy a hundred dollars in loose bills. Jimmy handed half of it to Elliot.

"Well, Mister Whistler, damned if you didn't get that fifty anyway," cried Denise, laughing. "You know you're never going to see that again, don't you, Jimmy? But what the hell! The missile crisis is over, I've got my master's degree, and we've got booze and hash galore. C'mon, it's party time!"

"Oh, yea, it *is* party time," piped Phyllis. "We should have a masked ball!"

GRAVITY FLOW

I

One snowy Friday evening, Jimmy Whistler took the Hudson Tubes, boarded a rickety old Newark bus for a half hour ride, and walked up Baldwin Avenue toward the house he thought of simply as "Baldwin," a big, gray, peeling, Victorian house, full of turrets and gables, with a large, sittable porch, and a short, overstuffed lawn, buttressed with a foot high wall of stone; the rooming house his parents ran, where the fallen came to rise and the risen came to fall; where nothing and everything mattered; where the incurably but, it was presumed, safely, mad were "mainlined" from gloomy institutions like Vineland for the hopelessly sad and sometimes mad and even bad, to build a little life the state was duty-bound to finance; where some committed suicide and others made incessant wars on phantasmal enemies; where the dipso- and the tulipomaniac smiled different visions from the porch; where all was well and well was ill; where life was crazily life, and death death.

For some, it may have been the dawning of the Age of Aquarius, but for Jimmy's parents there was nothing really new about the onset of the Sixties. They had been practicing a dressed-up, permanent-waved and clean-shaved version of Hippiedom ever since their son, Jimmy, could remember. Their knockabout life-style had been initiated with the Crash of Twenty-nine and developed to a fine art

126

during the Depression and the War, the best years of their lives. They had taken the job of superintending Baldwin while Jimmy was in the service. His mother, Fay, collected the rents, kept the books, and did the cleaning, as usual, while his father sat at the kitchen table, amid the debris, wearing one of his ancient, handsome, tailored suits, smoking a king-sized Chesterfield, and guzzling cheap sherry. But on this particular visit, there was a surprise for Jimmy.

"Where's Dad?" he asked, shaking out his coat and settling down for a cup of coffee in the small kitchen.

"Your father's moved out," answered Fay.

"Moved out! Where's he gone? Why?"

"I don't know. I don't know what's the matter with him. I think it's all those pills he takes. Or maybe he's getting senile. He's nearly ten years older than I am. He'll be seventy, you know."

"He's not senile. Far from it. If he's anything, he's hopped up. Is he drinking?"

"He hasn't stopped since your last visit."

Fay sat down with Jimmy. He was glad to be there, in that tiny place. Everything looked very clean and pleasant after his new place on the Lower East Side, a dump on Pitt Street, truly the pits. He had recently moved in there with his girl friend, Phyllis, who was a speed-freak artist, too hyper-active for housekeeping.

"He's been working on this new scheme of his," Fay went on, "about getting the Bishop to back him in a chain of charity stores."

"Yeah, he told me about that."

"What do you think of it?"

"It's crackers."

"Well, anyway, he says he has to be alone, so he can think. He says I'm a nay-sayer. But it isn't that, Jimmy; it's just that I don't see how he can do anything when he's

127

taking all those amphetamines and drinking all the time. How can he go to see a Bishop when he's drunk?"

"He *would*."

"Oh, I know he would. That's what I'm afraid of. Besides, that isn't the only reason he left. It's because he wants to be alone so he can drink. And do you know how much those pills of his cost him last month? Nearly a hundred dollars. I saw the bill, and I saw him take the money out of his cash box. He's not working at all, now. And there's only a few hundred dollars left. He had it up to nine hundred dollars when he was managing the Angels' Own Store. He was robbing them blind. That was the most money we've ever had at one time, and now he's spending it all. I don't know what we're going to do. He's too old to get another job. And I've got all I can do to run this house. It's a good thing we get free rent and his social security. Here, look at this—"

It was a note, scrawled in Elliot's large, aggressive hand. *My Angel*, it said. *I am leaving without saying good-bye because I don't want to wake you so early. But I'll be back tomorrow evening. Love and kisses from Casanova.*

"Casanova! Gee, that doesn't sound like Dad. Was he drunk, do you suppose?"

"I suppose so. But it was a nice note to get. It really cheered me up. He left it yesterday morning. He spent the night here. He came up to get his heavy overcoat out of the cleaners, and it was snowing so hard I talked him into staying. He doesn't look well, either, Jimmy; he's getting gray in the face from drinking. And did you notice his eyes the last time you saw him?"

"No."

"His eyes are all mixed bloodshot and yellow. And do you know what it's from? I found out. I caught him taking some new pills, things I never saw before, and when I asked him what they were, he looked so guilty. Finally I got it out

128

of him. The last time he went to the drug store to fill his prescriptions—he's got about twenty, you know, and they're all expired or faked—he asked the clerk if there was something he could take to . . . you know, to be able to make love. The clerk told him this bottle of pills would work. All they are is iron tablets—I read the label—but he's been taking them by the handful. They're turning the whites of his eyes yellow. That's what I think."

Jimmy couldn't help laughing, and Fay began to laugh too.

"I think that's why he's gone down to that hotel apartment house on Broad Street, the Margarita, where you and Phyllis stayed," Fay said, turning serious. I think he hopes he'll find some woman in that place who'll stimulate him." Then she laughed again. "But I don't think he will."

"Oh, Mom, I think he'll come home when he gets tired of it. This is just another binge."

"I don't know," Fay said, "he's got this bug in him about going some place. He's been talking a lot about Denver, and about the old days when he had money. He's been saying that he wants to go back out to Denver before he dies."

"He always says that when he's drunk."

"But I think he means it this time. I think he'd like to take the money and go out there. It's only that he doesn't want to leave you here in the East. He'd never go anywhere unless you went. He loves you so much, Jimmy."

"I know, Mom. I love him, too, but Jesus, he has a strange way of showing it."

"But what would we do out there? I don't know what he could ever do, at his age. It's just a dream of his. Another of his crazy dreams." They were silent for a few moments. Then she asked, "Do you miss Vera?" Vera: Jimmy's violent ex-wife.

"It's peaceful without her. I can write."

129

"I never liked her—you know that."

"I know. But let's stay off her, Mom."

"She calls sometimes, asking about you, but I don't tell her anything."

"Well, don't. She used to lay in wait for me outside the bookstore. That's why I quit. It's got to be a clean break. If I went back to her, it would just be the same old thing. She was always nagging at me about being an actor. But I don't want to be an actor, I want to be a poet. I've just won a prize. I'm beginning to get somewhere."

"But, Jimmy, poets don't make any money, do they?"

Jimmy changed the subject. How could he tell her he was going to be a bum? Bum. Beatnik. Hippie. Whoever didn't work in a factory or an office for a lifetime, and then retire, and be old, and be dead. Elliot was downwardly mobile. Fay was upwardly hopeful, but feckless. They had been hippies since the Twenties but they didn't know it, and would not have found it possible to have seen themselves that way. Fay would have said, "We always dress well," but they had been running away from bad checks for as long as Jimmy could remember. And yet Fay looked askance at Jimmy for being a poet, as had his former wife, Vera. How can you love someone who doesn't love what you love? Who despises you for loving it, and despises it as a rival? Jimmy being a poet was the one thing that those two, Vera and Fay, could agree on—both against it, against the only thing that really meant anything to him. Around him the world was coming apart at its seams; the Cold War seemed to be building to some terrible climacteric; but he didn't care. He knew others might disagree with him, but he felt that it was a rotten time to be young—a time when a few fools with bombs could subsume into politics every other noble human endeavor. At times he didn't care if the world blew up, although he doubted that the fools with the bombs had even the courage for a full-scale exchange. But he could take no chances. He had to write one lightening-struck poem before what may or may not come. For Jimmy, it seemed a time of double doom. Beyond that amorphous-end-of-the-world threat that seemed to permeate the air they breathed, there was a more definite, immediate, and frightening one. It was obvious to even the casual observer that Elliot Whistler was killing himself; and, if he died, Jimmy's sense of duty would demand that he take care of Fay, an ignorant, and, as Elliot would have said, *negative* force. This prospect represented doom to Jimmy's dream of being a poet; this was the secret fear that led him to live as if nothing mattered and every day was his last. He needed time to come to grips with his work, and Elliot's self-indulgent life threatened Jimmy with Fay's negative proximity. Elliot stood between them like a guard at a gate, whether Elliot realized it or not, protecting Jimmy from Fay's destructive capacities. Fay did not simply dislike, but *hated* everything she didn't understand, and she did not understand poets or poetry. Jimmy feared Elliot's death and Fay's proximity more than he feared an atomic Armageddon. Elliot's death would be Jimmy's doomsday.

Jimmy bid Fay farewell and took the rattletrap old Clinton Avenue bus downtown to see his father. Near Osborne Terrace a very recognizable neighborhood guy, Allen Ginsberg, climbed aboard. Jimmy felt a thrill at seeing the famous poet. It added to his conviction and lifted his spirit. He arrived at the Margarita just in time to be put to work. Elliot was moving. "I've been hoping you'd call so I could get you to come over and help me carry my bags. Otherwise I'd have to pay somebody. Do you want a drink?"

Jimmy said he did. He always loved having a drink with his old man. "What's that you're wearing?" Jimmy asked.

"What?"

"That. . . *tie*. It's got a hula dancer on it!"

"Oh, you mean Sweet Leilani. I got it at the Angels' Own. It's really something, eh?"

"But, Dad—my God! It's a piece of *trash*. I never saw you wear a thing like that."

"Well, how about this?" said Elliot, his eyes gleaming as he flashed a huge fake diamond ring under Jimmy's nose.

"Oh, Dad! What's the matter with you?"

"The matter! Why, my boy, I've never been better! Bright-eyed, bushy tailed, and free as a bird!"

"Your eyes are like two boiled eggs!"

"I don't believe that the ladies would agree with your assessment. Not by a long-shot," he said, winking. He went into the closet and reached up on a shelf and pulled down a little pinch bottle of whiskey. From where Jimmy was sitting, on a cardboard box packed with some of Elliot's things, he could see a whole row of pinch bottles, at least ten little soldiers, lined up and ready to fire, in formation. Elliot poured Jimmy a hooker of booze and Jimmy swallowed it. It was damned good to be out of the cold and muddy snow.

"Well, Dad, where are you moving to?"

"To where are you moving?" Elliot corrected, and told Jimmy that he had found a room around the corner, on Kitchen Street, in a house where they had lived twice before, once, when Jimmy was a baby, late in the Depression, and once later when he was about five, near the end of the war. It was the house they had been living in when Jimmy had started kindergarten. He remembered when Fay had forgotten to come and get him on his first day, and he had had to find his way home by himself. He was terrified, and, in his terror, had forgotten the address of the house, which Elliot had drilled him in. He could only remember the fact that the house in which he lived was the only one on the street that had shiny, curvy brass handrails siding its front

132

steps. With that information a kind, beautifully dressed lady was able to bring him home to his befuddled mother.

"But why are you leaving here, Dad?"

"It's too expensive, keeping an apartment," he said. "I can get a room over there and if I want to boil water for coffee I'll use an electric plate. I'll eat in restaurants, or up at Baldwin. You can fix this electric plate, can't you?" Elliot handed the contraption to Jimmy, who looked over the frayed wires.

"Yeah. It'll only take a minute. Dad," he said, "why don't you go home to Mom? She's lonely up there all by herself." He took out a pen knife and started fiddling with the gadget. He wanted Elliot to remain the guard at the gate.

"No, my boy," said Elliot. Jimmy could always tell that Elliot was drunk when he started my-boying him. "No, my boy; like Garbo, I want to be alone. My head is steaming with plans and I don't want any interference. Your mother is a nay-sayer. *I* am a *yea*-sayer."

"Dad, you know, she loves you so much."

"Well, she has a very strange way of showing it. You know, my boy, she can be a boundless harridan, an ignoramus who always thinks she's right. I can't stand it anymore. I'm too *old* for such indignities!" he almost shouted.

"She's awfully lonely," Jimmy repeated, for the moment having no other defense. If Elliot stepped aside, Jimmy would have to take his place. The prospect sent a chill of fear up his spine.

"I love her too; but I can't live with her. You should understand that. How many times have we offered you a free room at Baldwin, and how many times have you refused it?"

"I knew she wouldn't let me concentrate—let me do my work, study, write. She'd always be calling me to *eat*—interrupting me. She doesn't understand what I'm trying to do."

"She doesn't understand extended concentration. I read some of your poetry, you know. I don't understand modern poetry. I like Poe and Kipling and Tennyson—'Crossing the Bar'—but it seemed to me you knew what you were doing. Look, I have a typed copy of 'Crossing the Bar' here in my wallet." He showed Jimmy a stained piece of paper but did not unfold it—tucked it back in his wallet. "I want you to read it at my funeral, if I ever die." He laughed.

Jimmy shook his head. "The thought of living with her scares me to death, Dad—it would kill my chance to work—she's always interrupting; she won't stick to any agreement—but it's different with you."

"No, it isn't. That's just what I've been trying to tell you. I have my dreams, too. Do you remember Tennyson's 'Ulysses'? 'There's still some noble work toward the end'—or something like that?"

"Yes, that's it. But you'll go back when you've got all your plans made, won't you?"

"We'll see. Do you want another drink?"

"Sure do."

"All right. But don't get drunk. I want you to move me."

"Don't worry, Dad; I won't." But Jimmy did. They both did.

Fortunately, Kitchen Street wasn't far to go, just up the block and around the corner. When Jimmy saw the house he was disappointed, because those beautiful, shining brass handrails he remembered so gratefully were green and tarnished now. The place had become a fleabag for derelicts, drunks, and prostitutes. One of the places from which Jimmy had started out in life. The small apartments of the Depression and war years had been redivided with plasterboard into tiny compartments. It was just a flop house now, not that it had ever been anything so special, really, he sup-

134

posed. But he could still remember Mrs. LaSalle, the fat lady with the pince-nez who used to own the joint. Now in her apartment—the very apartment where Elliot had written the letter to the President of the United States that resulted in having Mrs. LaSalle's son released from a prison camp— there was a horrible old virago, gin-soaked and toothless, with a nasty-snouted barking bitch of a terrier in her arms. Elliot asked her to show Jimmy the room in the basement that he had rejected.

"What do you think of it?" Elliot asked. It was the only basement room; the rest of the basement was used for storage.

"This looks better to me than being way up on top. Suppose there's a fire? Down here you'd be safe. It's all cement. You could get out."

"But I like it better up there, even if it does cost a little more. Top of the Mark."

Jimmy saw what was on Elliot's mind. There wouldn't be any company down here. Upstairs, everybody kept the doors open and wandered through the halls sometimes half-naked. Jimmy thought, how ironic it was that all during his own early years Elliot always wanted a rent-free basement apartment and now he had to be up near the roof.

"O.K., it's your pick."

He hauled Elliot's bags up to the chosen compartment, on the fourth floor. But he was still sober enough to be thinking about safety, and he said to Elliot: "This place is a firetrap, Dad. Promise me you won't stay here very long. Promise me you'll go home to Mom as soon as you get your plans made."

"We'll see," Elliot said. "We'll see, my boy; we'll see." He looked haggard and gray of face, as Fay had said, but he was still a handsome old rake.

They drank together all afternoon.

135

The snow stopped falling toward ten o'clock in the evening, and Jimmy decided it was time for him to get back to New York. He had obligations, responsibilities. Work to do.

"Why don't you stay here and spend the night with me?" Elliot said. "The snow's getting deep out there. Your feet'll be soaked by the time you get to New York. You can go in the morning, can't you?"

"No, Dad. I've got to go. I've got to go." Jimmy was drunk. Could hardly walk. But he had things to do. He had things he just *had* to do. Just like Elliot. They each had to do whatever it was they thought they had to do.

II

A week later at Pitt Street Jimmy looked into a half-filled beer bottle that had been left opened and standing out and counted six dead roaches floating atop the stale, flat beer. He was disappointed because he could have drunk the stuff. He had no aversion to warm, stale, flat beer, and had learned to put a head on it by dropping an Alka-Seltzer tablet into it. But he wasn't about to drink any beer that had six dead roaches floating in it, bodies like boats and legs like oars raised up, so aimlessly. The place was filthy. In order to write, he needed some order!

He went out and bought some roach spray and sprayed the walls, up and down, back and forth, until there were billowing clouds of poison closing on him from every corner. It was bitter January cold out, but Jimmy knocked the cardboard out of the windows and let the air suck the poison out from under his nose. Then he blocked the windows again and started in the kitchen. But before he began in the kitchen he turned to survey the carnage. Roaches of all sizes and shapes were swarming over the walls, dropping with small, ticking sounds and rocking on their curled, chitinous backs, flicking, flailing, their feelers drooping. What a rout!

The kitchen gas range was a stronghold, a fortress of greasy grooves and baked-in crevices. He lit the oven and watched until the top of the stove glowed red. Out they came by the swarming hundreds, feet burned away, feelers melting into kinky hairs. They ran over the stove in desperation, panic, trying to find places where they could put their feet. Expectant mothers, their eggs in chitinous cases at their rear ends, struggled with their hindmost legs, as with an instinct to save their offspring, to force or kick the cases loose. Some had their cases dangling by only one side when they leaped from the top of the stove. As they landed on the floor and tried to crawl, with their burnt feet, their dragging, kinked feelers, with their wings askew, and their dangling, thread-hanging egg cases, he sprayed them madly then trampled, kicked, jumped up and down on them, only wanting them dead. Jimmy saw a fat, hideous albino roach, already like the pale ghost of its dead self, leap from the stove. He squashed it underfoot and swore he could hear its white shell crack and spray the pale muck of its insides out: squish! When he lifted his shoe it dragged itself, like animated pus, into a heap of glittering brownish bodies. Hundreds of crooked legs moved sluggishly—then, here and there, with sudden convulsive speed—over the place where the ghost had gone.

On the wall was a wooden plaque that held sets of false teeth, an exhibit, sold by a dental supply firm to dentists. It belonged to an artist friend who was to use it for some arcane artistic purpose but who had forgetfully left it behind. Jimmy grabbed the plaque from the wall and mashed it down atop this horrible mass of half life. Then he jumped on it, up and down, not distinguishing the sound of the breaking teeth from the sound of roaches snapping on the stove like popcorn. When he looked down there were rolling and bouncing human teeth among the slimy dead and still crawling. Sakyamuni says they will live again. Needed: Sneaky Pete, pot, peyote.

Next morning, across the Hudson in Newark, Jimmy's mother woke and heard a radio report of a fire on Kitchen Street while she was having her coffee. The report didn't frighten her, because the number of the house given was across the street from the rooming house in which Elliot was staying. Still, she was a bit concerned; so just to be sure she picked up the telephone and dialed the number of the superintendent of Elliot's building—the drunken virago with the snapping terrier in her arms. The line was dead. Then she went back to the radio and dialed around the stations, looking for a further report on the fire. At ten o'clock there was a bulletin the purpose of which was to correct the address as formerly given. The announcer's voice now numbered the house where Elliot lived, and apologized for the error.

Fay was struck with fear. But only six dead; six, and the house, as she understood it, held thirty, at least. He must be among the survivors. There was no way she could reach Jimmy immediately—he had no phone—so she called her sister, Myrtle, who lived nearby. Had she heard about the fire? Myrtle said that she had, on the morning news.

"That wasn't where Elliot was living, was it?" Myrtle asked cautiously. Fay told her that it was.

"Oh, my God, dear! Did you call there?"

"They don't answer!" Fay was weeping.

"Now, don't you be afraid, Fay. He probably wasn't even in the house. You just stay there and we'll be right over."

On the radio came a report naming two of the dead; but not Elliot.

"Oh, please come—yes. I can't get ahold of Jimmy. I don't know how to get him. He's over in New York some-

138

where with his hippie friends and I don't even have his new address. Have you heard anything? They say six are dead. Oh, Myrtle, please come over—hurry!"

Fay dressed and went and knocked on Moe Golden's door. Moe was a taxi driver who lived in a hall room upstairs, a sickly, kindly little bachelor, who considered Elliot his friend. Fay told Moe what had happened. "Oh, gees," said Moe, "was Elliot in there?"

"I don't know."

Moe's face, all bones and up-pointed chin, the sallow face of a man who had never been well, twisted with sudden fear, adjusted, resolved itself. "Come on," he said, "let's go down there and find what gives." When they got to the house it was still smoldering, hours after the time it was estimated that the fire had started. The big old house was roofless and nearly wall-less. Fay and Moe stood on the street in a crowd and looked into the cubicles, where, it seemed now, only insignificant lives could have been lived.

* * *

Jimmy had only been up for an hour, having slept late that day as a consequence of having been up so late the night before, murdering roaches. But, "Oh, blessed rage for order," he was in a room that had been swept and mopped. The stove (even its permanent stains) was glittering with the cleaning he had given it. And he was celebrating these surroundings with an early glass of cheap sherry of the type he called gasoline and a cup of black, instant coffee, when there was a rapping at the door, *rat-a-tat-tat.*

"Telegram for Whistler!" a voice called.

Jimmy went through the usual telegramaphobic reactions of persons unused to getting wired word of events. Then he read it. *JIMMY. CALL YOUR MOTHER. AUNT MYRTLE.*

He sat down. Maybe it was the roach-murdering spree

139

he'd been on, but he'd had an eerie feeling since getting up. He'd been doodling on a poem, and had nearly got it completed, just before Fear with bony knuckles knocked. He'd tagged the poem "Oncoming Company," because it was about such things—eerie feelings, telegraph messengers—

Swings pendulously now
that dark, that bleak o'clock
of place, the held in hell
ingrowing grave, the sea
of flooding tides, the fell
oncoming company.

Jimmy had a fit of the creeps, gulped his gasoline, went out, made the call at a nearby pay-phone, and Fay told him what was up.

"Oh, now, listen, Mom; don't get excited. He probably wasn't there."

"No, Jimmy—no. He would have called me by now. He wouldn't let me worry like this."

"What have you done?" he asked. "Did you go down there? Did you check the hospitals?"

"Everywhere. Moe's been so good. He drove me everywhere. They've got a refuge set up for all the people who were burned out. Moe drove me there, but your father's not there with the rest. Then a fireman called me and said I should check at the morgue. So Moe drove me down there. He went in and looked. He said Elliot wasn't there."

"Thank God!" Jimmy said. "If he isn't there and he isn't with the others he must not have been at the house last night."

"But where is he, Jimmy?"

"I'll come right over. Stay put."

"I will. I'm waiting for Aunt Myrtle and Uncle O'Toole. They should be here any time. I don't know what's keeping them."

140

Fay's family consisted of two sisters, one several years older than Fay, Jimmy's Aunt Myrtle, and one several years younger, Jimmy's Aunt Brenda, and Aunt Myrtle's husband, whom Jimmy referred to as Uncle O'Toole. Aunt Myrtle was a housewife who had raised five children, and Aunt Brenda was the widow of a suicidal butcher, a domineering woman. Fay had them, and she had Jimmy, and that was about all she had.

"O.K. I'll be right over. Now don't you worry. Dad'll show up and we'll all have a drink together."

Jimmy hadn't heard any report of the fire—just what Fay had told him—so he didn't know how much to make of it. He did figure that if Elliot wasn't in a hospital, wasn't at the refuge, and wasn't in the morgue, he probably hadn't been in the fire—there seemed small chance, considering the time, of any more bodies being discovered—probably had not gone to the house at all that night, but had been off at one of his other secret places, somewhere with some crony of his, drinking. But Jimmy was sure Elliot would have called Fay, no matter what, had he known about the fire and had he had a few of his wits about him. He wondered if Elliot could have been dazed and gone wandering off somewhere. Jimmy went to the Hudson Terminal to take the train through the tube to Newark. On the train, across the aisle from Jimmy, a man unfolded his *Daily News*. The headline read:

SIX DEAD IN BLAZE IN NEWARK.

When he got to Baldwin, Aunt Myrtle and Uncle O'Toole were there. Fay was already going into a kind of shock: she was unnaturally calm, very unlike herself. While Jimmy was on his way over, she received another call from the fireman with whom she'd spoken earlier.

The Fire Department had compiled a list of the tenants of the house and had checked them out. The count was complete: all living tenants accounted for and six dead

141

bodies added up to a full house. Was it possible (the voice was trying to be gentle) that a mistake had been made? Did Fay have any male relatives? Was there some man who could come down to the morgue and check—just to be sure?

"I tell you, he wasn't there," said Moe. It was clear that he was reluctant to press his (and Fay's and Jimmy's) luck with a second visit. Finally, Jimmy and Fay got him to take them to the morgue. His small, collapsed face was running with tears as he started the motor of his taxi. Aunt Myrtle sat on one side of Fay and Uncle O'Toole on the other, in the back. Jimmy sat up front with Moe. They stopped to look at the house, which was on the way to the morgue.

As Jimmy looked up at the ruin, with its blackened, still steaming timbers, and the great, jigsaw holes torn out of its walls, its roofless top, he remembered again the day his mother had forgotten to get him at school and he was brought home by the kind lady, and he remembered those jaunty brass banisters, which were black and crumpled now like the old horns found occasionally among the refuse heaps at the city dump, and how they had shined once, like beacons, when he was a child.

Aunt Myrtle waited with Fay and Moe while Uncle O'Toole and Jimmy went into the morgue. Jimmy could see Aunt Myrtle, round, plump, in her early sixties, sitting in the back of that idling, question-mark of a cab, hugging Fay to her, and Fay, after thirty years of marriage, just her frightened little sister again. The worst part was that Fay was not resigned, as he was, now. Part of her was still convinced that it was all some kind of mad nightmare mistake. "I know—I just *know*—that he's alive. Suppose he were to go home while we're here?" she said.

A man in a black suit rolled them out one at a time, each time pulling the sheet aside like a magician pulling aside his cape to display a bunch of flowers, or a rabbit.

After the second time Jimmy began to say "Voila!" silently, to himself.

Some of the bodies were burned terribly, literally roasted; others didn't show a mark of pink, or even a scratch, despite the fact that the roof had blown off and then caved back in on them (all of the victims had been living on the top floor). These unmarked were victims of smoke inhalation. Only one of the victims was young, about thirty; all were men; the others were old, showing emaciated, debauched bodies. Elliot's was the last they saw.

When the man in the black suit pulled the sheet aside, there he lay, stark naked. He had a big pink hand up over his heart in a familiar gesture. There was a triangular, second-degree burn on his chest. His bristly hair seemed pale.

Jimmy knew that it was Elliot before the sheet had been removed. He could tell by the feet; those big pink feet were sticking out. Jimmy had seen them when he came in, but was glad when the man in the black suit led him in a different direction. Jimmy leaned down at Elliot's side and touched his hair. He wanted to kiss him, as he had done so many times before, even the last time he had seen him, when he'd moved Elliot's things up into that firetrap, but Uncle O'Toole and the man in the black suit were there.

Back at Baldwin, after a long tearful interlude during which many drinks were consumed, much to Jimmy's consternation Fay asked Uncle O'Toole, not Jimmy, what should be done. This foreshadowed the future for Jimmy, this was how it would be if he and Fay were to live together. After many a few, that prospect seemed more impossible than ever. Jimmy chose to ignore them. He drank, smoked, and listened to the radio—"Twilight Time." His mind went passive, tuning out a conversation that seemed neither practical nor interesting. It was the best he could do in the circumstances. There was an empty room waiting to be rented in the basement of the house. He woke up several times on

143

top of the bed in that room, rejoined the gathering, a sort of wake, really, and pleasantly rejected it once again for the quiet comfort of the bed. Each time he returned to the gathering, it seemed that there were several more people present, each time night and day seemed to have reversed themselves. Oblivion rapidly followed, but, by all reports, he was walking and talking among the others, then he drew to a consciousness of cars, and a kind of slow motion hustle and bustle, and umbrellas and complaints. The rain came down like the silver nails in his father's coffin. Then he was being asked if he would say a few words and he read from his father's crumpled copy of "Crossing the Bar" by Tennyson.

> "Sunset and evening star,
>   And one clear call for me!
> And may there be no moaning of the bar,
>   When I put out to sea,
>
> But such a tide as moving seems asleep,
>   Too full for sound and foam,
> When that which drew from out the boundless deep
>   Turns again home.
>
> Twilight and evening bell,
>   And after that the dark!
> And may there be no sadness of farewell,
>   When I embark;
>
> For tho' from out our bourne of Time and Place
>   The flood may bear me far,
> I hope to see my Pilot face to face
>   When I have crost the bar."

Swaying on his feet, he stumbled over the words and got through the reading. But it didn't matter that it was a

144

bad reading, because this was all a dream anyway, wasn't it, a nightmare, from which he would awaken, *the* nightmare, the recurring nightmare that had plagued his sleep for months, if not years?

Fay hung like a broken doll between Aunt Myrtle and Uncle O'Toole. Sometime soon now they were going to turn her over to him and that moment would represent the end of his life, the end of his poetry, the end of his dreams. He began to do a little St. Vitus dance, a drunken man preparing to run for his life.

When they got back to Baldwin and the crowded little apartment, booze appeared from every side. Soon Fay had the radio blasting Chubby Checker's "Peppermint Twist." She shook like a Shaker. Really, she was hysterical. Overheard comments from the relatives caused Jimmy to remember Dylan Thomas's line, "After the funeral, mule praises, brays . . ."

"She's better off without him."

"He left her nothing."

Pale-faced Moe Golden seized Jimmy's arm. "Your father was a great tipper," he said. "A real mensch. You know what is a mensch? A human being. Someone of consequence. Someone to admire. Someone of noble character. Jimmy, your father was a real mensch, so don't listen to these gossip ghouls."

"An old reprobate," corrected somebody. "A spendthrift with nothing to spend. A bum!"

"Well, Jimmy will take care of her."

"Not him, he's just like his father."

Desperate to get out, Jimmy lurched toward the door, but in the hall an ancient apparition croaked condolences and Jimmy invited him in. The apparition was one of Baldwin's mainliners from the madhouse. Jimmy had already grabbed his hand in a half-shake, half-supportive motion that enabled them to stagger back across the room and into

145

chairs. Now they began to pump hands, so joyful were they to be firmly seated.

It was his old, moth-eaten and stained-stiff pajamas and robe that had caused Jimmy to take the old man for an apparition. Actually he was a handsome old duck in his eighties with tufts of white hair flopping wildly about on his head. Jimmy saw big, gnarled hands, and great, plumbeous eyes. For a moment it seemed that he had been delivered back to his father. But no, Elliot's spirit was gone from the air around them and Jimmy felt that not only he but every one on Earth remaining had lost an opportunity, a possibility, whether to know a good man or a bad didn't matter. But here was another, tenuously clinging to life's most important goal beyond survival, the manifestation of the spirit. Sobbing Jimmy of the crying jag could have taken him in his arms and danced him around the room, but his old legs would have broken and Jimmy's would have stumbled with drink and with rising sorrow.

*　*　*

A few lost days later, Jimmy emerged from the Bowery at Cooper Square, where stood the grim edifice of Cooper Union, and read the Con-Ed clock with blurry eyes. After ten, time for church; but he wouldn't go. He decided to borrow some money from his friend Marsayas, and get an eye-opener.

When he got to the door of the building his friend Marsayas superintended, one of the few renovated apartment houses in an otherwise dilapidated neighborhood, there stood Ape, the plumber, buzzing furiously away at Marsayas's bell. Ape was a short, powerfully built man of about forty who, as a result of his proclivity for the more kinky forms of sexual activity, preferred to frequent the more bohemian bars, where Jimmy and Marsayas hung out, rather than the sort of blue-collar joints where one might expect to find him.

Ape told Jimmy he didn't look so good, and Jimmy told Ape he was O.K. He didn't want to tell him that he had buried his father a few days ago, nor that he was blank on most of what happened since standing in the freezing cold at the gravesite.

Ape said he had an emergency job to do, something overflowing into a flood in a tenement on the Lower East Side, and that he was trying to get Marsayas to help him, his regular helpers being gone for the weekend. He said: "But as usual he ain't nowheres ta be found. How 'bout you?" he said, inspired. "Would ya like ta pick up a couple ten bucks say?"

"How long will it take?"

"Oh, nuttin'—a few hours. Do it for me, Jimmy. I really need somebody. I'm in a fix."

"Is it going to be hard? I don't feel so hot."

"Nah, nah. Listen, movin' a few stones, dat's all."

"O.K.," Jimmy said, and Ape changed a bit. He looked Jimmy over, said:

"But, do ya feel O.K.?"

Now Jimmy wanted the money, so he wound up selling Ape on the idea of using his services, and on the idea that he was fit as a fiddle. Off they went in Ape's overburdened pickup truck, through the sloppy, winter streets. They climbed out on East Third, and Ape yanked his huge leather bag of tools out of the back of the pickup. It had a long leather strap on it, so that he could stoop, put the strap over his shoulder, and stand up, hauling it up with him. He asked Jimmy to carry it. He had pipe, hoses, and shovels to carry. Jimmy threw the strap over his shoulder and heaved upward, but the bag did not budge.

Ape shook his head. "O.K.," he said. "I'll bring it. I don't want ya should bust sumpin." Up came the bag, and he walked with it and the pipe too.

The constipated building was a few doors down the block. Too bad that they couldn't get the truck any closer, but there was a vandalized car in the way. The trouble was in the basement, directly below a bodega. Above the store there were five human-infested stories. The Rat and Mice Arms, Lower East Side, Manhattan, New York, New York, U.S. of A, North America, planet Earth, the Universe. A lovely place to bring up children.

Ape dumped his load of iron and leather on the sidewalk and pulled open the cellar doors. Phew! Multitudes of foul-smelling molecules did a death-dance up their nostrils. Jimmy's stomach flip-flopped. He thought of the Rolfe Humphries' translation of the Aeneid. *Now, said the Sibyl, summon up your courage, for you will need it.*

Ape descended. Jimmy followed. *Before the threshold of hell they passed, and avenging Cares, pale Disease and melancholy Age, Fear and Hunger that tempt to Crime, Toil, Poverty, and Death—forms horrible to view.*

"How long has this place been backed up?"

"Couple days."

"A couple of days?

"Yeah. I had so many udder jobs, I couldn't get back to it."

"It's a wonder the Health Department hasn't been here."

"Hey, dis is New York."

The filthy ooze was a foot deep and jet black, anaerobic. "If anybody upstairs has a case of typhus, we've had it."

"Ah, I wade around in dis stuff all da time and I'm all right." Ape handed Jimmy a pair of rubber boots. "Here, put dese on."

148

They stood high up on a peak among peaks of the mountainous islands of rocks and gravel and mud that Ape had dug out on his previous visit. Sweat broke out on Jimmy's forehead as he pulled on the boots. His shirt and pants stuck to his skin. Outside was a cold winter day, and it was cool here, but humid, clammy. How the hell did he get himself into these things!

Ape put him to work at pulling up and stacking more of the slimy stones while he pumped some of the mephitic semi-liquid out from under them. Each time Jimmy plumped his gloved hands into the ooze to catch another slippery stone he thought of the possibilities of infection. Bacterial, protozoan, parasitic metazoan—words from books kept crawling into his head. Passages! *It is inevitable that these infections, so common to the alimentary tract of man, should be found in great numbers in the feces, and even in the urine.* Talk about the alimentary tract! He was wading around in the intestinal tract of a slum tenement.

"What are we trying to do here anyway?"

Ape was wrapping up some hoses in the cellarway. "Gravity flow! Dat's what we're after. Gravity flow! We gotta get dis shit runnin' out into da sewers. Dere's a block under dem stones somewheres. Dat's what's stoppin' it. We gotta find out what it is and get it out outta dere."

"What could it be?" Jimmy asked, using his interest as an excuse to stand up straight for a moment. He felt like vomiting.

"Never can tell," said Ape. "A few tings get trowed down da terlet and dey gadder up and make like a heap. Da pipes into da sewers is eight inches, but from what I can make out, dat drain you're clearin' is like one o' dem Roman drains—just a concave brick jobber, see, so it could happen. Den again a heavy flow might of moved a loose brick outta place. Hard ta say. Sometimes dere's biofoulin'. Dat's like when plankton forms up real t'ick. Hard part's findin' it. Rest is easy."

Not for another hour did Jimmy get the bright idea of tearing off the tail of his shirt and tying it over his face like a mask, stuffing the bottom down his collar. It relieved him a bit. He wished that he could pull it up over his eyes so that he couldn't see what he was digging in. He thought of Aeneas in the Infernal Regions, his only object being to see his father. He imagined how it would be if his father materialized. He'd be all dressed up, spick-and-span, neat as a pin, sitting at a little table on top of one of those mountains of slime, watching. His mother would be there, and she and Jimmy would dig together while his father watched them, kindly but superior, indulging their blessed rage for order. Well, unlike Aeneas in his Infernal Regions, he wasn't going to find his father down here. *O, how willingly would they endure poverty, labor, and any other infliction, if they might but return to life!*

"Here it is!" cried Ape. "Like I tought, it's a brick jam."

Jimmy crawled along a ridge of a slippery mountain of detritus and got shakily to his feet beside Ape. There it was. A half dozen or so bricks had fallen apart and melted down into a red stopper. It had caught eggshells, sanitary napkins, bits of glittering glass, a thing that looked like a skinny black snake but turned out to be a coathanger, and doubtful stuff packed in layers, packed in strata. *Here is the judgment hall of Rhadamanthus, who brings to light crimes done in life, which the perpetrator vainly thought impenetrably hid.* Ape picked up a shovel and gave the red stopper a couple of tentative taps, then one clanging blow, breaking it to pieces. "Woo-ish!" it went. The sewer was hungry! What an appetite!

"I'm gonna turn on da water," Ape said. "I wanna wash dis out so's I can see how bad da damage is. Just be a minute."

Jimmy sat thinking and dreaming, of Anchises and Aeneas. *Have you come at last, Anchises said, long expected, and do I behold you after such perils past? O my son, how have I trembled for you as I have watched your career! O father! your image was always before me to guide and guard me. . . . Then, he endeavoured to enfold his father in his embrace, but his arms enclosed only an unsubstantial image.* He rested his head in his arms. He could feel it burning through his shirtsleeves.

Suddenly a little stream of water, relatively clear, trickled down the Roman canal. Jimmy remembered what he'd read in Da Vinci's Notebooks, about man being only a passageway for food. Would that he were only that, and have some peace. He would have forgiven any man his meanness—his bloody devilish cravings—in the mood he was in. He watched the water purling away. No doubt it'd soon be carrying away nice loads of human excretion, the lost parts of bodies, dead cells, hairs, bits and parts of burnt energy, the stuff left over after the day's work, after the argument, the loving in the small bed while the kids slept fitfully nearby. Yes, there goes love. Off it goes, the domestic sewage, off to join the industrial waste, off to form the municipal sewage, to join the storm runoff, and there all to be wed and to become the combined sewage; off they go, through flush tanks and diverting weirs, through siphon spillways and sewage-treatment plants, through bar racks and fine screens and skimming tanks, through settling tanks and scum collectors, through grit chambers and sedimentation tanks, through trickling filters and activated-sludge units, through oxidation ponds and the centrifuge, through heat coagulators and into the incinerators, where, at last, all our loves go up in smoke. And the outfall works drop pure water, cleansed, unsullied

151

by any particle of humanity, by any watery history of the human condition, into the swaying receiving waters of river and sea. Out of the water we came, onto the land, and into the sky we go, and the smoke of our loves will crowd out the light of the sun, one dark day.

PART THREE

THE ORPHANED

By midnight, people lay about on the floor, some drink-drugged, some plain drugged. Harry Goldfarb, director of the Oh-No Soho Gallery, appeared at the door with big Denise, a performance artist, arm over shoulder, covered with blood. He had several dent-like cuts on his forehead, dripping in gouts. It seemed that Denise was having one of her bad trips. She'd wanted out. Harry had tried to help her down the long, iron-covered, loft stairway, she'd thrown a fit, and they'd both gone tumbling down. One of Harry's female assistants popped up, joined them, and tried to soothe Denise. They tried to hold her still, but Denise flailed on. Jimmy Whistler went over and took Denise by the shoulders and tried to pin her to a wall. She was a big girl, big as Jimmy, and very strong, and in her madness she broke loose and slapped him back and forth across the face with both hands, nearly unhinging his jaw with the first blow. He got her back in his grip, and held her there. Then she went loose and slid down the wall into a faint or a sleep or coma or God knew what oblivion. Harry and the assistant tried to wake her. Someone patted her face with a wet towel, and Harry fed her coffee. At last they got her on her feet. She was docile now, whimpering and pathetic. Harry led her out the door. He must have taken Denise all the way home. Neither of them came back. The place was a bloody shambles. Some Opening!

When Jimmy woke, scenes from the night before returned. He had poor Denise and her bad trip on the brain.

He remembered the early days, when Denise and he worked together at Barnes & Noble—how she had got her landlady to rent him a room in the Village—all of it was alive in his mind, bits and parts of his hangover.

Maybe it was just sentimentality, nostalgia—but he decided to find a place where he could get a couple of quarts of cold beer and take them up as an offering to good old Denise in what was probably her hour of need.

She lived in an ancient musty building. Jimmy climbed four flights of stairs and banged (cheerfully, he thought) on the door. Denise moaned from within, and called: "Who's there?"

"It's me, Denise; Jimmy."

She let him in, and lowered herself down on the floor, on a blanket, where she slept. She had her B.A. in Oriental studies, and it was her little resultant vanity to sleep on mats. She'd slept on a bamboo mat in the house where she'd got him his little room. She had used to play the recorder (the instrument, not the machine) and would play herself to sleep at night. She'd play until she dropped the wooden instrument in her lap, and, if she left her door open, as she often did, you could find her there in the morning, sitting up, mouth hanging open, holding the musical stick, like a child whose thumb has dropped out of its mouth. But, though she still slept on the floor, she no longer lived as she had in the earlier days. Her little shoe box of a room had been kept in fanatic order; its books, on neat shelves, floor to ceiling, had been arranged according to size and content; the pens on its neat desk neatly placed: a place for everything and everything in its place. This room looked like a small storage room for used books, bags of garbage, and other superfluities, and one in which all the shelves had broken and everything had caved in and commingled. It was fortunate for orderly eyes that the only light fixture was broken and ended in a frayed and dangling cord. The place was shadow-lit

and dreary, the room of a drinking and drug-taking ancho-
rite. Denise sat in the middle of this devastation like a big,
pale statue of Sorrow. She wore only a shabby pink slip,
most of the fluffy tops of her big breasts exposed, showing
blue veins. Her hair, which was thick, black, and kinky, was
in wild disarray. Her feet were dirty, and the little toes
black from sticking out the holes at the sides of her sneakers. (Jimmy thought she must have bought her sneakers
with holes in the sides.) The sneakers themselves, the
crumpled black skirt, and the blood-stained army fatigue
shirt, which she wore the night before, lay on the floor near
her feet. She held her knees in her hands. She looked like a
woman who didn't care what happened next, sad as an old
salad, just beat. A kind of young, frumpy Gertrude Stein.
Jimmy put the beer down on the floor by her feet, and said:
    "Here, kid! Here's something for the morning blues.
Want some?"
    "Oh, man," she said quietly, groaningly, "I'm so
ashamed."
    "Oh, come on now. What's this? Come on, let's have
some beer."
    "No, man . . . no . . . it was terrible last night . . . ."
    "What're you talking about. You got a little high,
that's all."
    She shook her head, slowly, side to side.
    "Oh, Jimmy . . . Jimmy . . ."
    "No. Really, Denise, you didn't do anything—" then
he gave her a big, stupid smile, and added—"except freak
out, fall down the stairs, and knock my jaw off its hinges—"
and then he made a face and said—"As a matter of fact,
your conduct was . . . *deplorable!*"
    She couldn't help herself. It started with a faint, blos-
soming, impossible-to-suppress smile, and then all the tension she'd been building up exploded into laughter, and
every time she looked up at him, she exploded again. While

157

the latest of these seismic fits was in diminuendo Jimmy opened one of the beer bottles. He wondered if what she had been on last night was still working on her. When her laughter had subsided, he stuck the bottle in her face, so that, before she could think about herself too much, she was tasting and swallowing. When she finished drinking, and put the bottle down, she looked at Jimmy seriously, and said:

"You mean you aren't angry with me?"

"Of course not. Why should I be angry?"

"I hit you."

"Oh, come off it, Denise. Drink some more beer. It'll help unscramble your brains."

She took another drink, then handed him the bottle.

"Look, kid," he said, "what are you trying to do with yourself? If it sends you away to the L.S.D. badlands, you should skip it."

"All my trips aren't bad."

"It looks to me like most of them are. Why push it? You're going to wind up in a bad way."

"I don't care. I don't care about anything. I just want to see something beautiful. Sometimes I see beautiful things."

"Doesn't look like you've seen anything beautiful lately, huh?"

"No, not lately."

"Then give it a vacation, why not?"

"Yeah, yeah, man; I will."

"Denise—you know, baby, you've got to take care of yourself a little . . . ."

She didn't say anything for a time. Then she shrugged; said: "I saw my mother, who had big boobs like mine, lean over a table so they fell free away from her body"—she got up and walked to a little table, on which books were unsteadily stacked, and demonstrated, placing her hands on the table, arms stiff, leaning forward and letting her breasts drop free beneath the slip—"like this, in such pain as I could never bear to see again. And six months after she'd died, my father—father—was killed in an auto wreck—"

She stopped abruptly, and, distorting her face, her eyes squeezed shut by a smile so tight she looked like an exaggerated comedy mask, trying to hold back the tears that were flying from them anyhow. She went back to the blanket and threw herself down on it, face away, without a sound.

Jimmy's own drink-agitated nerves allowed for it, and he felt the rising damp himself. He wiped his eyes on his sleeves, and sat on, waiting, trying to feel as little as possible.

About ten minutes later, Denise turned about, solemn, but dry-eyed. She said: "Pass me the beer, please."

Jimmy did, and she drank, and then she lit herself a hazardous cigarette, blew smoke, and smiled.

"I guess I can't do anything right," she said.

"Don't feel bad, kid," Jimmy said, "I can't either. None of us can. But we have to try, don't we?"

"What for?"

"Why not? If it don't matter, it don't matter either way, do it?"

She smiled.

He added: "Otherwise it do matter, don't it?"

She laughed. "You're a witty guy. I always liked that about you. You know what Auden said about wit?"

"What?"

"In his experience, he said, wit required a combination of imagination, moral courage and unhappiness. All three are essential: an unimaginative or a cowardly or a happy person is seldom very amusing."

"So you think I'm unhappy?"

"Aren't you?"

Jimmy shrugged. "But seriously, kiddo, one has to figure out what one's about. I remember in my downer days I used to say I was a puppet. It was true. I was living out my father's life for him. I was even afraid of my mother, because I knew she'd have told me I wasn't my father; and, though she didn't know it, what that meant to me then was, or would have been, that I wasn't myself, either; that I had no self, in fact. See what I mean? If I'd been myself, there could hardly have been any question as to whether or not I was my father. When you have a self, you're not afraid to take advice—even from parents."

"Well?"

"Well, this. If we don't find, or even make up, some kind of authority for ourselves, we'll wake up at death-time to discover that everything has been pointless. I saw that, when I thought I was going to die. I was sick, Denise, pneumonia. When you were away. That's why I'm determined, now, to become my own father. In this bloody world where no one else is willing to be your father, you have to become your own father; then you'll always have someone to look after you in your hour of need. Let me recite you a poem I wrote. It's called 'The Orphaned' . . .

When the mood comes upon him to die
of a loneliness deeper than death,

he must speak to himself like a parent
in a lecturing voice, but with love.

He must be his own father and mother,
and at night when he looks up at heaven,

where nothing of earth seems to live,
and the range of all things is so great

160

as to startle the love from his breast,
he must think of his father, the Rock,

and his mother, the Dead Sea, and of
the message he brings from the sun."

"Oh, Jimmy!"

"See what I mean? Be your own daddy and momma,
then you'll be all right all right. Be Big Momma."

"I dig, Jimmy; I dig."

"Good. Why don't you start right away. What would
be the first thing your momma and daddy would make you
do this morning."

"Stop drinking."

"Well, now, let's not be extremists. What's the second
thing?"

"Wash my face and brush my teeth."

"Good. Why don't you do that."

"Because I don't really feel like it."

"Good. Then don't. I mean, if that's the kind of
momma you are, I guess you're just going to have a dirty
kid—right?"

"Right!"

"Good," Jimmy said. "Pass me the beer."

"You haven't cured me, you know, with your poem
and your shitty jokes." She winked at him.

"Yeah, I know," he said, lifting the bottle. "It takes a
lifetime."

TONY'S HALFWAY HOUSE

Jimmy met Oskar at Stanley's, a lower east side dive that catered to the bohemian set—artists, writers, actors, etc. They got into a conversation about Dadaism one rainy afternoon. Oskar, he learned, was a young German painter. He was a handsome kid, in a black-maned, hard-featured German way: about eighteen, six-foot-five, a hundred-and-fifty pounds; wore horn-rimmed glasses, and looked intellectual. He had picked up the word "fluffy" somewhere and applied it to everyone and anyone as a sort of ambiguous term of ridicule and affection. Jimmy liked big, stringbean Oskar right off.

They teamed up, getting jobs at agencies with names like Strong Arm Labor, Inc., or Profit Power. Sometimes these agencies sent them out with a bunch of derelicts and winos to "knob 'em," to place samples of soap or fabric-softener on doorknobs in fancy neighborhoods. They loaded trucks, and washed cars. It was strenuous but it left time for both of them; for Oskar to paint and Jimmy to write. Then one day they found a home: a Long Island catering house where they were employed to wash dishes, change the sets in several banquet halls, etc. They worked weekends at Tony's Halfway House.

One Friday afternoon, Oskar arrived first. "Hi, dere, Fluffy!" he called from the kitchen door. "Looking for a job? We got lots of verk for you here. Know anything about shit?" He had a little cup of coffee in one big hand and a little pipe in the other. He stuck the pipe in his mouth

and made spitty sounds. "Gotdammit! It's gone out again."
He knocked the tobacco out of the pipe and stuck it in his
pocket. "Gimme a cigarette, Fluffy."

Jimmy lit the cigarette he had given Oskar, his lighter
with the Marine insignia of globe and anchor and fierce,
spreading eagle glinting in the evening sun under Oskar's
neatly trimmed and slightly silly black mustache. Behind
Jimmy and all around the sprawling, T-shaped stucco building that housed Tony's Half-Way House was a tarmac parking lot, and expensive-looking cars were already parked here
and there, glimmering in monied repose. Beyond the parking lot lay the greenery of a Long Island country town, and
beyond that the town itself, and the railway station by which
Jimmy had come and would go, fifty dollars richer, on Sunday night.

"Oh, here you are." It was Covetti, Tony's maitre d'.
Jimmy didn't like working with Covetti. They didn't click.

"Let's get busy here—Jim, Oskar—I want you to make
the salad for the first party; it starts at eight—we haven't got
any time for breaks. Come on, let's go!"

"Vhat da hell," cried Oskar, waving his long arms
and grinning, "der's plenty of time. Ver just having a
shmoke."

"Oskar—I said, let's go!"

"Gotdammit!" grumbled Oskar. But they went on
into the kosher kitchen.

Tony's had two huge fully-equipped kitchens, one for
kosher and one for non-kosher parties. There was actually
no difference between the two kitchens except that a few
rabbinical incantations had been said over the one, and all its
equipment, from spoons to tureens, and was jealously
guarded by Dr. Bloom, the attending rabbi. It would strike
the goyem as comical, how when the kosher kitchen ran
short of dishes or silverware, all that was necessary was for
one of the pearl divers to get what was needed from the non-

163

kosher kitchen and run it through the dish-washing machines in the kosher kitchen. Having been run through one
of these machines, the equipment apparently came out, not
merely Jewish, but kosher. The goy boys would say, as they
were waging steaming, soap-bubbling war on time and kosher appetites, "O.K., hurry up! Let's run these through.
They need spoons in the Bar Mitzva. Let's make 'em kosher! Hurry up! Hurry up! Let's make 'em kosher!" Then
they'd all begin to shout—the five or six, or maybe eight of
them, who were working the machines—"Let's make 'em
kosher! Hurry up! Let's make 'em kosher!" And they'd
heave racks filled with spoons onto the conveyors where
they'd rattle and splash through the washing machines and
the drying machines and then they'd heave them off again—
heavy, weighing twenty-five to fifty pounds, and lifted from
above waist height—shouting, in drenched clothes, through
steam like hot fog, "Let's make 'em kosher, boys! Hurry
up! Let's make 'em kosher!"

It was as though they'd gone insane with the mechanical processes of the work and the incredible labor demanded—as if they'd forgotten themselves and were trying to
remember again, by shouting, that they were there. And the
roar and clatter of machines and dishes and silver was so
overwhelming they had to scream to be heard above it.

"Hurry up, boys," they'd hector themselves, "let's
make 'em kosher!" and they'd laugh like lunatics. But that
hadn't begun yet. That came at the end of each party, when
the dishes and silver were beginning to run short. But before each party there was another rush, the preparative one.
The pace was frantic, maddening, exhausting, and somewhere before the end came in sight, and brought with it the
stimulation of hope, defeating.

Oskar and Jimmy were hosing out a garbage can in
which to make salad—others were frantically chopping ice-
berg lettuce and celery and green bell peppers, mixing salad

164

oil and vinegar—in would go the lot, and one of them stirring it with a broom handle.

From one of the five ballrooms they could hear music—a band warming up. There was the chapel to be prepared: a wedding, and therefore flowers to be arranged. A florist supervised this process, but they did the actual work, climbing ladders, spreading chains of roses from wall to wall. A Bar Mitzva required that great aluminum fountains be set up on tables in that ballroom, in order to spray sticky, bright-colored soft drinks into the cavities of semi-corrupted kids. Huge, round tables, like faceless targets, had to be carried from room to room, along with chairs by the hundreds; and hundreds upon hundreds of dishes had to be washed before they were used and washed as they came back in order that they could be used again, immediately, for the next course, for another party. Fruit salads had to be prepared, of canned grapefruit and orange segments and maraschino cherries, each in its individual bowl with cracked ice at the bottom, and before they were finished making these by the hundreds, the sticky, dirty bowls were coming back, waiters wheeling them in on twenty-tiered wheelers, the bowls on trays and filled with the dainties of fun—smashed green cigars, lip-sticked cigs.

"Hurry up, boys! Let's make 'em kosher!"

That was the call-to-arms. They might not even be in the kosher kitchen, now—they might not even be doing dishes—but they'd still scream it at one another. "Come on, boys! Hurry up! Let's make 'em kosher!"

First the fruit cocktail bowls came back, and they had metal top-pieces that had to be washed separately. Then came the big greasy soup-tureens; then almost immediately the soup bowls and under dishes. Meantime they had prepared the plates for the main dish, and now they'd be coming back, laden with leftover slop. If the boys were hungry they'd slobber down slices of beef or pieces of chicken as

165

they worked. Then would come the truly horrible, the gro-
tesque, dessert dishes. The standard dessert was a gooey
cake, of the wedding or birthday type, topped with ice cream
and overpoured with cherries jubilee. The icing was like
some form of pink cement, almost impossible to scrape from
the plates. Two or three of the boys became "scrapers,"
standing at the end of the conveyor, where there was a hole
in the aluminum top, beneath which, temporarily out of
sight, stood a garbage can, and, with heavy brushes, scraped
this abominable stuff from the plates, while the others kept
up the incredible traffic of the machines.

At this stage all of them were covered from head to
foot in parti-colored muck. The cement floor itself was an
inch-thicker with bright slime. Little pieces of meat, fat, and
bone came floating toward them. Tobacco, broken from
cigarettes and cigars, ran in among clots of pink icing and
chips of cherries; their clothes became slimy rags, their
shoes squeaked, and they could not see one another for the
steam. And now, just when they needed it most, the first
round of booze glasses would be coming in. First, the inevitable pink champagne, cheap stuff that was part of the pack-
aged party deal. Unless the boys were too impatient or too
thirsty to wait, they would scorn this. But then would come
the good stuff, the Scotch and bourbon and Irish whiskey,
glasses full and nearly full, any drink in the house.

"Hurry up, boys! Make 'em kosher!"

Shrieks of rowdy laughter!

Come four o'clock in the morning they'd stumble up
to the attic dorm where they slept, taking some beer along
with them. Soon the maloderousness of the room would become unbearable, and so they'd have to sleep.

"How's things going with your girl?" Jimmy asked.

"Not so good. Not so good," said Oskar, his long,
thin form sprawled on a cot next to Jimmy's. "I tink she's
sneaking out wit some prick." There was moonlight from

the window—stars, crickets—sleep. . . . Then they were scurrying about, getting themselves quick cups of coffee. It was two hours later, and there were tables to be moved.

"Why don't we get the hell out of this, Oskar?"

"You Gotdammed right!"

"I mean, what the hell are we living this way for?"

"Frog me?"

"Well, why don't you go back to window dressing?"

"No time. I got to paint!"

"Hurry up, boys, let's go!" It was that bustling bastard Covetti. "Come on, Jim, get that mirror polished! We've got a room to get ready."

Oskar and Jimmy vacuumed the rugs in the chapel. Oskar looked beat, his shoulders getting rounded, his chest hollow. "Listen," he said, pushing the huge vacuum as Jimmy held the cord out of the way, "let's go down to the basement tonight and get some shtuff to take home wid us— some meat and shtuff; we put it in a box and hide it in the parking lot, ja?"

"Das is nicht eine gut idee." Oskar had taught Jimmy some German.

"How come?"

"If these mob bastards caught us stealing they'd kick the shit out of us—"

"Bah! Dey don't catch us. Vhat you think, fluffy, I'm shtupid or somepin? Ve don't get caught if ve do it my vay. It'll give us somepin to do. Now, look; here's my plan. . ."

"Ha-ha-ha-ha-ha!"

"What's so funny in here, boys?" Covetti. "Come on, let's get this vacuuming done." He left.

"Ha-ha-ha-ha-ha!"

"Fluffy Sh-vine-hoont!" said Oskar, laughing. "He makes my ass shmile. Look," he said, suddenly, a serious expression appearing on his face, his big hands to his mouth, "one of my damn front teeth is loose."

That night Jimmy and Oskar crept down to the basement and took two big pieces of roasting beef from the refrigerator. Jimmy took a scrawny, uncooked chicken too. They hid their pelf in a cardboard box, outside the garbage room. It was a clear night and the sky was sprinkled with a mess of stars, so they sat and talked and smoked and never got any sleep at all. At six they went into the kitchen and made coffee. The others came down, and they started work. Then, with dreamlike suddenness, the parties were going full tilt.

Jimmy stood behind a partition and peeked out at the revelers. He didn't know if this was a Mafia wedding or a Protestant birthday party or a Bar Mitzva or what. All the parties had run into one in his mind.

The ballroom was roaring with people; the men were wearing black-trimmed maroon tuxedos; the women were wearing lavish, frilly evening gowns. There were a few with especially silly gowns. Bridesmaids, maybe. The music was blaring and many couples were Twisting. Jimmy saw something out of the corner of his eye and looked off to his left. Down the way from him, on his side of the partition, a bald blimp of a man was rubbing his bulk over a drunken blonde. He had a green cigar in his mouth. She was holding a glass of pink champagne in one hand and a lipsticked cig in the other. The big man had her pinned to the wall. But she wasn't fighting him; on the contrary. The big man kept grinding away at her, his chubby, hairy, beringed hands on the wall behind her, above her shoulders, his body shaking like jostled jelly. The man was beginning to get frantic, now; he was perspiring and shifting his cigar around with his tongue. The woman, with some difficulty, took a sip from her champagne glass. There was a tremendous roar of music and applause from the floor. The man,

168

heaving, panting, took one meaty mitt from the wall, reached down and, catching the blonde's dress by the hem, tore it straight up the thigh. He jiggled with himself a little, and then with her, and they both slid slowly down the wall and onto the floor. She dropped her glass and her cigarette. He spit out the stub of his cigar, and jostled—one, two, three, four—then let his weight go all over her, like a syrup.

Jimmy went back into the kitchen where he ran into Covetti, who told him to go and clean out the johns. There were two men's rooms and two ladies' rooms and all four were filled with vomit. Jimmy shoveled it up and mopped it away and wiped off the mirrors. He had a hard time with one of them in one of the ladies' rooms, where some dame had written "Dick me, Richard" in lipstick. A bit of ammonia finally got it off.

When Jimmy came back to the kosher kitchen, Covetti put him on pot walloping. He walloped them in the deep sink for what seemed a kind of tiny, Tin Pan Alley eternity. Then, deep in the evening, he was pulled off that.

There was a kind of commencement party for novitiate priests being held, and they needed extra tables. Jimmy collapsed the legs on a half dozen six-foot-in-diameter, eight-seater round tables and carted them, one at a time, out through the kosher kitchen and across the parking lot and in at another door. Inside, there were a couple of hundred rosy-cheeked, black-garbed, very drunken novitiate priests. They were sprawled about over chairs or tables, eyes-drooping or bulging, snoring or shouting. Two or three of the soberer ones occasionally carried out the bodies of their comatose comrades. The tables Jimmy brought in and set up were quickly loaded with pitchers of beer by the waiters. Bottles of whiskey were placed on each table. Joy and forgetfulness were being sung at a hundred tables around the room. At one table, "Carmina Burana" broke loose in seminary Latin.

Outside, the night was whipping up a thunderstorm.

Jimmy went to bring more tables, noticing, en route, the black-shod feet of novitiates protruding from the open windows of limousines. They reminded Jimmy of Parris Island recruits out of basic training, showing off how drunk they could get. "Onward, Christian Soldiers!" he saluted them. As he made his way out another door, a huge table in his grip, the wind caught it and gave his spine a sudden one-eighty twist. It sounded like six shots rang out from his spine, *snap snap snap, snap snap, snap!* That did it. The rest of the night he could hardly walk. He went about, bluffing everything he did, as his Buddhist pal Denise might say, in an ecstasy of agony with no Nirvana in the gloaming.

The sky broke open and the rain came straight down. It was nine o'clock, of whatever night it was.

"What night is it, Oskar?"

"Sunday," shouted Oskar, lifting a rack of scraped dessert plates onto the conveyor. "Let's make 'em kosher, boys!" Oskar took off his glasses and wiped them with his slimy apron. His face was pale and his light black beard was surfacing.

Jimmy threw down his brush and dug his nails into a particularly obstinate piece of icing. But his nails were too short and broken to do much good. He threw the plate into the hole. To hell with it! In a minute it was buried in muck. "Three hours to go, eh?" he shouted, or tried to shout. His voice was too weak to make much noise. He adjusted his stance to accommodate his back.

"What?" shouted Oskar, angry at having his numbing concentration broken.

"Three hours to go!" Jimmy shouted.

"Yeah!" shouted Oskar: then, "Let's make 'em kosher, boys!"—madly, madly—"Let's make 'em kosher!"

Covetti came in and sent Jimmy, who could hardly walk now, limping out again to see if the washrooms needed

170

cleaning. As Jimmy approached a ladies' room, the blonde who had been behind the partition came staggering out the door. She had the green, peaked look of one who has recently upchucked. He noticed that the tear in her skirt was bound closed with knotted bobby pins. She wore a diamond engagement ring and a diamond-studded wedding ring above it, and she was cling-clang with bracelets. Her face looked like an oil painting that had been wiped before it was dry. Inside, she left her calling card, in the form of several little heaps of pink vomit.

"That damned champagne!" Jimmy grumbled. He limped back and told Covetti that the room needed cleaning but that he wasn't going to do it. He said he'd cleaned it up once and let somebody else do it this time. He told Covetti he thought that his back was broken, and that he might sue. Covetti said that if Jimmy didn't clean it up, he could consider himself fired.

"Don't come back next week," Covetti said. Jimmy said, O.K., he wouldn't.

Covetti told Oskar to do it, but Oskar bluffed his way out of it. "Can't you see I got dishes shtacked up? I can't do dat now." His dark eyebrows were raised, as if to say there was something the matter with Covetti's brain.

"O.K.," said Covetti. "Harrigan, you do it."

"Christ, Mr. Covetti, I'm a mixologist, not a poil-diver. I don't know how ta clean good." Harrigan was an ex-bartender, permeated with alcohol, on the bum.

"Harrigan!"

"O.K., O.K.," said Harrigan.

"Now let's go, boys, make 'em kosher!" Covetti yelled, trying in his obvious way to be in, to be democratic. Soon as Covetti left the scullery, Oskar started howling with laughter.

"Dat ugly mutterfrogger—he didn't know vhat to say to me; did you see dat?"

171

Then, suddenly, it was midnight. They mopped up, threw off their aprons, put their jackets on, and stood about, waiting for their pay. Tony came into the kitchen with a bottle of whiskey and gave them each a drink before he paid them.

Outside, at the garbage room, Oskar and Jimmy dug out their box of contraband. They took turns carrying it under the moon. Two big beefs and a chicken were a heavy load for workers as tired as they were, and especially for Jimmy with his bad back, but they felt obligated to take the box along. It was a symbol of some kind. But it was a symbol for Tony's Halfway House, too. A city garbage truck caught up with them on the road. Two burly types explained that Mr. Covetti told them to pick them up and take them to the station.

"You boys get up there on the garbage," said one. "There ain't no room in the cab."

"Vell, vat de hell," said Oskar. "We stink like shit anyway."

"You'll have to help me up, Oskar," said Jimmy, "my back's broken."

The truck rumbled off into the night, Jimmy and Oskar bouncing amid the garbage.

"Say, ain't dis taking a long time to get to da station?"

"Yeah," said Jimmy. "Where the hell are we?"

The truck pulled between cyclone fenced gates.

"Vhat da hell is this?"

"I think it's the city dump," said Jimmy. "But it's so goddamned dark. I can't tell where we are."

The truck started backing up. It was a dump truck and it started lifting them high into the air and sliding them forward on mounds of garbage and dumped them into a mountain of garbage and began to bury them in more garbage. The truck pulled away and vanished in the night.

"Phheeew!" cried Oskar. "Dey've dumped us like garbage! I guess dis means dey don't want me back next week, either."

Jimmy's back-pocket, paperback edition of Orwell's *Down and Out in London and Paris* was spine-split and water-logged. He threw it on the steaming, mephitic heap.

"I told you, Oskar—the weed of crime bears bitter fruit!"

"Frog me," cried Oskar, flicking away several foul bits of gunk. Overhead, the reflected lights of the city shown, some distance ahead.

After a long walk to the station, Jimmy and Oskar rolled in from Long Island and hit the downtown subway. "I gotta have a drink," Jimmy told Oskar, "my back is killing me."

"Look at dis shit all over us! I'm going home and soak in the tub for a week, and burn dese clothes," said Oskar.

"You handle it your way, I'll handle it mine," said Jimmy. "I'm going all the way down to Brooklyn, see Marsayas and Joan and get drunk as the skunk I smell like. They're back from Frisco and I heard they brought some chick with them."

"Ja. I'm sure you'll impress her, fluffy," he said, smiling, as he stepped off the D Train. "I heard she's a looker," he called, and swooosh, he was gone.

Jimmy's friends, Marsayas and Joan, had settled in a little dump of an apartment over a funeral parlor and a Mafia bar. Joan was trying to make their new friend and roommate from Frisco, Lani Kona, feel at home.

"I can help you fix the place up," Lani said.

"It'll give you something to do," Joan said, "when you aren't trying to get back in school."

"And I'll finally get to see Kimo," she said, hopefully. Lani had discovered, back in Frisco, that

173

Marsayas and Joan actually knew that same young Jimmy Whistler she'd known all those years ago in Hawaii.

"Why do you call him Kimo?"

"Hawaiian for Jim."

"Kimo-the-Poet," Joan tried, then laughed. "No, honey, it just doesn't work."

"You think he'll come by sometime?"

"Yeah, he knows we're back. He might pop in at any moment. He's just like Marsayas, like all these guys, totally undependable."

"That isn't how he seemed in Hawaii. He seemed . . . he seemed . . . staunch. So military, so . . .together."

"That was a long time ago, honey. And he's had a terrible marriage."

"What was she like?"

"A show-biz bitch, eye-lashes out to here, all kinds of paint—oh, I suppose you could say that she was pretty good looking, in a cheap sort of way."

"He was such a clean boy. He seemed to shine."

"Well, don't expect him to be the same. He is a poet, you know, and crazy as hell, like all of them; but a lot of fun when he's not too far gone. He was an actor for a while, you know, and he can recite beautifully."

"Yes, I remember how he used to read poetry to me. I thought he was the most beautiful thing I'd ever seen." She laughed, shrugged her shoulders. "I think I'll have that glass of wine, now."

"How 'bout some pot," Joan said, lighting up, and passing the joint.

After a pit stop and five boiler makers, Jimmy limped across Brooklyn Heights toward Marsayas's and stumbled into Chic's mafia bar, downstairs from the flat. Marsayas, himself not a serious bather, did not rise from his bar stool to seize Jimmy in the usual bear-hug that was their standard greeting, but sat with a wondering look on his face, then the gleeful gargoyle appeared.

"What in hell's happened to you? You looked like you climbed out of the town dump—worse—pheeewwey—you *smell* like you climbed out of the town dump."

"That's because I *did* climb out of a town dump, you dumb son-of-a-bitch! Why else would I look and smell like this. The mob boys out at Tony's Halfway House dumped us in the town dump." The denizens of Chic's perked up their ears and gave him the once-over. The bartender appeared to say to Marsayas, "I'm not serving him in here."

Jimmy overheard. "For God's sake, I had an accident, man. Give me a boiler-maker, quick!"

Marsayas said, "Can't you see he's had an accident? He's got cuts all over him. Look!"

"O.K.," said the bartender and drew a beer and a shot for the victim. He handed them over at the greatest distance his arms could manage. "God, you stink like—"

"Hey," said Jimmy, "I'm closer to it than you are."

The bartender shook his head. "You got an egg shell in your hair." Marsayas reached over and carefully picked it out of Jimmy's matted hair. "There seems to be a lot of other stuff in there, too," Marsayas said.

"I don't wanna know," the bartender said.

"Another one, please," Jimmy said. The bartender repeated the order. Perhaps it was sympathy, which is hard to come by in such hard rocks, proving how pathetic a sight Jimmy must have appeared, but the bartender continued to serve him after that. Suddenly Jimmy had to go to the bathroom desperately. He had climbed aboard the bar stool somehow, but now he couldn't get down. "It's my back. I think I broke it."

"When they dumped you?" asked Marsayas.

"No. Before that. A table got caught in the wind and twisted my spine. Lift me down, will you?"

Marsayas lifted him down, then realized that the only way Jimmy was going to make the men's room was to be carried. "If I'm going to carry you, I might as well carry you upstairs." He lifted Jimmy in a fireman's carry and out of the bar and up the stairs to his place, kicked the door open and sat him down at the kitchen table, Jimmy moaning and groaning in agony throughout.

"Look what I found," he said to Joan and Lani, who were seated at the kitchen table. "Lani, this is your poet."

"Oh my God," said Joan. "What's happened to him?"

Lani rose from the table. This was not Kimo, this bunch of stained rags with goo in his hair and a three-day growth of beard. She leaned across the table trying to find the young Marine that she remembered. He seemed to be passing out and coming back and passing out again.

"What's happened to him? What's the matter with him?"

"I haven't slept in three days," Jimmy said, "I've broken my back, and I've been dumped in a town dump. I had to walk miles to the station to get the train into the city. And I've had a few drinks for the pain."

"More than a few," said Joan.

"O.K., many a few." Jimmy started laughing hysterically, then screaming as his back gripped him, then laughing again.

"Do you know who this is, Jimmy?" asked Joan.

Jimmy tried to focus. "A beautiful Hawaiian girl," he said. "I knew one just like her once. She was a child and I was a child in a kingdom by the sea."

Lani almost started to cry, saying, "I think he remembers."

"Give me a cigarette, will you, somebody?"

Joan said, "I'm gonna give you a bath, that's what I'm going to give you." She started to lift him, but couldn't.

"Marsayas, get him in the bath tub. I don't go for that crap, but we could use some air freshener around here. Lani, light some incense!"

In a half-hour they had Jimmy back at the table, dressed in Marsayas's clothes, which were too big for Jimmy and made him look like a rumpled clown. Joan had shaved him while he was in the bath tub. At least he looked clean. She forced some hot coffee down his throat. He looked around. "Where the hell am I?"

Lani said, "Kimo, do you know who I am?"

"I think you must be my sweet Leilani all grown up," he said, squinting. "Am I right?"

"Yes, Kimo, yes! I'm your sweet Leilani all grown up. Your little sister, remember?"

"It's like a dream," he said, and his eyes rolled back in his head and nearly disappeared. He shook his head and looked vaguely at them, grinning, and with a pale face of exhausted idiocy shouted, "Make 'em kosher!"

THE MONDRIAAN

When Jimmy Whistler's father died, Jimmy and his mother, Fay, decided to superintend a house in New York, in Chelsea or Greenwich Village, wherever they could find one. Jimmy had to help take care of her, and, at the same time, the move would alter his situation with his girlfriend, Phyllis, with whom he'd been involved for several years. He wasn't being fair staying with this girl when he had no intention of marrying her. He was attached; it was difficult; he just didn't have the guts to break up.

The plan, as it evolved, was to move all of Fay's things to Phyllis's apartment, so that both Jimmy and Fay would be in New York to look for a house. They'd rent a van in Newark, and hire Moe, a taxi driver they knew, to drive it and to help carry. Finding a super's job shouldn't take more than a week or two, Jimmy reckoned. Then they'd move their stuff from Phyllis's to the new house, and that'd be it. He was willing to help Fay, but he had to do it in his own way. He had to stay close to his own life in New York. That wasn't asking too much, was it?

Phyllis had agreed to this plan. Of how she felt, Jimmy wasn't certain. She seemed to approve, in general. She knew very well what the situation was. She had known Fay for several years, and liked her well enough, with qualifications—Fay could be difficult. Jimmy reminded himself that one never knew exactly what Phyllis was thinking, or how much she knew. Jimmy felt like a husband who cheats on his wife, but needs her, not exactly loves her more than he does his mistress, but feels obligated in time to her. Making this move with Fay might let him off the hook, let him worm out of having to make a final decision. He could just end up spending more time with Fay than he did with Phyllis—but Fay could be difficult.

They were leaving Newark then, leaving Baldwin; that old rooming house that had been their home, of sorts, for nearly a decade—the longest permanent address they'd had as, what one might call, a small family. They said goodbye to the many nameless life-mad men and women who had passed their way as they'd officiated over and under that unofficial, memory-filled madhouse where most of the tenants had been sent from the State loony bin at Vineland; but mostly they thought of Elliot, Jimmy's father, that strange, self-made failure, who'd had everything once, in another world, the world before the Crash.

The cab doors of the big rented van swung shut, Fay sat between Moe and Jimmy, and the winter wind was blowing on them, blowing their hair. Jimmy wondered what Fay was thinking. He knew she was afraid. He knew she was sad. But he suspected that, now it was done, she was looking forward to the future, too. One of her endearing as well as maddening qualities was that she neither dwelt on the past nor learned from it. By the time they were humming on the highway she was smiling, looking about, chattering, pointing out across the choppy, lordly Hudson at the Manhattan skyline, and he could see that it was still there, the spirit, the life.

At night Jimmy went to his job on the docks and hauled crates of cabbages about. When he'd get in, in the morning, he'd hit the sack for two or three hours, and up, shower, eat breakfast, and stand about smoking while Fay fastened her earrings or brushed the cat hair from her skirt. Despite the cat hair, she managed to look nice. Enthusiastic, buoyant, she was wearing pastel woolen suits. She looked almost glamorous, at least fifteen years younger than her age of sixty. How it was that she could look positively glamorous and appealing, really girlish and pretty, after all the scrubbing she had done in hotels and rooming houses over the years, was a mystery. In certain respects she'd never matured. She was ambiguous, changeable, by turns enthusiastic and easily discouraged. After only a few days of looking for what they wanted, she said: "Maybe I ought to go back to Jersey." And it was this that Jimmy worried about. He feared she hadn't the will to see things through.

Jimmy passed a real estate office in Greenwich Village late one Friday afternoon, on his way to his job on the docks. He stopped in, told the rental agent what he wanted, his qualifications, and that his mother would take the house with him. Jimmy told the rental agent her qualifications for such an important post. Think of it! A mother and son who had both been in the hotel business, who had run rooming houses, both of them able to keep transcripts and ledgers, veritable bookkeepers; people unafraid of wielding mops and brooms; attractive, well-spoken, appear to be somewhat educated—then a frown: odd, very odd!

"You say you can do electrical work?"

"Yes. Just about anything like that."

"How did you come by that knowledge?"

"I studied electrical engineering," Jimmy lied. He had read a How-To book.

"You went to college?"

"I quit. But since then I've steeped myself in autodidactology. Of course, there are a few holes, but nothing that can't be corked, as the Dutch say."

"Well—huh—may I ask just why you want to take a job as a superintendent?"

180

"It's my kind of work. My mother and I were made for it. *Partus sequitur ventrem,* you know. I've been doing it all my life."

"Mmmm. I see." Of course he didn't; he looked foggy. But when he met Fay the next day he took a real shine to her, though he was worried about whether she'd be able to do such hard work. Jimmy assured him that he'd do the heavy stuff.

"O.K. then, I'll take you over to the house. I think you people should fit right in there. After all, this is Greenwich Village."

Jimmy wondered—was he being sarcastic, or honest?

It was one of those big, sham-quality joints that had recently appeared all over the Village. They had names like the sedate "Van Dyck" and the ultramodern "Picasso." Theirs was a big refurbished brownstone building now called "The Mondriaan," located in the block-length curve of Morton Street, between Seventh Avenue and Bedford, a quiet, quaint, tree-lined street, just out of the way of the booming Seventh Avenue shopkeeping, restaurant, and night spot area, and three minutes from the Bleeker Street stalls, stands, and Italian markets. The big front doors were thick plate-glass, which meant a great deal of cleaning. The vestibule consisted of ten wide marble-veneer stairs, and they meant a great deal of mopping. Inside, it was just narrow hallways, lined with doors with imitation brass imitation knockers that were actually doorbells that rang when the knockers were lifted, red wall-paper up the walls, an elevator full of stainless steel, and that meant a lot of wiping, and narrow marble stairs spiraling upward around the elevator to the eighth floor, top of the mark, and they meant a long trip down pushing a broom or a mop.

Near the stairwell, on every floor, there was a door opening to an incinerator chute. The agent—Bradhurst—took them down to the basement to show them the big incinerator. He asked Jimmy what he thought of it, and Jimmy told him that he'd seen many incinerators in his day, but that this one was unquestionably the finest. Jimmy told Bradhurst he thought he could work with this one. He looked it over carefully, patted it approvingly, and smiled at Bradhurst.

"You like it, eh?" Bradhurst queried, apparently needing reassurance.

"I think it's just great," Jimmy said, and patted it again. "It could turn a body to dust in just five minutes."

Bradhurst looked at him quizzically.

Jimmy winked.

Bradhurst smiled doubtfully. Apparently he was satisfied. Then he took Jimmy and Fay into the laundry room, where both of the machines were doing a fat, bubbly, white jiggle, and making sucking noises like a fat child eating spaghetti.

"There's a kickback switch, so instead of the fuse blowing, the power just goes off, and all you have to do is switch it back on again. But I guess you know more about than I do, knowing electrics and all, eh?"

"Oh, yes—yes—" Jimmy said, hurriedly, "I know all about kickbacks."

"Good. Good. Very good," said Mr. Bradhurst.

Fay said: "May we see our apartment now?"

"Oh," said Mr. Bradhurst, "there's just one more thing I'd like to show you first. But, on second thought, this is really more for your son—I want to show him the boiler room—so I'll let you into the apartment—it's just down the hall from the boiler—and you can look it over while we take a peek in at the Big Boy—ha—that's what we call him—the boiler, I mean—the Big Boy."

He let Fay into the apartment, and took Jimmy on to the boiler room. It was about thirty paces down the cement floored basement hallway from their apartment door (their door had an imitation brass imitation knocker on it too, just like the doors of the big people upstairs); but Jimmy was not listening for doorbells, but was feeling great clongers at a distance; clunkers, bongers, and—was it screams? Bradhurst was leading him toward these sounds. They came to an iron door, with a large red-and-white sign reading *DANGER!* on it, and from inside of which emanated an ominous, pulsating sound, which encouraged Jimmy to believe that the sign had not been placed on the door for nothing. Dapper Mr. Bradhurst bravely threw open the door and gingerly climbed down a rusty iron ladder, indicating with a nod that Jimmy should follow. Jimmy didn't care much for the idea of going into a pit with a thing that made such hideous snorts, but if Bradhurst was game, he expected it would be O.K. So he followed.

The boiler was a huge, squat black thing, which, when seen from the side, as one saw it from the door, looked like a blocky, crouching sphinx, and when seen from the front (one had to walk along a narrow cement catwalk, and put oneself practically into its chops to see it from the front) truly depicted a monster out of one's worst dreams— Moloch, a red, fire-spitting mouth with jack o' lantern teeth, that were grates; crossed, angry yellow eyes, that were lights (the crossed look having been caused by one of them being bent inwards on its metal stem), and black, zig-zagging pipes sticking out of the top of its head like crazy Medusa hair. Obviously a thing of foul disposition.

"Have you a boiler license?" queried Mr. Bradhurst.

"Why, no; I haven't. Do I need one?" In his childhood, Jimmy had lived so intimately with boilers he'd never considered a license to touch one necessary.

"Oh, my! I thought you most certainly would have a boiler license, what with all your experience in other houses. Well, we'll just have to arrange to get you one. Mr. Kreigsgeld, the owner, will come to meet you and your mother next Saturday. He'll take care of that then. And that gives you a whole week to move in and get yourselves settled before assuming your duties. Now then, shall we go and see how your mother likes the apartment?"

It could have been bigger; it consisted of one large room, one small room (Jimmy's), and a kitchenette and bath. But it was a neat, clean, cheerful, modernistic little place, done in white (and that was good, because it was a basement apartment, and needed light), and the flooring was black rubber tile throughout. Yet, it did get plenty of light from the row of high little windows that looked to the street and the sun in the mornings.

"Curtained," Fay said, "they'll be beautiful." The bathroom was of blue tile, and clean, and nothing was chipped, for a change, and the kitchenette was functional and clean, and, surprise of surprises, everything worked.

Jimmy saw that Fay was delighted. He knew her to be thrilled at the prospect of having an apartment that offered her some chance of exercising her "not inconsiderable domestic skills," as Elliot had called them. The place was partially furnished, and Bradhurst told them that they could use any of the furniture that the former tenants had left behind, now in storage; and Fay was very busy, as Jimmy could see, thinking about where she would put this, that, and the other. In short, she was sold. She hadn't realized yet how much work there was to be done in such a building, and Jimmy didn't want to discourage her before they got started. He figured they'd find another place if this one got to be too much. But he wished that she could have been more patient, given him time to find something smaller, easier to manage. This was a very big house, and that boiler was—was—a monstrous humdinger!

Outside, Fay said: "Oh, it's a knockout, don't you think? But I didn't want to act as if I liked it too much. I was afraid they'd cut our salary if they saw how much I

184

liked the apartment." She laughed mischievously. "Let's go and have a glass of beer and celebrate."

The "salary" to which she alluded, was fifty dollars a month. Fay was now collecting Elliot's social security check, as widow's may, but that was merely a widow's mite. Jimmy figured that would be all hers, and that, plus the salary, plus fifteen a week or so, out of his paycheck, would give her a pretty sizeable grand total—and no rent. It more than doubled her present income and it improved her circumstances in general. When she wanted to, she could go over to Jersey and visit with Aunt Myrtle and Uncle O'Toole, and Jimmy would stay behind and mind the house. Then, at other times, she could watch the house and let Jimmy take off for a day. Trouble was, he'd have to hit the docks steadily three nights a week and take care of the heavy work in the house, too, every day, all day. But he had two other evenings free, during the week, and the weekends, too, or at least part of them, in which to do some writing, he hoped. Jimmy, a poet, had been planning a novel. He didn't think it would be too bad. The Mondriaan wasn't what he'd have taken, had he more time, had Fay not rushed him. But he didn't have time. Fay had been chomping at the bit. And it was fun that first week, when nobody knew they were there; before the house came down on them.

Owner Kreigsgeld was a sly, waxen little creature, with mean, protuberant frog-eyes, and a fishy, puckered mouth. His body seemed that of an undernourished child. He sat in their living-room with his legs neatly crossed, so as not to muss his creases, his little black patent leather shoes glittering, and rubbed his nose with his thumbs, now and then, as he talked. He was a pompous, condescending little business-ghoul, who asked: "Do you understand that I expect this house to be kept clean?" and, "Do you know how to make out a receipt?" He might well have asked: "Can you read?" Bradhurst, obviously embarrassed, ventured now and then, though carefully, sycophantically, to say things like, "Oh, Mr. Kreigsgeld, Mrs. Whistler and her son know all about that. They were in the hotel business. They're very able people," and "Jim, here, has been to college—right, Jim?"

"What do you take a job like this for, then?"

"I like the work."

"Like the work?"

"Yes, Mr. Kreigsgeld, Jim is very handy with tools. He studied electrics."

"Electrical engineering," Jimmy corrected.

"Yes," said Bradhurst—"You see?"

"I . . . don't . . . know . . ." said Kreigsgeld. Then: "But we give you a try."

Kreigsgeld gave Bradhurst fifty dollars in an envelope for Jimmy to take with him to the Fire Department Licensing Bureau, which he, in turn, was to give to a certain Fire Captain who would make himself known.

Several days later, Jimmy sat in a waiting room beyond the partition of which a huge, examination room hummed and tested, and ran over in his mind all the details—the valves and inlet pipes and so on—of a number six-oil boiler. Then a big, burly man, with iron-grey hair and a face the color of the fires he had fought, came in. He wore no coat or hat, but the rest of his garb was that of a Fire Captain in full-dress regalia and Jimmy thought he saw gold epaulettes on his broad shoulders—but no, it was only the flickering fluorescent light that portrayed the unreal. He snapped: "You Whistler?"

"That's me."

"You wanna take this test for the boiler license—right?"

"Yes, sir; I do."

"Have you studied?"

"Yes, sir—all week."

186

"Follow me." The Captain led him out of the office and into the hall.

Jimmy was standing now, and what he was standing next to—aside from the fire-faced Captain—was a warning at least five feet high and three feet wide, the substance of which was an indication that anyone who should entertain the idea of bribing a public official, such as the Captain, could expect to be caught, drawn-and-quartered, and have his parts sold, at a small profit to the city, to a dog food factory. So when the Captain said: "Have you got the fifty bucks?" Jimmy hesitated, having, for a moment, the eerie sensation that he was being entrapped.

When he didn't answer, the Captain said: "You know, kid, the examining clerk has a lot of work on his hands. He might not be able to see you today."

Jimmy looked up at the sign, read:

WARNING!!!

and handed over the hot little public service appreciation donation envelope.

"Just a minute," the Captain said, and turned his back. At the count of fifty he turned back. He put his hand on Jimmy's shoulder, said, "Good luck, kid," and went back into the office again. Ten minutes later Jimmy was called in for the test. He was asked one question: What number oil does a number-six boiler use? Amazingly, Jimmy passed.

The super across the street had been taking care of The Mondriaan temporarily. Of course, he had his hands full with his own place, "The Dali," and wasn't doing very much for The Mondriaan, so when the notice was put up on the front door that there was a super in residence, Fay and Jimmy were hit, as if by the stuff from the fan, with complaints, requests, and demands, all of which had been neglected for months on end.

As the onslaught subsided, life at The Mondriaan took on shape and regularity. A day began at nine o'clock

187

in the morning with Jimmy going up and sweeping the halls and stairs all the way down, through the vestibule, and on out to the sidewalk, where he gathered up the trash and sweepings to bring in and burn in the incinerator. He tended the boiler, and, if it were a day for the garbage men to come, got the twenty cans out on the street and dragged them back in when they'd been emptied. Then it was a matter of fixing light switches, unclogging toilets, installing new tiles in bathrooms where the old tiles had been chipped or had fallen out, putting new washers in leaking sink spigots, and such like odd jobs; and, of course, always waiting for the next complaint.

On the third Saturday Kreigsgeld came around, just after Fay and Jimmy had finished cleaning the house from top to bottom, banged on their door, and complained that he'd found a cigarette butt in the vestibule. Somebody had dropped it there since it was swept. They told him so, and a few other things, too, and he retreated.

Fay helped Jimmy with the cleaning, and cooked them meals that they were rarely able to eat, for the constant buzzing of doorbells, ringing of phones, etc. On Saturday mornings they did a heavy-duty cleaning job on the house from top to bottom. Jimmy'd take a five gallon pail with a wringer attached and a ten pound mop up to the eighth floor and push them, clanging and plopping, all the way down through the basement, and into their own apartment, which deserved to be kept at least as clean as the rest of the house. Ideas of Order.

While mopping, Jimmy often encountered the tenants in the hallways. And most of them proved to be perfect snobs. He hated these bucket-in-hand encounters. If he were to say "Hello," he'd get a grunt and a sidelong look, and be made to feel like an Untouchable. On the other hand, if he didn't speak, and kept his head down and his mop moving, Bradhurst would tell him later that So-and-So found him to be a rude young man. But to be got up at three o'clock in the morning to hear a drunk make complaints about his lost keys was nothing in any way unusual. Jimmy discovered that a superintendent, in one of these slick city apartment buildings, is lower than the low.

All the tenants weren't like that, of course, but the majority were. Most of them could scarcely afford to pay the exorbitant rents they were paying. Kreigsgeld, a type of man most of his tenants would look down their noses at, and for the wrong reasons, was to be admired in so having arranged things that he could get blood from such turnips. The books in their bookcases showed a slavish devotion to whatever was the fad, the prints on their walls were the selections of persons who have read only the latest, trendy intellectual claptrap and pop psychology. They worked in offices and got out their berets and sandals on weekends. It was La Boheme on a full stomach. Jimmy threw one of his extra manuscripts into the incinerator's fiery chops in their honor. "Well, this is your life, James Whistler," he said, and he thought he heard the house applauding.

One Monday morning the sidewalk in front of The Mondriaan was strewn with litter, as if a garbage truck had lost its balance. If Kreigsgeld had seen it in a mess like that he'd have raised hell. Not only that, but there were fingerprints and smudges and kid's soap-mark graffiti all over the big plate-glass doors. Jimmy pushed one open and peeked into the vestibule. Cigarette butts, cigar butts, candy wrappers, and—the master stroke—a little heap of vomit on the third stair near the wall, a pet's regurgitation, probably.

Just as Jimmy was about to make his way into the house, by the basement entrance, he was accosted by the superintendent from across the street, the one who had taken care of The Mondriaan before Fay and he took over. The superintendent of The Dali had "gas heat," or so he had informed Jimmy several times, great pride ringing in his

189

voice. To have oil heat was to be a superintendent who had to get dirty, but to have gas heat was to be a superintendent of higher standing, an aristocrat among superintendents. He-who-has-gas-heat wears frilly bright pink shirts, a cravat stuck in his collar, stands about all day and has nothing to do but to smoke colored cigarettes in a long ivory holder. He-who-has-gas-heat is always organized, is efficient, is never in the kind of fix Jimmy always found himself in.

He-who-has-gas heat said (speaking in an unidentifiable, middle-European accent): "Say, when if you're gonna sweep here? Dis paper blows on me. How 'bout it?"

Jimmy told him he was going to get right at it.

"Good," he said. "You know, but son-of-a-bitch, I couldn't get my front clean."

Jimmy said, "As soon as I get it cleaned up, I'll come over and do your sidewalk, too. O.K.?"

"Sure, O.K." He smiled at Jimmy, and looked at his crotch. "Pretty busy you got, eh?" He smiled again, and motioned his head disdainfully at the Mondriaan. "That's a tough joint to be. Goddamn, she drived me nuts. Had nay trouble wid da boiler?"

"No, not so far," Jimmy lied, not wanting to give ruffles the supremacy he was seeking.

"Ho, gees. Dat t'ing out all winter. The pipples go crazy. No hot water. No heat. My God! I scaired dey would kill me. She's no good, da Big Boy. She break, all time, watch!" He pucker-smiled and looked down at Jimmy's crotch again. "Lottsa work, eh?"

"Looks like I've got a week's work out here alone."

"Ya," he said. "Nice day, though. If tomorrow bees like today, son-of-a-bitch, dat's what I hope!"

"Me too."

"Well, see you, keedo. O.K.?"

"O.K.," Jimmy said, and descended the steps.

Inside the basement door stood one of the long-faced horsey girls (there were two of them: Fay and Jimmy called them the horsey girls because they often wore riding dress, and in their apartment they each had an English saddle, a collection of riding crops, and the sets of dull little spurs they hooked to their boots to kick horses with: the walls of their apartment were covered with pictures of horses, and the biggest picture was a painting of a horse, executed in such a way as to make the horse indistinguishable from any other horse who ever proudly galloped, and underneath which was written, on a brass plate attached to the frame: Seabiscuit). This young equestrian woman had a sour look on her face that morning, and, when she saw Jimmy, she said:

"Mr. Whistler! I have troid and troid to locate you. These washing machines have simply been a terrible nuisance. One of them isn't working at all. And the other overflows every time it's used. You simply must do something about this. And there hasn't been any hot water *all* weekend, I-ther."

"I'll get right on it. You say there hasn't been any hot water?"

"Not a drop."

"Boiler must have gone on the blink."

"I should say!" She stomped off in her boots, slapping a puff of her jodhpurs with a riding crop, and in a few seconds Jimmy heard the elevator clanging and wheezing as it lifted her, temporarily, out of his hair.

"Christ!" he said aloud. "The whole place has gone to pieces at the speed of light!"

He went in to look at the incinerator, thinking that he'd just as well set fire to whatever was collected in it before he swept up the front. He opened the incinerator door and looked in. God! There wasn't room for enough air to get in there to start a fire with. He'd have to pull half of that

191

stuff out, burn the other half, and then stuff the rest back in and burn that. He thought he'd do that as soon as he got the front of the house swept up, but he had to change his mind on that score, because he couldn't get the incinerator door shut again. So he kept on pulling the trash out of the incinerator. He was beginning to get frantic, thinking that old Kreigsgeld might show up.

He pulled and tugged the stuff out of the incinerator's mouth: an old girdle, a fluffy pink slipper, a milk container with a condom on it, a half empty box of doggy biscuits, an empty caviar tin, a five pound bag of rotten potatoes, a Teddy bear, a broken riding crop (ah!), an old pair of men's shoes, tied together at the laces, an empty can of crabmeat, foot plasters, an old stained jockstrap, a framed photograph of Harry Truman, an empty six-pack of beer cans, a sewing kit (Jimmy set that aside); and before long he was knee-deep in mephitic rubble. He reached into this heap, that completely surrounded him, and filled the little incinerator room, grabbed an old newspaper, set fire to it, and threw it into the incinerator's mouth. *Whoo-ooooosh!* Up went the flames!

He stood there for a couple of minutes, sweat dripping from every gaping pore, looking like the chimney sweep he was, to see that the fire was burning properly, then closed the incinerator door, leaving the grate open so that the fire could get air, and waded through the debris, on out into the basement. He hurried into the apartment, got the keys, opened the storage room door, where were located the kickback switches, and pushed the fallen one back up. There was a gurgling sound, a roar, and then a sweet and steady jiggling noise, meaning that the washing machine that didn't work had been overloaded, causing it to throw the switch mid-cycle, and now it was, like any dumb machine, completing the job it had started by doing the second stage of a phantom laundry.

Jimmy was in a sweat for fair, now.

He grabbed a broom, a mop, and a pail, and pulled them out of the storage room, locked the door, and took the works into the apartment. Stepping in, he almost broke a leg slipping on the stack of complaints that had been shoved under the door. He dropped his equipment, grabbed the phone, and called the boiler repair service. Fortunately, he was told, there was a service truck equipped with a radio in the neighborhood. Jimmy could expect help at any time. Then he made another hurried call to the washing machine repair service. Be around that afternoon, he was told. He grabbed the pail and took it into the bathroom, to fill it at the tub. He caught a fleeting glimpse of himself in the bathroom mirror and looked away. His face was beaded all over with perspiration and smeared with soot. An egg shell was clinging to his shirt like a leech. He needed a shave. His eyes were red. His curly, disheveled hair caused him to look more like a Medusa than a man. In fact, that glimpse he'd caught of himself very nearly stopped him in his tracks. He wondered, for an instant, if Kreigsgeld would rather find *him* looking nice and the house a shambles, or him a shambles and the house looking nice. How long would it take him to shave? He decided that he'd better stick to cleaning up the house. He hopped into the elevator and rode up to the eighth floor and began sweeping and mopping down in lightning-like strokes. By this time, he wasn't thinking too clearly. Everything had to be done and it all had to be done at once. That was all he could understand about the situation. He didn't even stop to wonder why everybody had left bags and boxes of trash outside their doors. He didn't even stop to think about it, when on the eighth floor he tried to put one of these bags in the incinerator chute and found that the chute was stuffed. Instead, he took the bag and put it in the elevator, and all the rest of the bags and boxes went into the elevator, too, as he worked his way down the stairs.

In the basement, when he rang the elevator buzzer and it dropped down to him with a squeak and a shudder and he opened the door, he found it as full, it seemed, as the incinerator had been; only, unlike the incinerator, one of the items in the elevator walked out of the door under its own locomotion. It was the horsey girl, and she had a bag of garbage in each arm, each bag filled with unburnable bottles.

"I have never seen anything like this," she complained. "Why is all this garbage in the elevator?"

"To get it down here," Jimmy said, in short temper.

"Well, she said, "if you would unclog the incinerator chute, you would be able to get the garbage to its proper place in a more convenient and expeditious manner, don't you think? I, personally, don't care to ride in elevators full of garbage, and I doubt if the rest of the tenants would appreciate it I-ther. Is the washing machine working yet?"

"One of them is," Jimmy said, stuffing garbage in a garbage can.

"Thank heavens!" she exclaimed, and went to look.

Jimmy loaded four garbage cans with the stuff from the elevator, and left them standing there as he ran outside to sweep up the front. He was plying the broom like a madman, sweeping everything up, including poodle and Great Dane droppings, when he heard a scream from the basement. He looked behind him and saw that there was smoke billowing out of the basement door, which he'd left propped open.

"Fire! Fire!" It was the horsey girl.

Jimmy looked around him, his wits scattered. What to do? He saw the dainty super across the street bob up out of his basement and disappear again. Jimmy made a beeline for his own basement door, held his breath, and dove in. But it seemed that this was not to be his heroic day. Instead of finding the damsel in distress, he ran into her, and both of

194

them went sprawling on the floor. It appeared that if Jimmy had just stayed out of the doorway, she'd have found her freedom. Now they floundered about, not able to see, and held onto each other in a most familiar way. Jimmy wondered if she didn't take advantage of the situation.

They finally groped their way outside.

"My Gawd!" she said, standing next to Jimmy, watching as the smoke beclouded and darkened the street. Jimmy heard a voice and looked up. A tenant that Jimmy had dubbed "The Countess" for obvious reasons, had her head stuck out of her window (he could see the two heads of her two poodles, too). She wanted to know if the house was on fire.

"Just the basement," Jimmy called up to her. He felt a bit unhinged. Then, sirens wailing, bells tolling, two fire trucks pulled to the curb. In they went, the men of whatever squad it was: hoses criss-crossing the little street. Dogs barked. People stared. Firemen cursed. Bells rang. Sirens screamed. Cars pulled up. Traffic snarled. And Jimmy wept.

Then, suddenly, it was over.

"You didn't have any fire there, sonny," he was told by a uniformed expert with a big fireman's helmet, called The New Yorker, he discovered. "Your incinerator backed up. Chute was clogged; pushed the smoke back down. You gotta keep that chute open." He turned to a fireman who was standing nearby. "I told you that was it, didn't I? Hell, this place is famous." He turned to Jimmy, and added, "Long before you, son. An owner who won't pay for proper repairs."

Behind the fireman to whom Mister New Yorker had been speaking, lurked the super of The Dali. Mister New Yorker looked over at him. "Happened three times when you were taking care of the place, didn't it?" he called to He-who-has-gas.

"Yes, sir, Captain. Three times backs she up on me. I the one who called now."

"Good man," said Mister New Yorker. He turned back to Jimmy. "You're new, eh? Well, I'll give you a break, sonny. I gave Frilly-Front there a nice ticket the third time out. But I don't want to be called out to this damn place no more, got it? I got real fires to fight."

"Yes, sir," Jimmy said, and snapped to salute.

By five o'clock that afternoon things were under control. Jimmy'd got most of the mess the firemen had made cleaned up. He'd got all the trash burned (making certain first that the garbage chute was clear), and he got the front walk and the vestibule cleaned and shining. The washing machine repair man came a bit earlier than expected and fixed the broken machine. The boiler repair man had come and had got the Big Boy growling properly, so as to make heat and hot water, and Jimmy had got all his soot and grease cleaned up after him. Cleanliness and Order had been restored. He straightened up the apartment at odd moments, so that Fay wouldn't find a mess. He shaved and showered and put on clean clothes; and, not having to go to the docks on this Monday night, he felt momentarily relieved, and had a cold beer.

But he was disgusted, discouraged, exhausted, undermined; in short, feeling rotten. He'd expected Fay to be back by now. She'd probably decided to stay on an extra day. Probably having a few drinks and a good time with Aunt Myrtle and Uncle O'Toole. It was better that she hadn't come home, in the middle of all this commotion. But Jimmy wished she were here now, so he could go out without feeling that the place would cave in while he was gone. He felt like walking out on the damned place for good and ever. It'd been wrong of him to stay the whole weekend with Phyllis, and not come over to check on things. But any house that can't be left alone for a day and a half ought to be razed, buried—in short—shoveled under.

A month or so later, Fay left on a Thursday afternoon, intending to spend the remainder of the day and Friday, Saturday, and Sunday with Aunt Myrtle and Uncle O'Toole. She said she'd be back from Jersey before noon on Monday. Just after she left, the Big Boy boiler had a nervous breakdown. Jimmy barely had time to get the repairman in to doctor it up before he had to leave to go to work on the docks. And when he got to the docks, more bad news was waiting for him. It seemed that, as a result of a union shake-up, they would no longer hire extras; this was to be his last night. Furthermore, due to bookkeeping complications, there would be no pay that morning.

Then Fay showed up. She was tired from her trip over and wanted a tall, cool drink. That was fine. But after a *few* tall cool drinks Jimmy found himself with a tipsy Fay on his hands, and that wasn't so fine.

"I can't take this anymore . . ." she cried.

"What do you mean, Mom?"

"This place is no good for me. All I do is work around here . . . and you're always going off and leaving me all alone . . . always out with one of your hussies . . . I want to live in Plainfield, where I have friends . . . I don't like this place at all! I don't like Greenwich Village and all these peculiar people!"

"Well, I'm a grown man, Mom. You don't expect me to stay home all the time, do you?"

"You could stay home with your mother once in a while," she said. "You leave me here with this whole house on my shoulders."

"Well, you leave me here alone all the time, too; don't you? You've just got back from Plainfield, haven't you?"

"Yes, and now you'll walk out."

197

"Well," Jimmy fibbed, "I've been stuck in here all week-end, haven't I?"

"I'm doing you a favor," she said, "staying here. I just want to see you get on your feet, otherwise I'd live over in Plainfield."

"Well, what about me? Aren't I doing you a favor, too? I thought I was. You have more money now, don't you; and you have the freedom of the City, of all of Greenwich Village."

Fay banged her glass on the kitchen table and started wailing at the top of her lungs about being unloved and mistreated and deserted. Jimmy was afraid that somebody would call the cops. There were a lot of people in the house who didn't like them, and who would leap at the chance of putting them on the spot. Then Jimmy thought that he might be able to scare Fay out of her hysterics by pretending to call Aunt Myrtle and Uncle O'Toole and asking them to come and take Fay back to Jersey. But before he knew it, he was actually putting the call through. Fay was still wailing in the background when Aunt Myrtle came on the line. Jimmy looked at Fay, and decided to go ahead with it. He told his aunt roughly what was happening, and, after considerable hemming and hawing, she agreed to drive over from Jersey and take Fay back. Jimmy figured that, if he could get Fay quiet by the time Aunt Myrtle and Uncle O'Toole arrived, he'd just ask them to come in for a visit. He didn't want to send Fay away, really. It didn't seem right. But he wasn't quite able to handle the situation either. And he was afraid they'd be fired out of the place before they could get themselves stabilized. They especially needed the house, right now, with his job at the docks closing up.

Finally, Fay quieted down and just sat and sobbed. Jimmy tried to console her, but it wasn't much good. She had it in her head that he was the cause of all her troubles, whatever they were. He was her only resource, and he'd

198

failed her. She believed that she was unwanted, unloved, lost and alone, and there wasn't anything Jimmy could say to shake her out of it. It was a good plain crying jag. But finally even the sobbing subsided. She went into the bathroom and washed her face, and came out all made up again, and aglow.

Jimmy asked her if she didn't want some coffee and she answered that what she wanted was for him to fix her a nice drink in a clean glass and to put some ice in it. He did that, and gave it to her, and then she asked him what he'd told Aunt Myrtle.

"I told her you were sick," he said, lying.

"Is she coming over?"

"Yes, she and Uncle O'Toole."

"Do you want me to go back with them?"

"I think it'd be better if you did, Mom. And as soon as you feel better—in a day or two—I'll come over and get you."

"What about the house?"

"I'll take care of it."

They had a few more drinks together, and talked on, reasonably, until Aunt Myrtle and Uncle O'Toole arrived. They didn't bother to come in—just honked the horn outside until Jimmy heard it. He took Fay out to the car.

Fay was all submissiveness now. She'd completely worn herself out. At the last minute, Jimmy wanted to make her stay, but when he saw Aunt Myrtle scowling behind the wheel, he thought better of it. His aunt and uncle would be sore as hornets, coming all the way to New York for nothing. Fay was thinking the same thing. Jimmy had a feeling that she wanted to stay but thought it was best to go along. Leading her to the car, he felt like an Aztec priest taking a human sacrifice to the altar. But he knew too, that Fay could handle herself with Aunt Myrtle. She was Fay's big little sister, after all.

199

It was clear that Fay wanted to be in closer contact with her family, to live in her home town, where things and people were familiar. She didn't like the people who lived in The Mondriaan. They were foreign to her, alien, snobs. Besides, The Mondriaan was too demanding. The O'Tooles had a nice room for her. They'd let her have it cheap, if she wanted it.

Well, there it was.

Jimmy couldn't keep the house going by himself; and, even if he could, as soon as the owner discovered that Fay had gone, they'd certainly ask him to go, too. The Mondriaan was a two-person post. So there was no question about it, Jimmy was going to have to leave—and pretty shortly. But where was he going? Even if Kreigsgeld let him stay on alone, he'd have to be at The Mondriaan by day, and he was losing his night job on the docks, and where could he get another job that was near the house, that paid well, and that occupied him only three nights a week? He couldn't see himself working five nights a week on one job, and five, or really seven, days a week at The Mondriaan, and writing too. That was a bit much, he thought. Besides, the house was a nightmare. He wanted out of it himself. But then, perhaps Fay would change her mind, as she often did. He looked through his beer glass darkly at an uncertain future, and chug-a-lugged.

AN ACTOR PREPARES

The actor must use his imagination
to be able to answer all questions.
—Constantin Stanislavski

Jimmy Whistler's neurasthenic girlfriend, Phyllis, called him in the middle of September to tell him that her parents were coming East from Seattle for a visit—just a week-end—and she wanted him to go with her to show them the Big Apple. In fact, she wanted Jimmy to play husband, which is what those two poor deluded people still thought him to be—their never-met son-in-law. Jimmy and Phyllis had been living together for a couple of years, but now Jimmy divided his time between Phyllis and his mother, sometimes staying with Phyllis, sometimes staying with Fay.

Phyllis's father, of course, had been in and out of New York often in the past few years, being, as he was, a pilot for a major airline, and having had, for a time, a regular run between New York and Seattle. About a year and a half ago, he had been switched to a run between Seattle and Tokyo, and that had saved Jimmy and Phyllis a great many headaches. Before that, when in New York, he'd tried to meet Jimmy several times, but Jimmy had always somehow avoided the encounter. Phyllis had met her father uptown several times, but had told him that her "husband" was called away, was sick, had to work, was drafted—any lie she

201

could think up to save Jimmy from the meeting and still not make her father suspicious. But this time her parents had written:

"We are coming East to see a few shows, but more especially to meet Jim. We sincerely hope that nothing will happen to make that impossible."

"You've just got to meet them, Jimmy," Phyllis said. "I don't think they believe me anymore when I tell them about you. Please, just this once. Oh, how I hate this bullshit!"

Jimmy couldn't find it in his heart to refuse her. But, on the other hand, he didn't like the idea of pulling off such an imposture. He was an actor, not a liar. He didn't want to lie to a couple of (probably) nice people, to make them think he was their son-in-law. Phyllis shouldn't have told them that they were married in the first place, but surely she should have told them by now that they weren't.

The fact was that Jimmy and Phyllis were scarcely seeing each other nowadays—for Jimmy had a new love; but he wasn't sure as to whether the new love loved him. She was a beautiful Hawaiian girl whom he'd first met when, as a Marine, he was stationed in Hawaii. Upon seeing her again, only recently and rather magically, he realized that he had always loved her, but had suppressed this emotion for years. She had taught him to float. He was a strong swimmer, but couldn't stop. If he stopped in the water he would immediately sink, but for Lani he could stop and float, lose the troublesome idée fixe and float.

Jimmy had always considered Phyllis more of a friend than a lover, though that had been part of their relationship for a while, the result of Jimmy enjoying her intellectual companionship, and his affection for her, but she was not Jimmy's type when it came to amorous affairs. Phyllis was careless in the extreme about her appearance—she'd let her teeth go bad, though her parents would have been delighted to send her to any of the best orthodontists; she did not eat

202

well, and she experimented with some of the lesser drugs, so she was undernourished and sallow of complexion. She loved getting clothes at the Salvation Army and other thrift shops and often wore a hodgepodge of odd garments. Many things had conspired to cause Jimmy to want to keep his distance from dear little Phyl, for whom he otherwise felt a great warmth of genuine affection, perhaps even a touch of love. She had a wonderful witty quick mind and a charmingly skeptical view of life. She said it was "a bullshit world," and that she could prove it anytime she liked.

That was the situation. Well, that was the half of it. Jimmy, a struggling actor/writer, and his widowed mother, Fay, superintended an upscale apartment building, named The Mondriaan, in Greenwich Village. And, as if things weren't complicated enough, Jimmy's "in-laws" were coming to New York on the same weekend that Fay had invited her sister, Jimmy's Aunt Myrtle and her husband, Uncle O'Toole, as Jimmy had always called him, to visit. They couldn't be stopped. It was going to be a busy weekend.

Fay worked very hard on their super's basement apartment all week. She had polished the furniture, put up new curtains, waxed and rewaxed the rubber-tiled floor till it was gleaming—in short, she had prepared it for the inspection of her fastidious big sister, Aunt Myrtle, and for the enjoyment of her equally fastidious brother-in-law, Uncle Albert O'Toole, a factory leather worker. It was Fay's intention to show her lace-curtain Irish relatives how well she was doing—and, indeed, the apartment looked very pretty, entirely satisfactory for that purpose. By Friday afternoon, she had a roast pork in the oven, three pies baked, hors d'oeuvres on a platter on the table, drinks mixed, etc., and was in the process of getting herself dressed to receive her visitors.

203

Jimmy, too, was getting himself dressed in his best bib and tucker. He'd accumulated a few clothes in the past year, and was now able to make himself fairly presentable in a well-cut, good-fitting suit, a chocolate shirt, cream-colored tie, and a new pair of oxblood loafers. He was slimmer, now that he'd been working night-shift on the docks, and he had a good tanning machine tan, and his hair, like the Washington Square grass of that summer, was bleached, with strands of bright gold running through it. He had gone to college on the G.I. Bill, majoring in journalism, attended a couple of top-ranking dramatic schools, and was now appearing with an off-Broadway repertory company. Jimmy was dedicated to the art and craft of acting, and couldn't help but feel that this weekend presented him with a challenge, even if there was a lie involved. After all, acting was lying, of sorts—well, pretending—but it was lying to tell a greater truth

Fay and Jimmy had discussed the situation, and decided upon a plan of action. Since Fay had no intention of meeting Phyllis's parents and palming herself off as Phyllis's mother-in-law, Jimmy would tell Phyllis's parents that his Mother was away, visiting her sister in New Jersey, and that he had been unable to get in touch with her in time to have her back in New York to meet them. It was a frail story, but Jimmy thought he'd be able to bluff it through. Furthermore, he'd tell them that he'd volunteered to help keep the house that she superintended in good shape while she was away, and that would give him an excuse to spend some time with Fay and Aunt Myrtle and Uncle O'Toole. A lot would depend upon what Phyllis's parents wanted to do; and, of course, upon what Aunt Myrtle and Uncle O'Toole wanted to do.

First, Jimmy was to wait and meet and greet Aunt Myrtle and Uncle O'Toole when they arrived at five, then he'd make some excuse or other and leave and go over to

204

Phyllis's apartment to pick her up, and, from there, go uptown to the hotel where her parents were staying, and meet them.

At ten minutes after five the doorbell rang, Jimmy pushed the buzzer, asked who was there, over the speaker, and heard Uncle O'Toole, his voice full of static, say, "Jimmy? Is that you, Jimmy? Uncle O'Toole here. How do we find you?" They were in the lobby. Jimmy went upstairs and led them back down.

Nervous laughter.

Confusion.

Hugs and kisses.

"Say, this is a pretty fancy building," said Uncle O'Toole.

"What a lovely apartment!" said Aunt Myrtle.

"Do you mean you get this apartment free?" asked Uncle O'Toole. "Do you get tips, Jimmy? Well, let *me* give you a tip. Save your money. Ha-ha!"

"What lovely curtains!" said Aunt Myrtle.

"What smells so good?" asked Uncle O'Toole.

"Fay, you look lovely!" said Aunt Myrtle.

"You're lookin' good, Jimmy," said Uncle O'Toole. "Lost a little weight?"

"Do you get a salary here, too?" asked Aunt Myrtle.

"Quite a deal you've got here," said Uncle O'Toole.

They all sat down and had a couple of Irish whiskies together; then Jimmy excused himself, saying that he had to go over to the docks to pick up his long-awaited final pay check, and that he'd be back as soon as possible.

He grabbed a taxi out on Seventh Avenue and scooted over to pick up Phyllis. When he got there, she was all aflutter. She was worried about how she looked, but Jimmy couldn't remember the last time he'd seen her looking so nice. She had her fine, pale hair in an upsweep, and was wearing a pretty teal suit. She wanted to know if she looked nice, and he told her that she did.

"Oh, this is such a lot of bullshit," she said nervously. "If only I didn't have to pretend with them."

Jimmy's sentiments exactly. Then she donned her tan raincoat and picked up her little native-American beaded pocketbook, and spoiled the whole thing.

"Haven't you got another purse to carry?"

"What's wrong with this one?"

"It looks like you picked it out of an ashcan somewhere in New Mexico," he said.

"Well, it's the only one I've got," she snapped.

When they got out of the subway in midtown, Jimmy stepped into a store and bought a plain black pocketbook for her.

"But what'll I do with this one?"

"Put it inside the black one."

"Bullshit!" she said, as she did so.

Jimmy stopped her again, taking his handkerchief and wiping off some of the excess rouge from her face. He hadn't noticed it in the house, but out in the sunlight she looked like she had a target on each cheek. Ordinarily, she never wore makeup, and, surprisingly, for a girl who could paint pictures, was considered by some to be a serious artist, she had developed no skill whatever in the use of makeup. Jimmy, on the other hand, had been taught to do theatrical makeup. He stood, dabbing at her with his handkerchief, trying to tone her down a bit, while she cursed and complained, full of impatience.

"To hell with it!" she said. "Come on; let's go!"

"Well, you don't want to look like you're ready for a war dance, do you?"

"To hell with it! It's just a lot of bullshit."

The poor little thing. She was more nervous than he was, and he wasn't exactly calm. Her parents were staying at a good hotel in the upper-midtown area. At the desk, Phyllis called their room. They were told to come right up.

Jimmy felt embarrassed getting into the elevator. The incongruity of their situation struck him. He disliked himself for feeling it, but Phyllis embarrassed him. She hadn't stood still for his treatment, and her makeup was smeared. The black pocketbook he'd bought her in such a hurry seemed far too large and awkward for her (still, it was an improvement over the beaded Indian one that was contained in it). And Jimmy could see, now, that her pretty teal suit had black cat hairs all over it; and her stockings hung loose and twisted on her thin legs. Some of the upsweep of her hair had come tumbling down, and despite the cool evening, she had beads of nervous sweat on her forehead, corrugating her face powder. Little Phyllis was not beautiful, but had she had the instinct for adornment of a primitive, she could have made herself appear quite attractive. But the instinct for adornment was completely missing from her personality. Makeup was missing from her makeup. Looking at her, Jimmy wondered what her parents would think. Here he was—tall, well-built, and, by most accounts, good-looking. Would they think he was some kind of fortune hunter, taking advantage of their little Phyllis? Some kind of rogue? How could they ever understand how it was that Phyllis and he had got together? How could they understand the tenderness he felt for her, his admiration of her gutsyness and her artistry? How, perhaps, theirs was a case of friendship gone too far?

The elevator stopped: they got out and found the appropriate door and knocked. "How do I look?" Phyllis asked.

"Fine," Jimmy said. "You look fine."

The door was opened by a round-faced, good-humored-looking man of medium height, wearing a grey pilot's uniform. He had a ruddy complexion, blue eyes, and

207

close-cropped salt-and-pepper hair. He was holding a cock-tail glass in his hand.

"Daddy," Phyllis said, and threw her arms around his neck. Then she pulled away and turned to Jimmy, saying: "Daddy, I want you to meet my husband, Jimmy. Jimmy Whistler."

The pilot, smiling, extended a hand to Jimmy. Jimmy took it and shook it. "So you're my son-in-law, are you?" he said; and Jimmy thought for an instant that he doubted it. "Meet your mother-in-law, Jimmy." A slim, attractive woman stepped forward.

"Mummy!" Phyllis cried, and threw herself into her mother's arms as she had into her father's. When "Mummy" had disengaged herself, she came to Jimmy, put her arms around his neck, and planted a kiss on him.

"My, Phyl, but your husband is a handsome young man," she said, and then to Jimmy: "I want to welcome you into our family, Jimmy. Do you realize that you and Phyl have been married for over three years and this is the first time I've laid eyes on you. Well, I certainly like what I see."

Jimmy felt crummy. How could he have ever got himself into something like this?

"Have a drink, Jimmy?" asked the pilot.

"Yes," he said, "please."

"Canadian Club?"

"Fine."

"Soda?"

"Please."

"Ice?"

"Please."

"Well, Phyl. . ." said the mother, holding her daughter at arm's-length and looking at her, "you look just fine. Married life seems to agree with you."

"Yes," said the father, handing Jimmy a drink, "you look well, kitten. You know," he said, speaking to Jimmy, "Phyl was a sickly little girl. She had one thing after another. Not like her sister at all. Her sister was a regular little butterball. But Phyl looks like she's putting on some weight, now, too, dear," he said, addressing his wife, "doesn't she?"

"Yes, she looks wonderful."

"I bet," said the father, "that you make her eat; don't you, Jimmy?"

"Yes, I try." It was true; but Phyllis was anorexic.

"Oh, I can see it," said the mother.

"Why don't we eat now?" said the father. "Let's go down to the restaurant and we'll all have a nice dinner. How's that sound?"

They went down to the hotel dining room and ate. The mother had fried shrimp, and Phyllis and the father and Jimmy had Lobster Newburgh. Jimmy was so nervous during the meal that he choked. All he could think of was getting away from these good people before he tipped his hand. They weren't unusually inquisitive, but naturally they had a great many questions to ask of the young man whom they thought to be their son-in-law. That was what they took him for, it seemed. And they seemed to like him, too. Jimmy wondered how Phyllis was going to explain this away in years to come. She'd probably tell them that they'd got a divorce on the grounds of mental cruelty and Jimmy's stock with them would hit bottom. Even now, that future time troubled him. Being an actor, he liked to be liked.

Phyllis was ecstatically happy. Jimmy could see that she was very proud of having got herself married, in their eyes. Probably she never thought the day would come when a young man whom she could claim as her husband would sit at a table with herself and her parents and please them so. For her sake, Jimmy was very attentive to her, and tried to

209

show the parents that he loved her, which, in fact, he did. But he felt that the whole thing was not only preposterous, but sad. He knew in his heart that he wouldn't be with Phyl much longer, and this seemed an awful crime to commit near the end of their time together. His new heart's delight flashed forward, he blinked, and she vanished.

They left her parents that night with the understanding that they would meet at ten the next morning and that they'd take a tour of New York together, and, later, Saturday evening, they'd all go to a play, and afterwards have a few drinks and a snack somewhere. Phyllis knew that Aunt Myrtle and Uncle O'Toole were at The Mondriaan, so she didn't object to Jimmy taking a different train and going straight there. When he kissed her goodbye on the subway platform, she thanked him for going to meet her parents, and said: "Wasn't it really nice? I mean, they're real squares, but aren't they nice? Do you like them, Jimmy?"

Jimmy said that it was and that they were and that he did.

"Oh, Jimmy, why can't we be really married?" she asked wistfully.

He felt like a criminal.

When he got to The Mondriaan, there was a party in full swing. Fay was dancing with Uncle O'Toole, and Aunt Myrtle was engaged in a monologue about Greenwich Village. They were three sozzled sheets in the wind. Jimmy sat down, nervously exhausted, but relieved to be at home, and let Aunt Myrtle chatter at him while he drank a good stiff drink.

Aunt Myrtle was only about two years older than Fay; but Fay, who'd kept her figure, looked about twenty years younger. Uncle O'Toole, who referred to himself as "a tough guy from Joisey," was a lean, dapper man in his late sixties. He did not have the same settled appearance as his wife. He was a wiry, energetic man, full of fun.

"Let's go out somewhere," he said. "This is Green-wich Village, ain't it? Let's go out and get a look at some Village characters, whatdaya say?"

"Now, O'Toole," Aunt Myrtle put in, "we can't afford to spend—"

"What the hell, Myrt!" said Uncle O'Toole. "You only live once, right Jimmy? Whatdaya say, Fay? Shouldn't we go out and see the characters?"

Uncle O'Toole won the day, or the evening. Jimmy took them out to a place on Seventh Avenue where beer was served in pitchers and a banjo-band played Gay Nineties music. They loved it. They sang with the band and drank the beer until none of them could talk or walk normally, and then Jimmy took them home in a cab. Fay gave them her bed and she took Jimmy's and Jimmy left them all there, puffing and snoring, and went over to Phyllis's to sleep. He set the alarm, and next morning, bright and early, he was there when they came to.

Uncle O'Toole leaped out of bed as full of energy as he'd been early the day before. Aunt Myrtle seemed grog-gier, but came around fast after an eye-opener. Fay had a hangover, and felt sick. She spent some time in the bath-room, throwing up. Jimmy felt like he was sleep-walking.

Aunt Myrtle wanted to know if there was much of that "mess-sin-ation" around Greenwich Village. Jimmy gath-ered that she meant the mixing of the races.

"About as much as anywhere," he told her, never hav-ing thought much about it.

Uncle O'Toole said: "I don't approve of that; do you, Jimmy?"

Jimmy told him that he had nothing against it. "I wouldn't go out of my way to marry a black woman," he said, treading where the ice was thin, "but if I fell in love with a black woman, and we wanted to marry each other, I'd marry her."

211

"You *would*!" exclaimed Uncle O'Toole, shocked. "But suppose you had a daughter," he said, explaining the problem succinctly, "you wouldn't want your daughter to marry one, would you?"

"Well," Jimmy said, "it looks like if I had already married one, and I had a daughter, I couldn't offer much of an objection to my daughter marrying one, too, could I?"

"Mmmm," said Uncle O'Toole, thoughtfully. "I see your point."

"You're not going to marry one, are you?" asked Aunt Myrtle, genuinely alarmed.

"I haven't been asked."

"My God, Fay," cried Aunt Myrtle, "Jimmy isn't thinking of marrying a colored girl, is he?"

"He's only teasing you," Fay said.

"Oh," said Uncle O'Toole, "I get it," and laughed.

Aunt Myrtle said: "Well, for a minute there, I thought my poor sister was going to become the grandmother of a pickaninny. And me the great-aunt of one. You mustn't do that to her, to us, Jimmy. I know you've got some weird ideas, but she's had a hard enough life as it was, with your father." The thought inspired her. "Oh, what a strange man your father was! I wouldn't have put it past *him* to marry a colored girl."

"Now let's leave him out of this," said Fay. "He's gone to his rest. Let's not talk about him when he's not here to defend himself."

"Well, I was thinking of the life he led you. My dear Albert has never treated me in such a way. He's worked hard all his life. He always supported his wife and children; didn't you, dear?"

"Yeah," said Uncle O'Toole devilishly, "but sometimes I think maybe old Elliot had the right idea."

"Oh," said Aunt Myrtle, turning red, "to say such a thing!"

212

Jimmy left them there to hash that out, while he went uptown with Phyllis to meet her parents. When he got back from taking a scenic cruise around Manhattan Island, from looking at the "ant-like" people from atop the Empire State Building, and from climbing into the Statue of Liberty's head, the same discussion was still underway back at The Mondriaan.

"Why did that man wear his hair like that?" asked Aunt Myrtle.

"He looked like a girl," Uncle O'Toole said.

"Why do you live over here?" Aunt Myrtle wanted to know.

"Was he queer?" asked Uncle O'Toole.

"I'd like to see a lesbian," said Aunt Myrtle.

Next thing Jimmy knew, he was coming out of a theatre on Forty-sixth Street, having just slept through a Rogers & Hammerstein revival. Years before, his acting coach, Dr. Zolauf, had introduced him to them at Carnegie Hall. Hammerstein's line, "You've got to be carefully taught," came to mind.

Phyllis and Jimmy walked hand in hand, ahead of her parents. Phyllis said: "They really love you, Jimmy." He'd been turning on the charm. Once, in drama school, he played the Hairy Ape, and he felt suddenly swept with nostalgia for the part.

Then he was at The Mondriaan again, sitting at the table, and Aunt Myrtle, now thoroughly sloshed, was saying: "Let's go out and see if we can find a lesbian bar."

"Let's go out, Jimmy," said Uncle O'Toole. I want to see some bohemians."

Jimmy took them to the White Horse Tavern.

"This is where Dylan Thomas drank himself to death," he said. "There's a picture of him on the wall. See?"

But it cut no ice with Aunt Myrtle. Far as she could see, it was just a dump. And who was this Dylan Thomas and where did he get such a funny name?

"He was a famous Welsh poet," said Jimmy.

"Famous for getting drunk and not supporting his wife and children," Uncle O'Toole said, showing a dumbfounding knowledge of modern literature. "I heard all about the bum." This turned several poetic faces in the crowd. The White Horse was a shrine to the Welsh poet.

"Your Uncle O'Toole knows just about everything," said Aunt Myrtle with pride and conviction. "Go ahead, ask him about something. Ask him!"

Jimmy sat, dazed, smiling, his head nodding approval, his mouth in a frozen smiling rictus.

Phyllis's parents left on Sunday afternoon. "We are so glad to have you in the family, Jimmy," her mother said. And to Phyllis: "You take good care of our son-in-law, Phylly, do you hear?"

Aunt Myrtle and Uncle O'Toole left on Sunday evening.

"See you all of a sudden," Uncle O'Toole said waggishly.

"We've had a wonderful time," Aunt Myrtle said, "even if I didn't get to see any lesbians."

Exhausted, embarrassed, and ashamed, but having completed the greatest performance of his life, and one that he vowed would have no encores, Jimmy collapsed on his bed at the Mondriaan. It had been an epiphany. Now he thought he knew the difference between acting and lying. He hoped he did. Stanislavski had never clearly explained it.

THE GOLDEN FLEECE

"Hail to thee, blithe spirit!" Jimmy shouted, spotting Marsayas in the dusty parking lot at a country station in Pennsylvania. They hugged each other and Marsayas drove them across the countryside and then through Doctor Brazil's farm and finally to his own outlying cabin.

"Who is this Doctor Brazil, anyway?" asked Jimmy, as he bounced along, trying to light a cigarette.

"Why, Christ, Jimmy, where have you been? He's famous! Didn't I tell you? He was an old pal of Aldous Huxley's and knows Timothy Leary. He's a medical doctor and a terrific painter. His paintings are psychedelic. He uses what he calls glow paint. When he came back from the Amazon a couple of months ago, he brought all the ingredients needed to make a wonderful spiritual potion. We'll try it later. Sorry you won't get to meet him—he's off somewhere making a documentary."

That evening Jimmy drank what felt like gallons of home-brewed beer with Marsayas and Joan, patty-caked with little Marsayas, who used his daddy's gargoyle grin to charm him, all to the strains of Ravi Shankar. After Joan and the toddler went off to bed Marsayas and Jimmy sat together drinking deep into the night. Jimmy told Marsayas about a job he'd been offered. Of course Marsayas saw writing for television as a "damned freaky sellout. You're a true damn poet, you jerk, why on earth you'd want to do that, I can't figure. Me, I've given up writing poetry completely, I haven't got the stuff. But like I said years ago,

215

you're among the elect, you dope, a true poet. I'm sticking with my painting." Marsayas gurguggled some beer and rumbled internally.

Jimmy felt drunk on Marsayas's home brew. Something happened to the night. It vanished. Jimmy slept peacefully that night for the first time in a long while—until the sun burst through the window like a golden glove, punching him in instead of out.

He still held a mug of splashing instant coffee in his mitt as Marsayas drove them all in his bouncing, shaking old rattle-trap jalopy off to what he called the waterfall, explaining that it was a swimming hole whose cold water would soon wake Jimmy up and snap him out of his hangover.

"And I hope you're up to trying some of Doctor Brazil's yagé potion. It's only a mild hallucinogen, but, believe me, it'll make the whole experience miraculous. It's all about nature, Jimbo, inside and out. It's about more than getting close to it. It's about *being* nature. It has removed from me the ugliness of the residual of any ambition. You need it. You'll love it!"

They left the car creaking in the sun and stumbled down the embankment—Marsayas leading the way. Joan feared for the toddler a bit because the embankment was steep, but they dropped into the shallow from the rocks without incident. It was a smooth shallow pond, purling slightly, only a foot deep. On a lower level, was a kind of natural slide that had been worn into the rock by the rush and rub of the water.

One could slide down this into a deeper pool, perhaps four feet in depth. It was too small to swim in, they could get only about three overhand strokes and they were up against a smooth wall of red rock. Jimmy and Marsayas tried to deepen it by throwing up the stones at the bottom, but they could go on doing that forever and they were here for fun and not work, so their labor was short.

216

The toddler had to be kept up in the higher, shallower pool, Joan attending. Marsayas and Jimmy joined them and sat down on the hot stone to enjoy some cold beer from sweating cans.

"How's your hula girl? Why didn't she come?"

"When I first met her she might have been called a hula girl, but she's not like that any more. She's tall and svelte, wears business suits and is a communications genius. She was too busy to come with me. The world is too much with her. She's heavily involved in what Phyllis would call the 'bullshit world.' Sometimes at night though she turns back into a hula girl for an hour or so, and that's magic."

Marsayas lit a joint. "Joan has become more of a mother than a wife." Marsayas took a deep hot drag and held it while handing Jimmy the joint.

There was a small concrete bridge down below the deeper pool and a pickup truck whizzed by over it, otherwise no sound but water and talk and the child's laughter. Below the bridge the water dropped in a steep fall and then, after a rushing meander, into the lake. The lake was very large and dark and Marsayas claimed that a phantom chief beat an ominous tattoo upon a tom-tom out there at night.

Marsayas chanted in a low mysticism-packed voice– *"The voice of the white birds from every quarter cried out, You have lost your country, You have lost your country!* The whole tribe was wiped out by the white man and the chief was out for justice. Of course scientists say the night rumblings are made by natural gas, a less impressive explanation, don't ya think?"

After the pot they took a plunge in the water and then Marsayas said he'd heard that somewhere upstream was a great waterfall, one that fell for perhaps a hundred feet— "not a Niagara, but a fair cataract" and it was supposedly located in a canyon of considerable beauty—and would Jimmy like to hike up the stream with him to find it.

217

"What are we after? Just the waterfall?"

"C'mon, man! We're argonauts and we're after the golden fleece."

"And you're Jason, I suppose?"

"Of course, c'mon! Take one of these." Marsayas handed him a sugar cube. "You'll need energy."

"I'm out of shape," Jimmy said.

"That'll take a little while to work," Marsayas said. Jimmy shrugged and they started off up the shallows.

Marsayas had been roughing it in a woodland way for over a year now and moved along at a good pace over the slippery rocks, sometimes through the water, sometimes along the bank, but more often wading through the knee-high water, because the bank was quite steep most of the way and often it was non-existent, only a sheer wall of rock in its place.

He looked a mythological figure of a man, tall and broad and beefy of shoulder, red and bushily bearded, sharp-eyed, visored cap pulled low for the sun: he moved sure-footed as a goat—or not quite, for he did slip occasionally, but even a mountain goat might have slipped on these watery stones.

Jimmy kept apace about twenty yards behind and it took his whole attention focused upon where he was next to step to keep him from dropping farther behind. They were no longer boys and this delicate goat-walking on watery stone was an effort, of the body but then more of the will. Jimmy wished Lani were here to see this beautiful place.

Where were they going? Where? And why? Why make the effort?

Back at the lower pools near the bridge there was rest on the hot stone with beer, kept cold by the cold purling water and the shade of the rock over it; so why this little odyssey, this minor quest? Why be Argonauts? What was the grail they were after?

218

When Jimmy looked up Marsayas had disappeared ahead of him and he saw a long gently rising glassy piece of water, reflecting mountains, bushes, trees, and below the crazily slanting mountains, bushes and trees, all the little gems half buried in a slippery silt, as if the flow of the water had discovered a sunken treasure, brightly colored arrow-heads, axes, peace pipe fixtures, as yet all unmanufac-tured—the raw material of a stone culture, the proud stuff of the phantom drummer of the lake and casting over it all, over the reflected, layered escarpments, over the faint tiny rock flowers, little bits of bright blue, scarlet, and gold, fool's gold, the reflected sky and the mysterious shadows of unseen birds, wind-caught leaves, swaying lazy branches and Jimmy wondered where was Marsayas: had he fallen so far behind in this fantastic world, was all this sudden glare and shadow too much to be accepted, was he no longer any part of it, that could flow with it all at will, or without will, without the consultation with will, as Jimmy imagined the red shadows who were men and women that had flashed here once had been able to do? But those men and women had had to fight the chaos around them, too, the gravity flow.

Then Jimmy saw Marsayas, as he came wading knee-deep in water around the long bend and he was standing on a rock his arms akimbo and breathing hard; Jimmy could see his glistening back heave; he turned toward Jimmy and mo-tioned and pointed up through the trees and Jimmy followed his gaze and saw deeply hidden a small cabin grayed by weather.

Marsayas grinned and pointed. "A poet!" he called and turned to his task of getting from one rock to another, the mountain goat.

Again they came upon a small waterfall with a sharp declivity and they had to work their way around it up the steep embankment of black mud and moss. Their feet and fingers ripped and upheaved the fine smooth moss as they scurried, a bit fearful of taking a long uncontrollable slide backwards and on to the jutting rocks and then they were able to drop down again into the cool water at the top of what Marsayas said he thought was the penultimate fall and the mud was washed from their feet and Jimmy dipped his hands in the water and rinsed the mud from his knees.

The water here was only about four inches deep but stepping into it he was alarmed by its pressure and for an instant thought it might over topple him and send him headlong down the fall to crack his head on the rocks below, but he was learning already that to deal with nature one must relax: it is the only "safe" way, Marsayas had said.

Marsayas was teaching him not to fight the stone under his bruised feet but to put down a foot with all its muscles loose and to let it find its shape on the earth: otherwise it wouldn't be accepted and rejection was the danger. How much of this damned chaotic world was he fated to endure?

Had he begun sliding down the muddy bank he should have forced himself to relax, to go limp and to accept his fate and he was already winning a faith that helped him believe that he should have merely slid over those jutty rocks like a piece of mossy mud and gone on sliding down and down and down the great fall under the bridge and meandered, making with his body some mystic hieroglyphs in the water, until he fell gently into the lake without hurt.

He might have passed Joan and the toddler and called good-bye to them. He might have been ushered into that dark frothy water by low drums at twilight. Would life be so bad? Life? Life without Lani?

But now Marsayas and Jimmy came upon an exceedingly long and narrow place which, except for the fact that it was all moss and stone and gurgling, rushing water and the fact that it was so terribly deep a trench in the high mountains, reminded Jimmy of one of those canals that city workmen dig in which to lay pipe for sewers (he'd had first-hand knowledge of such labor) and he felt like a workman on break as he and Marsayas sat, panting, and smoked another joint, kept dry by a plastic container in the pocket of Marsayas's raggedy cut-short jeans. "Are you feeling it?" he asked Jimmy.

"I feel kinda weird."

"That's the sugar cube. Doctor Brazil's hallucinogenic stuff. Smoother'n peyote, more friendly than L.S.D." Marsayas saw that Jimmy had a far-away look in his eyes. Then Jimmy began to speak, hypnotically, to no one. "Water is naked but for its diaphanous gown, which can best be detected when the water falls over an escarpment. Then the gown shimmers like silk in the sun or at night with the glow of the moon. She who is underneath the gown is Water, who is always a dancer, and is then a hula dancer, or a belly dancer, but can be at other times a ballerina, an adagio dancer, or whatever, but always a dancer, at least always ready to dance. The Water in your glass, if it is not a glass made opaque by color, seems to be sleeping (in a black glass it seems dead). But Water does not sleep for very long. It catnaps, but is as ready to swing into action as is a cat who has detected the slightest creeping of a mouse. Water appears to be feminine, but a great, broad-shouldered wave, one of those that come from the sea and flow over land, destroying whole cities, Water in that form would give us the sense of powerful masculinity, like a football player. Everyone knows that Water is graceful—a fountain spray, for instance—but it can also seem clumsy, as in a stagnant flood of several weeks duration, when dead animals float on it, and its lovely perfume dissipates and is replaced by a sulphurous stench, the odor of the dead. This is when Water seems to be connected to the warriors of the wasteland, and distinctly masculine, the destruction men make, which is so unlike the fecundity of the sparkling, egg-rich stream full of

221

fish, which seems feminine. So Water is both Yin and Yang, the Lingam and the Yoni, or appears in such aspects, apparently at will. Of course how it is contained tells the story, in a tall clear glass or falling between two jutting rocks. Water, then, tends to conform to its surroundings and is coy in its pretenses. So, if we think of Water at all, it is as an hermaphrodite, as he-she or she-he Water, a sideshow trickster, like that star one can point to, that glittering dew drop in the night sky, which has been gone for a billion or more years."

"Wow! Are you all right, Jim?"

"Yeah, yeah, I guess so."

"It must have been Doctor Brazil's potion. You went off on a rant."

"Did I? I just got to thinking about all this wonderment of water. I'm O.K."

They sat awhile, listening to the splashing waters, drying, soaking in the sun. Light seemed to bounce from the multifoliate greens surrounding them and streak back upward toward the radiant sky.

"What do you think, Jim? Should we keep on going?"

Jimmy didn't know what it was that made him sense the larger fall beyond the smaller, perhaps it was some accurate unconscious reading of the lay of the land, or something vibratory in the rocks, but it seemed something else which he was forced to say was a kind of indescribable sensation. Jimmy sensed a great booming mystery that was also a sort of magical silence beyond and he said, "Yes, let's go on. Yes, he thought to himself, I'm going on. The word "yes" felt like a mantra and he found himself thinking or saying "yes, yes, yes!"

This was a treacherous place, for the water was deep and rushing with great, foaming force down its narrow confines and there was just moss-slippery rock edging steeply up into the thickest bramble and tangle of green life Jimmy could remember ever having seen, even in Hawaii, but somehow they found their way onto a wide open flat place and the water was gentle again, almost still but for a slight observable upper purling, a rippling and it was all open here, wide and open again and Jimmy felt as if he had been in a tunnel and was now out again in the open.

But there was yet a sense of being low. It must have been due to the sense of height ahead, because they were already quite high up. They had come nearly two miles steadily upward and that was from a high place itself.

Yes, the feeling of being low must have been because of the great height Jimmy sensed ahead. Or because of the mountains rising all around him: or because the azure and pink-streaked sky still seemed to be so high above. He had an image of men casting for trout with long, flexible poles, men with wading boots and colorful flies pinned all over their hats: pipes in their mouths. And when he looked up Marsayas was gone—gone again!

And for all Jimmy had learned his feet were badly bruised, cut even and he would have been limping had he been walking on soft grass, so he had to take ridiculous delicate little painful steps, like a baby's steps and he'd probably be left so far behind he'd be ashamed to be such a tenderfoot.

And Jimmy wondered, with his Zen Master, what were the punishments of them that serve the Evil One, of those who cannot make their living except through violence to Being. And he saw Marsayas, ahead, standing in the center of a great open place and the water up to his knees and he pointed up, crying over the natural sounds "Look! Look!"

And Jimmy took one last look at his poor wretched feet to see that they were well placed on the slippery-as-ice rocks and looked up to where Marsayas pointed and saw an over-awing escarpment circling round them in deep beautiful folds of rock and placed them in a kind of canyon.

And his feet slipped and up they went most idiotically into the air and down he went plunging and thrashing and laughing like a fool, but he kept his plaid slouch hat that Marsayas had given him above the water and a bit of his forehead and he came up making an absurd joke of how the beauty of the place had knocked him over and Marsayas at first afraid Jimmy had hurt himself began to laugh and Jimmy looked in his hat and best of all his smokes were still dry, and so he scampered on in the sun drying off and caught up with Marsayas and right around a bend in this enormous place—there was the waterfall.

The waterfall came down for a hundred feet or more, then hit an odd rock and fell out like an opening fan across itself; so it was like two falls, one down, one crossing that, like translucent lovers entwined and undulating and above them, below a deep blue twilit heaven, a great cliff hung, weighted with trees.

Jimmy knew a mystic place when he saw one; a tabernacle. "The rock looks like an Indian chief," he said, panting. "See, he's in full regalia. He's smoking a peace pipe. He's smiling."

THE CARTESIAN DIVER

Darkling, I listen . . .
Keats

Jimmy Whistler recognized the moonstruck Beta at once. It was just as his friend Porter had described it—not more than two or three feet high, built right in the earth, and about six and a half feet long. But for the small skylight on top, that looked up through the trees, and the small lifting door on the lake side, it looked like a coffin regurgitated by its grave. Porter had said that his brother, the family hermit, had built the tiny cabin for himself one summer so that he could "keep his space. At first," Porter had explained, "there was only Alpha, the family cabin, then Matthew built Beta, so Dad decided to build the rest of the cabins to rent to lake vacationers and fishermen and make some money."

Jimmy kneeled and lit a match. Inside lay a soggy brown army blanket and a camouflaged sleeping bag. He put his can of beer on the damp ground and got in, stretching out on his back. Above, through the narrow window, he saw the twisted black interstices of the trees against the thick clusters of the stars, and the fancy struck him that he had fallen from above and had lodged in the narrow part of an hourglass and that he was looking down at billions of sparkling grains of time that rested on the bottom, below him; that he would eventually dislodge and join those grains and become fixed, somehow, in the bottom of the night.

The sound of Bach rolled over him, expressed in melancholy organ music, come from distant Delta, and Jimmy thought, "Suppose I should just stay here and let time drift away without a struggle?" Then he heard the rowboat bumping against the shore, the clanking of oars and oarlocks, not twenty feet off in the gloom, and Lani calling for their little boy, Semper Fi, to be careful.

"Mommy, here's Daddy, in a little house."

As Lani came upon him he was getting to his feet. "Just trying it for size," he said.

"How is it?"

"Cozy. How did you know where I was?"

"A chain smoker like you? In this dark? Listen, Jimmy, you're just being dramatic. Melodramatic. It's nothing to fail. Besides, five rejections of a novel isn't failure. Everybody fails, but they keep trying."

"I've never succeeded. At anything. A failure since birth when I made my mother suffer, as she's told me often enough. A thousand hours in labor. Ten thousand! Apparently, I didn't want to be born. I didn't like her milk. I don't like anything. Everything eats everything. Any God who would create such a place must be a monster. Everything reeks of pain and death."

"You've had more than one too many beers, and if you write that, nobody will read it. And think of Semper Fi and the new baby coming now—what are you going to call him or her? You're drunk. You've got to wean yourself into sobriety. You never used to drink so much."

"It's deep pain—and all these responsibilities scare me."

"A melancholy romantic—is that it, Shelley?"

"Shelley stopped swimming and drowned. That's not so bad. But Keats! I prefer Keats. I lie in the darkness and listen into silence sometimes, outside the stream of time where life hums and burns with its moths and flames, its

226

mechanical tropisms of desire and death; I listen to the silent voice of the nightingale with my friend Keats, the dead boy, the poet."

"But he was tubercular, Jimmy, not just peculiar!"

"Ho, ho! Thank you for appreciating my thoughts."

"Snap out of it! You have a child of your own to think of and another coming. Don't forget, just because I don't show yet, I'm pregnant." Her voice seemed disembodied in the darkness.

"I don't think I'm strong enough to lift all that weight," he said. Then he smiled a rueful little smile that she could barely see in the moonlight, and said, "Echo to Narcissus, but your feet still crunch the leaves, my heavy-with-child." He looked for Semper Fi, silhouetted, for an instant, in the moonlight, but flashing in and out of view. Now the five-year-old was crawling out of Beta with the blanket wrapped around him, a ball of childish, male energy.

"Where's Porter and Cecily?" Jimmy asked.

"They're still at Delta. Can't you hear? Isn't it some-thing, having an organ up here in the woods?"

"But he's stopped playing."

"Having a drink, probably. Your charade, your anat-omy of melancholy, didn't work. We all just kept on having fun after you left. Porter shrugged and said, 'Well, he's a poet.' You can't bring everybody else down with you, you know."

"But you came looking, my love."

"You're sozzled. I was half afraid you'd drown, like Shelley—quite unintentionally—or not."

"Not what?"

"Not unintentionally, you idiot; you've got us all worried."

"Let's go pick them up in the row boat."

They rowed along the bank of the dark, deep, shimmer-ing mountain lake, easier than climbing through the gloomy

227

woods, and returned to Alpha first, a full-sized, well-accoutered log cabin, where Jimmy filled a jar with Porter's homemade wine and, at Lani's insistence, put on a life-preserver. "I still worry about that fixation of yours. Are you sure you can float?"

Then they groped their way through the moonlit gloom down to the dock and pushed off out on the lake. The moon broke through the glowing clouds full as the plunging back of a white elephant and shown on the lake in broken, swaying pieces. In front of the patched black and moon-drenched blue of the night sky there was a dense beribboning of sparkling stars.

"It's a Van Gogh heaven," Lani said.

Jimmy pulled at the oars, sending the boat rapidly out toward the lake's abysmal depth. It was the thought of freedom, of relief that propelled him. But he wasn't going in the right direction. One of the oars was longer than the other and the boat kept drifting away from the middle where a tiny rock island stabbed upwards through the water. At first he thought his coordination was off, having drunk so much. "Why can't I make this boat go straight?" Then he realized what was wrong and managed by compensation to get the boat away from the shore. Porter had begun to play again, something somber that came over the lake in waves of sound, perhaps another Bach, which meant that he was still at Delta, the cabin where his father, the Bishop, had chosen to build the organ. "Hardly a little night music," Jimmy said.

"Oh, Jimmy," Lani said, "it's so beautiful up here. I wish we never had to go back to New York."

"So do I. Back to the bullshit world."

His hateful novel, so filled with the pain, real and imagined, of a lifetime, had been rejected, and no wonder, he thought, no wonder. Who would want to read such a shapeless agony of a thing? And yet it was the shame of failing,

228

of failing, of coming from nothing, from less than nothing, from an ugly childhood spent with drunken and irresponsible parents, with humiliation at every turn, at school, in the streets, at home, which was no home, ever, but demon basements criss-crossed with pipes, rat-sat-upon; brick walls oozing bed bugs, of coming from nothing and describing it as accurately as one could, and then going back to nothing with it, another unwanted item, another way for God to reject his life, him, thank you, thank you, your Majestic Cruelty, and to hell with all!

When they landed on the opposite shore, Lani called from the dock at Delta for Porter and Cecily to come out for the ride back to Alpha.

*   *   *

Porter's father was an Episcopal Bishop. Cecily's father was a Port Authority lawyer. Lani's father was a successful businessman in Hawaii, all acceptable. But Jimmy remained the downstart son of a downstart father; a thief, a liar, and a drunkard, that man. Even Jimmy's grandfather had married a rich woman and gambled her wealth away. His mother, who now lived in a nursing home, was a moral idiot from a family of moral idiots. Guilt, shame, humiliation rocked him. His drunken blood coursed through him bearing the dagger of the mind. He felt cut up inside. But how could anyone ever know? And who should care? God didn't. God wasn't. God couldn't be—be God and be evil, Locke said. For that was the world and the world said No.

Cecily came alone. "Porter wants to walk back. He's got a flashlight. But it's still too dark for me. I don't want to get all scratched up in the bushes." she said. "Push off, Captain!" And back out onto the brimming lake went the boat, four aboard, the two women, the boy, and Jimmy.

"They went to sea in a sieve, they did," sang Jimmy, cueing Semper Fi.

"In a sieve they went to sea!" the boy cried.

"Far and few, far and few. . ." said Jimmy.

"Are the lands where the Jumblies live!"

"Their heads are green. . ." said Jimmy, stopping to drink wine from his jar.

"And their hands are blue. . ." Semper cried.

"And they went to sea in a sieve," Lani finished the Lear poem.

"And there's the Dong with the Luminous Nose!" cried Cecily, pointing toward the woods, where Porter was making his way along the dark shore, in and out of the undergrowth between Delta and Gamma, his flashlight bouncing before him.

"A little wobbly," said Cecily, "after an evening of beer, wine, and Bach."

"It's true, Daddy, Daddy," Semper shouted. "It's the Dong! Daddy, look! He's real!"

"The Dong with the luminous nose, the love-sick Dong," said Jimmy.

Next morning after breakfast they went for a walk in the woods, which rose steeply, with trees standing in uneven tiers, higher and higher, and Jimmy could almost see them, growing beneath the water, lower and lower, mirrored into the blackness, as if there were no bottom to the lake at all, the valley of drowning darkness.

Here they were in the Laurentian mountains of Canada. What were they doing up here in paradise, anyway? He should be back in New York, doing something about his failed novel, not vacationing in Canada with a couple of spoiled rich kids who had never had a problem in their lives. But that wasn't fair, either. They were friends. Good friends. But what did that mean to him? Cut no ice.

He and Lani couldn't afford to spend money for a trip like this. Lani had won the money on a television quiz show, of all things, and he had been able to watch the show in the market research office where he worked. She had been quite good, quite enterprising, winning while he was losing. New York, Montreal, the mountains, and the deep bottom of the lake—what did it all mean?

Now he brought up the rear, an ex-Marine out of shape from offices and drinking, puffing and panting in an effort to keep the others in view. Some way ahead of him he could see Lani, lifting herself by the low branches of the trees, pulling herself up the steep embankment. Ahead of Lani was Cecily, who held Semper's hand, and Porter led the way, like an Indian scout, somehow marvelously untouched by all the drinking they had been doing. When Jimmy caught up with them, the others were standing at the edge of a place where the bank dropped sharply for about a hundred feet, and where could be seen the whole lake, smaller now and far below. Porter jumped up and down, smashing puff-ball mushrooms for Semper's delight and edification, Jimmy supposed, for Porter taught at a private school in New York. He claimed he would be its headmaster by the time he was thirty-five. Jimmy believed him. Hell's bells, Porter could converse in Latin!

Cecily showed Semper a large, spreading shelf mush-room with an underside so smooth and velvety that a very clear drawing could be made on it with a small stick or twig.

"This is what a unicorn looks like," Cecily said, hand-ing the mushroom to Semper. "And unicorns can only be captured by little girls and boys like you. They'll come and put their pretty heads in your lap."

"And it has a horn like that?"

"Yes—and I think I see one now!"

"Where? Where?"

Cecily pointed through the trees. "There," she said. "But oh—he's gone now. Vanished."

They climbed on, among poplars and mossy elms, slipping and sliding on the thick matting of ancient gray leaves that lay moldering, bat-winged ashes; through nettles that brought quickly disappearing red blotches to their hands; and over slippery, green, moss-covered rocks that crouched like ancient unmoving animals, petrified life; and finally back down to Alpha, Semper crying out at the sight of numerous unicorns, scurrying among the trees like shy deer.

The others had lunch. Jimmy was still unable to eat, though the climb had invigorated him, somewhat. The beer tasted better now, and he drank some of the homemade wine, bottled by Porter's dad, the Bishop, and soon his hangover had partially metamorphosed into the mild safety of a glow. After lunch they took the boat and the canoe and went out into the middle of the lake to the great domed rock the Bishop had named Whalehead. There they lay on the rock, sunning, Jimmy sipping wine from his jar and watching Porter skim pebbles off the water.

"Tell me a story about a unicorn, Daddy."

"Well . . ."

"Yes?" Semper looked up at him, expectantly.

"Once there was a unicorn," Jimmy improvised, "who only had an ice cream horn . . ."

"Yes? Yes?"

"It melted in the sun one day . . . and . . ."

"What, Daddy? What?"

"And the poor unicorn passed away."

"That's cute, Jimmy," Cecily said, laughing.

"What does it mean that he passed away, Daddy?"

"Oh, he melted away, son, from the horn down."

"Oh," said Semper, knitting his brow, "that's sad!"

"The Bishop thinks you're a very good poet, Jimmy, but he disagrees with your theodicy," said Porter. He says

232

you don't look around at the joys and beauties of life enough. He respects you, though—very much."

"It's the habit of a lifetime—not looking at the good side. I'm tired of it, myself."

"Gloomy Gus," said Lani. "Jimmy used to be a very risible guy. When I first met him he was always full of fun. In Hawaii he was a member of the HASP—Hawaiian Armed Services Police. That's how we met. He got me out of a dangerous situation and my father threw a luau for him. He was a laughing hero then. I fell in love with him. I didn't know he was a manic-depressive."

"I'm not," said Jimmy. He wanted to change the subject.

Lani had been sunbathing, face up, an arm across her eyes. Jimmy had thought she was dozing. She was the good side of life, the beautiful side, she and little Semper. They were the good side, and he was part of it, now, wasn't he? They loved him, even if his own mother and father hadn't, didn't.

Suddenly, Cecily shrieked, jumping up, pointing at Jimmy's knee, and Jimmy looked to see what he thought was a sparrow jump from his knee and fly off in a crazy elongated spiral over the lake, into the trees.

"It was a bat, Jimmy!" Cecily said. "It was right on your knee."

Porter laughed. "It must have been asleep in that crack," he said. "You probably woke it when you sat there."

"Oh, I *hate* them," Cecily said.

"They're harmless," Porter said. "Some of them do carry rabies, though. That's the only danger. He didn't bite you, Jim, did he?"

"No, no, he just flew off," Jimmy said. "No harm done." He quickly drained the remaining wine from his jar.

"Let's make Cartesian divers," Porter said, turning to Jimmy, "our version, anyway. Like this: We put some water in those empty wine bottles on the porch and plug the tops with corks and throw them up in the air and into the lake. We keep filling them a little more each time until one goes all the way to the bottom and sticks. It's a question of fine-tuning. I win, if yours stays down and mine comes up."

"Mine will be the first to drown," said Jimmy.

"Oh, Jimmy," said Lani, "don't be so negative."

"Let's get those bottles. All aboard!" Porter cried.

After depositing Lani and Semper on shore, and picking up a case of empty wine bottles, and a basket of corks, Porter and Cecily took the canoe, Jimmy the rowboat, and in the middle of the lake, directly across from Alpha, they began sinking the divers. At first the bottles weren't filled enough to hold them down even for a few seconds, but soon they had reached the necessary refinement and the divers went down and remained below surface for some time, then one or the other of them would pop up, jumping out of the water.

The game was carried on by adding more water and sending them back down, whether to return or not no one could know. Jimmy thought it a silly, senseless game, but then what wasn't? And Cecily and Porter seemed to think it great fun.

Jimmy took a drink from his renewed supply of wine and pitched his diver high into the air. It smacked the water. He pulled at the oars until he came to the spot where the diver had hit, and there it was, magnified to look as if it were just below the surface. He watched the bottle, soon a mere swirling fleck of light, scarcely distinguishable from the countless other flecks that were caught momentarily by the sun-drenched surface before they rayed down and diminished in darkness.

"He's through," Jimmy thought, as the boat rocked gently. "He can't take anymore. Can't take anymore."

The rowboat sank deeply on one side with his over-leaning, his peering. It floated gently sideways through water that rippled with a sound like tiny, muffled bells.

Darkling I listen; and, for many a time
I have been half in love with easeful Death,
Call'd him soft names in many a mused rhyme,
To take into the air my quiet breath . . .

Keats's words ran over and over through Jimmy's mind, transporting him from the lake, the sky, to the beckoning darkness deep below. His breath came in short light whispers. Suddenly his elbow slipped off the side and the boat rocked violently, then steadied. He caught his breath. He had drifted down as far as Delta. He was nowhere near where the diver had gone down. He regained his bearing. Cecily and Porter sat off at a great, wavering distance, in the canoe. Lani and Semper, even farther, smaller, on the shore. All of them were waving to him, smiling at him, waving to him. He belonged to these good, lost human beings. He belonged to them. They needed him, too. There was green and gold everywhere. Even the glittering water was gold. The water was gold.

He took a cigarette from a pack, lit it, placed it between his teeth, and pulled hard at the unmatched oars. The boat angled about, spreading in its wake two curved waves in different directions. Then he saw his diver break from the water, dripping, high, shining, some distance ahead.

www.ingramcontent.com/pod-product-compliance
Lightning Source LLC
LaVergne TN
LVHW092037030225
802888LV00003B/13/J